THE MILLENNIAL ARK

THE MILLENNIAL ARK

A novel
by
Michael R. Seymour, MA.

The Millennial Ark

Copyright © 2015 Michael R Seymour, MA.
Printed and bound in the U.S.A. All Rights Reserved

ISBN-10: 0-6924-6206-6
ISBN-13: 978-06924-6206-5

Published by Valley View Enterprises LLC
1564 S. 700 Road
Council Grove, KS 66846
785-466-1327

Prologue

William Howard Bennett, Senior Vice President of Operations for Richman Oil pushed a button on his desk and the great window blinds opened. He rose and walked to the floor to ceiling windows that comprised the west wall of the room. He looked out upon the city wishing that the entire landscape could be covered in oil. "Another lovely day, Patrick." He spoke as if there were someone else in the room. "Shall we see if everyone made it to work on time?" Since there was no response from the empty room he walked slowly back to his chair and pushed another button.

"Yes sir?"

"Come," Bennett demanded.

A young man with a red bow tie and carrying a legal pad entered the room and remained standing.

"We want to get a jump start on the tree huggers, Richards. I've given this a lot of thought and there are three areas we need to concentrate on. We're at the end of the line here; we've taken all the easy oil and burned it up. The stuff that's left is going to be hard to get and expensive, we need to keep our prices low enough that those renewables are still uneconomical. We are trying to figure out a way to have a monopoly on the sun and the wind but we aren't there yet.

"We know that those rigs in the Gulf are ticking time bombs. We know that sooner or later one of them is going to fail. We know they have the potential to pollute the entire Gulf and kill every living creature in those waters. We don't care. It is important that we appear to care, can you do that Richards?"

"Certainly, sir," Richards answered.

"That pipeline across the country. We know that those tar sands only amount to a pimple on a gnats' ass as far as world oil consumption is concerned. We know that it has the potential to destroy the fresh water that is used for irrigation and drinking throughout the Midwest. We used existing pipeline wherever we could so we could lay off those pipe fitters. We know that it is going to leak and we don't care. It is important that we appear to care, can you do that Richards?"

"Certainly, sir," Richards answered.

"That fracking we're doing. We know that it is destroying all the fresh water on the planet. We know that it is taking all the fresh water and contaminating it and injecting it in the earth where it will never fall as rain again. We know that our fracking is causing earthquakes that are destroying roads and bridges and buildings. We even know that our fracking is causing earthquakes that are destroying our own pipeline but we don't care. It is important that we appear to care, can you do that Richards?"

"Certainly, sir," Richards answered. He waited. Bennett looked up at him without saying a word. Richards turned and left the room.

The angry voices pounded at Bennett's temples. They started when he was just a child; right after his mother abandoned him.

She hates you; they hate you; they will always hate you.

His mother, upon learning her husband was a Nazi, chose to abandon her baby and save her own life. He could never forgive her.

Bennett sat back in his chair and addressed the empty room. "You know Patrick I won't be happy till this Earth is covered with oil. I won't be happy till all the clean water is polluted and those idiots have to pay us for clean drinking water. I would be happiest if those earthquakes were a lot more powerful and I could watch these buildings crumble and fall and be covered in ashes."

Soon, he would get his wish.

Chapter 1

Adam leaned against the front fender of the red 1993 half ton pickup truck. He read the words on the sheet of paper for the tenth time. It was a printed copy of an email, and it read:

Adam Lee Thomas_____
From: "Justin Williams"
jwilliams@richmanoil.com
To: "Adam Thomas <adamt@penmail.net>
Subject: Job offer
Adam
I heard they were going to try to use that old pipeline instead of building a new one. Now you need work. We thought that might happen. I was able to get hold of the guy I was telling you about and you need to give him a call. His name is Tom Hendrix and his number is 555-454-9211.
I put in a good word for you and he said they had a couple of openings that might start at $38.50/hr. with a lot of overtime. Call him quick.
Tell Annie hi when you see her.
Justin

He folded the piece of paper and placed it back in his hip pocket. He walked slowly around the truck checking the tread wear on the tires. A cold wind blew from the north; he turned up his collar and turned his back to the wind.

Adam stood six feet one inch tall and weighed nearly 230 pounds; he was wearing a plaid long sleeve work shirt with a jean jacket, old work jeans and well-worn cowboy boots. The old straw cowboy hat concealed his mane of long sandy colored hair. He was standing in front of the Atlas Tire and Rubber Company and as he completed his inspection of the tires he was approached by another young man of slightly smaller build who was twenty-four-years old, wearing a greasy blue uniform. They had graduated from high school together, and had been good friends since grade school.

"Hey Adam." The young man waved his right hand as he approached.

"Hey Tim," replied the cowboy. "You suppose I can get a few thousand more miles out of these old rags?"

"Let's have a look," offered Tim, as he began to run his hand over the tire treads one tire at a time.

As he was checking the last tire, he looked up. "You told Annie yet?"

"Not yet," replied Adam, he lowered his head and kicked one of the tires.

"She is not going to take the news very well," Tim spoke as he slid under the truck on his back to check the spare tire.

"What can she say?" Adam pleaded, "We can't get married without money, she doesn't work now and it's the only job I can find, and I refuse to take her daddy's money."

"She'll probably just bust you up a little," Tim removed a tire gauge from his pocket and began to check the air in the tires.

"She could beat up a lot of guys we know, that's a fact," Adam walked along beside his friend. "I still remember Ted Martin from fifth grade, served him right, but he'll have that limp the rest of his life. What a girl, she's big but I love her."

"You can probably get five thousand miles out of those, watch the left front one, keep the spare aired up and watch the potholes," advised Tim. He patted his friend on the shoulder and walked back toward the building. "You ought to sell tickets for when you're going to tell her you're leaving town, we'd pay to see a good ass whippin'," He chuckled. "When you leavin'?"

"Soon I hope," Adam replied as he started his truck. "The sooner the better. Thanks buddy." He backed out of the parking lot and drove toward home.

The City of Fort Pearson got its name from the fort of the same name that had been built 150 years before to keep peace with the Indians. Wagon trains stopped there on their way to the Santa Fe Trail and a good part of the old historic community had been preserved. It was a quiet little community sixty miles from Wichita, the people were friendly and there was a lot of community pride.

He drove on to his parents' house. He felt terrible moving back home but when he got laid off, he had to quit college and give up his apartment. It wasn't bad living at home; just like when he was a boy; he stayed in the loft above the garage and his parents let him do household chores to make up for their trouble. Of course, if you had asked either of them they would have said it was no trouble at all and they were glad for the opportunity to spend time with their only child.

As he crested the hill he saw the old home place, it was in a middle class neighborhood at the north edge of town; it was built on five acres and Dad had built a large building in the back that served as garage and workshop.

His immediate problem now was that the pipeline work that had kept him busy for the last two years had ended. The contract was finally completed and he found himself suddenly out of work. No way would he even consider asking John Williams for permission to marry AnnaBelle without a steady job. This economy sure messed up their plans. The two of them planned to finish school, get married, have some babies and live happily ever after. Now this. With enough money saved he was convinced that he could persuade Old Man Meeker to sell him that land and those buildings. With that land and a college degree to back him up, Mr. Williams would not refuse; that according to AnnaBelle's older brother, Adam's best friend, Justin Williams. Adam was convinced that if he took that job with the oil company and if he could save the money, that by the time AnnaBelle was graduating they would be real close, maybe close enough for her daddy to say yes.

He pulled the red pickup into the long driveway beside the house, past the garage; then backed in to the door at the rear of the garage that led up a flight of wooden stairs to the loft where he was staying. His bags were already packed. Besides a few close drinking buddies no one in his family yet knew that he was going south to Louisiana to work in the oil patch.

Mr. Tom Hendrix had been happy to hear from Adam. Justin had indeed put in a good word for Adam and Tom said he could start whenever he got there.

Justin was AnnaBelle's older adopted brother, the son of her father's twin brother who had died; now he was the one Daddy hoped might manage the ranch one day. Justin had other plans. He hated to farm, hated to plant and sow, hated to work with animals and loved to travel. He was two years older than Adam. When he graduated from college with a degree in mechanical engineering he headed for the oil patch and got a good job with Richman Oil, he was now on the fast track toward management in that company; he traveled a lot, and now wanted Adam to come aboard as well.

As Adam carried his suitcases down to the truck he began to worry about how he was going to break this news to AnnaBelle. She was a sweetheart and he really loved her but she had inherited her grandfather's temper. Lord what a temper that girl was cursed with. And she was a big girl, not as big as Adam but really big for a girl. He never wanted to marry anyone else, not from the time they were small; he didn't want one of those silly sissy city girls. He was planning to need a woman that could raise strong sons and daughters that could tend their land.

He finished packing the truck and walked around the garage to the back door of the house to say goodbye to his folks. No sooner had he entered the door than he heard a lovely voice.

"Go back and wipe those feet, Cowboy!" Jerri Thomas worked part time in the office of the utility company where Ken worked and made a decent living as a part time interior decorator. The front room of her house was a constantly changing showplace for her clients and she had worked a deal with a local furniture company to use their place to help sell the new stuff.

Jerri was a small woman and not at all suited for farm life. Adam decided that he must have gotten his love for the land from his father.

"How's it going, Mom." Adam caught his mother in a bear hug in the living room. She looked down at his feet and smiled when she saw that he had removed his boots at the back door.

She hugged him back.

"Pot roast for supper." She knew it was his favorite.

"Can't stay, Mom" he apologized with disappointment in his voice. He could smell the rich aroma from the kitchen. "I need to get down to Pittsburg before dark."

"What's the hurry," she questioned. "AnnaBelle's not going anywhere."

"I'm going to be gone for a while," He finally broke the news. "Justin found me a job down south and I need the money."

Jerri stepped back with a questioning look on her face. "You can't just up and leave like this, have you talked to your father? How long will you be gone for?"

"No and quite a while, where is Dad?" He started walking toward the kitchen.

"Your father had to work late again, something about a blown transformer or something. Surely you don't expect to leave without saying goodbye to Ken?" She pleaded. "And pot roast is your favorite."

He hated to disappoint her but he needed to get on the road. "Can't wait Mom, the sooner I get down there the sooner I get back."

"And where pray tell are you going exactly?" She followed behind him, but stopped a moment to straighten a picture.

"I'll be in Lake Charles, Louisiana to start with." He was at the back door and putting on his boots.

"You're just like your father, once your mind's made up there's no stopping you. At least let me make you some sandwiches for the road." She opened the refrigerator and began to dig inside.

"Thanks Mom, but I'll get something on the way." He stepped over and hugged her.

"Do you need any money?" She asked with resignation in her voice.

"I've got plenty, thanks." He walked out the door. "Tell Dad I'll be in touch, love you both.

He walked quickly around the garage to the truck and as he drove past the house, Jerri was standing outside the back door and waving. He could tell that she was crying. He knew that would happen and he hated to see Mom cry. He waved and wondered if he would ever be here again, not for the last time.

Chapter 2

As Adam drove out of town, he took a right on a country road. Patches of snow remained in ditches and shaded areas; they might be there till spring. He drove for two miles then turned back to the east. On the northeast corner of the intersection sat a small house built of stone, it was over a hundred years old and was surrounded by many old trees that would shade it all summer. Beyond the little house were several outbuildings in a state of disrepair: they needed painting and many of the roofs showed signs of wear. To the east of the house were many long, low, metal-framed buildings, also in a state of disrepair. Some of the glass was broken, but much of it remained in the steel frames. These dilapidated buildings covered several acres of land and at one time would have been a showpiece. Ben Meeker inherited this place from his uncle and during the whole time he owned it, never did one bit of improvement. Adam thought this place had tremendous potential, and when he had enough money saved he would buy it and those greenhouses would be filled with plants. He and AnnaBelle agreed that it would take a lot of work but it would be worth it. Besides, this piece of land adjoined the Williams property and would be a nice addition to her inheritance.

John Williams began to manage his father's property before he left high school. This land had been handed down for four generations. Those generations were of the belief that land acquisition was key to success in farming and the farm was always expanding; never selling. They raised cattle and row crops, corn and milo and soybeans. The Kansas farmland was perfect for this combination. His hope was that his eldest adopted son, Justin, would one day take over the reins and it was hard to accept the truth that Justin was not destined to be a farmer. AnnaBelle on the other hand seemed to enjoy farming, she was in college now majoring in business; there might still be hope. He demanded that his children finish college and since he was paying the bills they shared this belief.

The only time that John had ever spent away from the farm was when he went away to college to get a degree in agriculture. An adventurous part of him wished that he could have worked in a big city. That part of him yearned for fast cars and fancy things. His duty was to the farm so after graduation he returned home and never left again.

It wasn't that he didn't like Adam exactly, there was that one little fire event, but other than that; well, you shouldn't blame the son for the sins of the father. Besides, AnnaBelle seemed to care for him. It was difficult for John to show much emotion toward anyone one way or another and sometimes people thought that meant he didn't like them. He was simply a task oriented individual. If you needed something done; he could do it, but if you needed someone to kiss your baby he wasn't your man.

He had spent the morning feeding cattle, carrying those giant bales of hay out into the pastures and unrolling them so the cattle could eat. As he turned into the field he saw a red pickup stopped in the road at the crest of a hill, he didn't give it much thought and continued into the pasture.

Adam drove slowly past the old Meeker place and up to the crest of the hill that marked the end of the property line. He sat for a moment on the hill and gazed at the land, he could see for miles. To the right was the Williams ranch, a sturdy stone house with many outbuildings, several pole barns, three grain silos, and one large blue metal building. John had constructed this large building so that AnnaBelle could practice her barrel racing. She rode a four-year-old Sorrel Mare named Trixie and one wall of her bedroom was covered with ribbons and trophies.

The leaves on the distant trees were thinning with the cold weather but some of them still held their color, in a couple of weeks they would all be gone. The several ponds in the distance would all be frozen over and it would be a struggle to keep all of those cattle fed and watered. He wished he could be here to help, he wished AnnaBelle's daddy liked him better. Adam had taken the blame for that fire, even though he was covering up for the girl. If her daddy knew she and her friends had been smoking and set all those bales on fire he would have been so mad at her that he would probably have cut her off and then she never would have finished college. It would be alright once he saved a little money and fixed up the Meeker place.

In the distance he saw a man in a green flatbed truck, feeding hay to the cattle; it must be John. He wished they got along better. He put the truck in gear and drove past the farm buildings, as he passed the truck in the field he made a point to raise his left hand in a wave. There was no response from the man in the truck; surely he was busy with his hay bale.

John was watching the big hay bale roll out on the ground and the cattle run to eat it. As the big roll emptied out he looked up at the road just in time to see the man in the red truck waving, he waved in return, too late

Chapter 3

AnnaBelle Williams wanted nothing more than to please her father. This man was known to have sacrificed many times so that his children could have a better life. Both of the children agreed that all Daddy expected was for them to finish college and then get on with their lives. They knew that it was his hope for them to come back to the home place and help to preserve what their parents and grandparents had worked so hard for.

As a dutiful daughter, AnnaBelle was enrolled in a good college and would work hard to complete her degree in business. She was in her third year of a four-year program and her grades were good. Daddy was happy. All she really wanted to do was to marry Adam, raise a passel of children and live happily ever after. Marriage and children would wait until she finished school. By then, Adam would have also finished college and been able to get that piece of property next to Daddy's. Her hope was that those two bull-headed men in her life would finally get together.

AnnaBelle had no real preference for schools, but her best friend, Debra Sturgis, talked her into coming along with her. Debra was an art major who wanted to teach art in elementary school. The two girls took as many classes together as their different majors would allow and today their English course finished at 3:20. The two girls shared an apartment together on North Rock

Road and since they both had an easy schedule on Thursdays, this was their day to party. Today was AnnaBelle's turn to drive and when class was over they drove together east on 21st street. She drove a small four-door bright yellow pickup truck that Daddy bought her for school. It had distinctive chrome railings along the sides of the bed and a front bumper sticker that read, "EAT BEEF."

"Have you noticed those two guys that sit together in the back corner?" Debra asked as she buckled her seat belt.

"They are kind of cute," answered AnnaBelle. "But remember I'm taken."

"Doesn't hurt you to look," replied Debra, "That one just makes me want to say screw this class, let's go get some beer and party."

"I'll go so far as to buy the beer," AnnaBelle pulled into a big shopping center parking lot. "But I'll reserve the partying for you and me and Adam."

"You're no fun," Debra took the twenty that AnnaBelle offered and jumped out of the parked car and walked into Twenty First Street Wine and Liquor. She returned a short time later with two sacks.

"What did we get?" asked AnnaBelle as she drove back out into traffic.

"A little beer, a little wine," Debra turned around in the seat and placed the sacks in the back seat. "Let's get a couple of burgers to go with the egg salad, I'm hungry."

As they entered the drive through Debra continued. "So, have you heard from Adam since the big layoff?" This was a touchy subject with AnnaBelle but Debra needed to know.

"He moved out of his apartment, moved back with his folks, cancelled his phone and his Internet, and hasn't called me for four days. I have no idea what he's up to, but he'll come up with something." She sounded a little worried.

"Have you tried to call him at his folks?" Debra persisted.

"Jerri works all day. I left a message, but Adam hasn't called me back. I'm sort of pissed right now." There was anger in her voice.

"If you'd marry the guy, Daddy would surely support you both." Debra was digging into the sack of food and began to eat a French fry. "I am so starved."

"Adam would never take money from Dad. He's too proud. He'll make it on his own or die trying. The problem is that he is so stubborn he won't talk to Dad about us getting married until he thinks we're set, and we might never be set enough for him." She pulled into the apartment complex.

They gathered the food and drink and books from the truck and walked to their second floor apartment. Debra stopped to check the mail on the way.

When AnnaBelle opened the door, a long haired yellow cat rushed out the door. "Go ahead out you slut," she chided the cat, "get yourself knocked up and see what happens."

"At least one of us is going to party tonight." Debra laughed as she sorted through the mail, tossing the junk mail in the waste basket and placing the bills in a wicker basket on a shelf.

The apartment was a two bedroom, two bath affair with a front room, a kitchen/dining room and a large balcony. The bedrooms each had a private bath and were at either end of the apartment, separated by the living area. A bar with three bar stools separated the kitchen area from a comfortable carpeted room with a fireplace, large TV/stereo, couch and two reclining chairs.

Debra removed a Tupperware container from the refrigerator and placed it on the bar along with two plates and silverware. AnnaBelle filled two glasses with wine and placed the fast food on the counter and the girls began to eat.

"So, does your dad still hate Adam?" Debra struggled to ask with a mouth full of egg salad. "This stuff needs more salt or something."

"Dad doesn't hate Adam," AnnaBelle insisted. "He still hasn't gotten over that fire that burned up those big hay bales."

"Why didn't you tell him you started that fire and Adam took the blame for it?" Debra scolded. "I wanted to tell him at the time but you wouldn't let me, remember?"

"I remember and you know how Dad feels about smoking and he would have disowned me if he found out. It should be good enough that I never did smoke after that." She was finishing the last of her fries and stood to refill their wine glasses.

"Do you think you ever will tell him the truth?" Debra insisted. "You should you know."

"I'll wait till I'm out of school,"

"Didn't I remember hearing something about a rift between your dad and Adam's dad?" Debra pushed the empty plate away and stepped into the living area and curled up on the couch, still sipping on her glass of wine.

"Adam and I have talked about that on several occasions, nobody wants to talk about it, not Mom or Jerri. It's sort of like an old family secret that no one wants to talk about. There might have been something going on between Dad and Jerri and Mom and Ken, but nobody talks about it. Whatever it is, it's like those two guys just really don't like each other, so it sort of reflects on Adam." AnnaBelle brought the bottle of wine into the room and refilled both their glasses.

"I'll ask my mom," Debra said, "She was in high school with them, if anybody knows what the deal is she will. I'm supposed to call her tonight and I'll ask. More wine please."

The girls were well into the second bottle of wine when there was a knock on the door. Debra rose too quickly and stumbled against the table, the empty wine bottle fell over but she was able to save the less empty one.

"Whoa," she said as she stumbled toward the door, "I'm not used to this."

She opened the door and exclaimed, "AnnaBelle, it's your knight in shining armor, Hello Cowboy." She hugged Adam.

AnnaBelle did not rise from the couch, she turned and waved for Adam to come to her.

"Hello lover," Adam sat beside her on the couch, they hugged and kissed.

"Why didn't you let me know you were coming?" AnnaBelle punched him on the arm. "I've been worried sick." She meant it.

"I didn't want to get you all disappointed if I couldn't come." Adam explained.

"Want a beer Cowboy?" Debra shouted from the kitchen.

"Sounds great. Thanks," he replied.

"What's going on now," AnnaBelle asked, "what about your phone?"

"Still no phone, can't afford one yet," he replied, while he took the can of beer that Debra offered.

"Thanks Deb." He finished half the beer in one long pull and set the half empty can on the table.

AnnaBelle immediately raised it from the table and placed a coaster under it. "Your mother would skin you alive."

"So, what's your plans? Got a job lined up?" AnnaBelle asked.

"Yes I do," he replied. "Got any more beer?" He rose, finished the beer and as he walked toward the refrigerator, he removed the piece of paper from his pocket and laid it in AnnaBelle's lap. He picked up the two empty wine bottles on his way to the kitchen. "You two must be half lit?"

"Plenty of beer Cowboy. Help yourself." Debra chuckled. "I believe we're lit all right."

AnnaBelle was laughing along with Debra but the joy seemed to leave her as she read the email.

"Surely you're not going to consider trying to get this job?" AnnaBelle asked with fear in her voice.

"Done deal," Adam said, as he pulled on another can of beer. "Called the guy, got the job, I start as soon as I can get there. You can thank Justin."

"What's the job?" Debra asked.

"Oil field work," AnnaBelle said with disgust in her voice. "Damn dirty, greasy, dangerous job, and half way across the country." She turned to Adam. "Did you tell this guy you'd take the job? What about us?"

"Of course I told the guy I'd take the job," Adam countered. "There's no work back home right now. I can make $38.50 an hour, with a lot of overtime. If I save all my money, we can still get married when you get graduated."

He sat beside her on the couch and tried to hold her hand. She pulled it away from him.

"What about getting on with your dad, like you said?" She asked.

"They're not hiring, and no one else is either. Look, Annie, it's only for a little while, then I'll be back and we will be able to afford to buy the Meeker place, and we can have those babies and live happily ever after," he pleaded.

"Not if you're dead, you fool." AnnaBelle was angry.

"It is dangerous work," Debra agreed.

"And so is ranching, and farming, and walking down the street." He rose and took the paper from AnnaBelle's lap. "Look, my mind's made up, I'm going. I've tried every other option; I'm tired of being poor. I'm packed and ready to go to Louisiana and I can leave right now if you want me to."

AnnaBelle rose and hugged him. "Look Adam, I'm sorry, I've had a little too much to drink. Why don't you get your bags and come on in and eat something and tomorrow morning when I feel better we can talk about this, what do you say?" She was rubbing him on the back.

"That's settled, Cowboy's staying," Debra rose and walked to the kitchen. "Want a beer Annie?"

"We all need another one," Adam said, he kissed AnnaBelle and walked out the door.

"Is he leaving?" Debra asked as she returned with three beers.

"I hope not, I shouldn't have jumped on him like that. He feels bad enough already what with losing his job and all. I am such a bitch." She popped the top on the beer.

The door opened and Adam returned with two suitcases. "Daddy sure keeps you in style," he said as he looked around. "This place is fancier than your last one."

"Daddy read the papers and thought we needed to move into a better neighborhood," AnnaBelle explained. "Take your stuff down that hallway; you'll probably want to clean up a little."

He carried his bags to the bedroom, took the beer from the counter and soon the shower was running.

AnnaBelle walked back to the bedroom and changed into a baby blue nightgown. She was seated on the bed when Adam stepped from the bathroom; he was wearing only a pair of gym shorts.

"What happened to Deb?" He asked.

"She knew we wanted to be alone," AnnaBelle explained.

He sat next to her and they began to kiss.

"Look Adam, you're going to be leaving for several months and that's going to leave me here all alone." She stood. "You know how I'm going to miss you."

"And I'll be all alone and be missing you too," he explained.

"Here's the deal, I promise to let you go without making a fuss on two conditions. First, you take my cell phone and I'll get another."

"And let Daddy pay for my phone, no chance." He was irate.

"Just till you can get a paycheck, then you can pay me back, but in the mean time I worry if I can't get hold of you. Deal or not?" She was firm.

"Ok, deal. But first paycheck I'll pay you back," he acquiesced.

"Second, I want to tie you to that bed and blindfold you and have my way with you." She smiled.

24

"No problem, babe." He flung himself onto his back and spread his arms and legs wide.

"You have to promise that no matter what happens, we have a deal." She was firm.

"Ok, deal." He shut his eyes.

"Don't struggle." She kissed him, here and there. "I might get used to this." She chuckled.

Chapter 4

Adam was seated at the kitchen counter sipping a cup of morning coffee. The air was filled with the pleasant aroma of bacon and eggs and coffee.

Debra entered the kitchen, dressed for her morning run.

"Feeling OK, Cowboy?" She joked. "You guys kept me up all night, so you must not have any permanent injury."

"Everything seems to work if that's what you mean," He was able to joke about it now.

"Smells good," she walked into the kitchen and surveyed the food. "Enough for three?"

"And then some," he walked to the stove to stir the eggs. "I always cook enough for Coxey's Army."

"Good," she walked toward the door. "I'll run for twenty minutes or so, I need to watch my girlish figure." She shut the door behind her.

Minutes later, AnnaBelle walked into the room rubbing her hair with a towel. She walked to Adam and they hugged and kissed.

"I forgot how much I missed your cooking," she began to dish food onto a plate.

He joined her at the bar.

"How soon do you have to leave?" She questioned.

"The sooner the better. The sooner I get there, the sooner I can come home." He finished several large bites of food and took his plate to the sink and rinsed it.

"We don't have class till this afternoon, can't you stay at least that long?" She pleaded.

"It's supposed to rain and it's about seven hundred miles, I'd like to get there before dark." He stepped into the bedroom to get his bags.

AnnaBelle opened her phone and began to punch buttons:

To: 555-555-6731
justin
if u get adam killed i will never
forgive
you. he will have my phone so call
him at this number. when I get a
new
one ill text you.

She rose from the table and poured a cup of coffee; before she sat down she opened the phone just as Justin's response came through.

Message (1/103)
Fr: Justin
? what?

She thought a moment then began to type.

To: JUSTIN
Adam came by here last night and he is
going to go to work for some friend of
yours in Louisiana.

She waited for a reply.

Message (1/104)
Fr: Justin
Good. He needs the money have him call me and let me know when he'll get there. I will try to meet him. It's a good thing.

To: Justin
K

Adam carried his bags to the front door and set them on the floor. He returned to the counter and sat next to AnnaBelle.

"I texted Justin," she explained, "he said to call him when you know when you will be down there and he will try to meet you there."

"Really," Adam said with a smile. "It'll be good to see him. Now give me a hug."

She stood and hugged him for a long time.

"Just a minute," she ran into the bedroom and returned with a small sack.

"Here's the charger and the book," she handed the bag to him. "You promised, remember. Deb and I are on a calling plan and we can add another three numbers, unlimited text and no long distance. You can pay me back." She put the phone in a little black leather holder and worked to fit it on his belt. "Justin's number is in the contacts list. I had them put all my numbers on a travel drive so that won't be a problem."

"Now you won't have any excuse to call me, so I don't need to worry."

He took the phone from the case and looked at the new keyboard. "Never had one of these before."

"Thanks, I'll call." He kissed her. "Love you lots."

"Love you back," she replied and they walked hand in hand to the door.

Debra was just coming up the stairs as Adam was leaving. "Bye Cowboy. You be careful now, ya hear? I'd hug you but I'm all sweaty."

"Bullshit," exclaimed Adam as he crushed her in a bear hug.

"See ya soon." He carried his bags to the truck and the girls waved goodbye.

AnnaBelle was crying, she felt she would never see him again.

Chapter 5

"Stop crying," Debra demanded. "He'll be just fine. I called Mom last night and got the poop on your folks. Want to hear?" They walked to the kitchen counter and Debra filled a plate with food.

"Back in the day, your dad and his dad were like best friends. They were like joined at the hip, been friends since grade school. It started when his dad was dating your mom for a long time. This new girl moved to town and she was a hottie. Pretty soon she was a cheerleader and all the guys wanted to date her. This would be his mom. Your dad was unattached and started taking her out."

"But he was dating Mom, right?" AnnaBelle interrupted.

"Don't confuse me, it's confusing enough," Debra scolded.

"But I always thought Mom and Dad dated all the way through high school?" AnnaBelle persisted.

Debra finished her food and carried the plate to the sink.

"They dated after high school, according to Mom. I need a shower, follow me and I'll tell you the whole story as told to me last night while you two were humping like bunnies and I wasn't."

Debra walked down the hallway toward her bedroom disrobing as she talked.

"Mom said it all started back when they were in junior high." Debra finished disrobing and tossed her clothes into a clothesbasket by the bathroom door. She turned on the shower to adjust the temperature and raised her voice above the sound of the running water. AnnaBelle seated herself cross legged on the freshly made bed and listened.

"Your mom, Susan had the eye for Ken, Adam's father." Her voice rose as she washed her hair. "It was at a basketball game, Ken was sitting with his friends in the bleachers and your mother forced my mother to go down and tell Ken that she liked him."

"That your mother liked him?" AnnaBelle yelled.

"No dummy, that Susan, your mother liked him." Debra stuck her head out of the shower curtain, her hair covered with foam.

"So, what happened?" AnnaBelle finally yelled in frustration.

"So, I guess Ken thought about it for a minute, looked back to the top of the bleachers and told my mother that he was going to go up there and sit by himself and to tell Susan that she could come up there and sit with him if she wanted to." Debra turned the water off as she stepped from the shower and began to dry her hair.

"Okay, so what happened?" AnnaBelle pleaded.

"So, Ken gets up and goes to the top of the bleachers and sits down. My mom told Susan what he had said and she thought about it a minute and then got up and sat next to him. Mom said Susan told her that he didn't say a word to her just smiled and held her hand through the rest of the game. I guess it was pretty noisy but she said it was the sexiest thing that ever happened to her." Debra dressed quickly into jeans and a sweatshirt and began to comb her wet hair in front of a full length mirror, while AnnaBelle began to chew her nails.

"Stop that," Debra ordered.

AnnaBelle sat on her hands.

"So, Susan and Ken were a thing in high school, what's the big deal?" Debra walked barefoot into the living area sat on the couch and began to put on her socks.

AnnaBelle followed and sat next to her.

"It means that I never knew that Ken and Mom had a thing, all the way through high school and I never knew. I always thought Dad and Mom dated forever." She was obviously upset. "So, what happened?"

"This new girl showed up in town during their sophomore year, see; it was Adam's mom, Jerri. She was cute and sweet and got to be a cheerleader in their senior year. Now your dad, John starts to date this new girl and they begin to have a thing." Debra walked to the front door and returned with a pair of black boots with brown tops, she sat and put them on.

"So, this new girl is dating my dad, but has the hots for Adam's dad? How do we know this?" AnnaBelle asked.

"This is according to my mother, who knows all things. Just hear the rest of the story." Debra finished with the boots and took a few steps around the room to get them seated then sat back down. "John and Ken, best friends since grade school; are dating your mother Susan and Adam's mother Jerri and this went on for a while."

"There was this big graduation keg party thing going on right after the graduation ceremony, see and everybody's getting drunk."

"Mom doesn't drink," AnnaBelle interrupted.

"Maybe not now, but she did then," Debra continued. "Everybody's getting shit hammered and your mom, I guess, has had enough of little miss perfect putting the moves on her boyfriend, Ken, so I guess she lets her have one right in the mouth. So, the party's over for Jerri cause she's bleeding, my mom drags Susan out of there and that leaves Ken and John who don't give two shits about the little cat fight cause their drunk. Mom said the rumor was that Ken and John decide to go swimming and they've been drinking on this big old half gallon of bourbon and they're way too drunk to drive and besides the girls have taken the cars. The boys in their inebriated state decide to liberate Old Man Meeker's new truck and drive down to the creek to swim. Before they left they told everyone they were sick and tired of women and they stumbled off together with their bottle. An hour or so later they come driving past the party in Old Man Meeker's new truck, they are whooping and hollering and they drive that new truck straight through the barbed wire fence, up over the pond dam and sink it smack in the deepest part of Meeker's pond. Everyone sees this and runs over the fence and to the pond thinking that they both have drowned. By the time everyone gets there your dad and Ken are swimming back to the dam and climb out of the water and they are both naked. You know how rumors start; they left the party hating women and ended up naked together in a stolen pickup truck. They said they lost their clothes but people will believe what they want to." Debra walked to the kitchen. "Soda?"

"Sure," AnnaBelle accepted the bottle from Debra, "So, what happened next?"

"Remember this was all hearsay," Debra continued, "because Mom and Susan left the party when she punched Jerri. The next day after the party, Ken leaves town and goes off to join the Marines."

"What about Old Man Meeker?" asked AnnaBelle, "Didn't he press charges?"

"Don't know for sure, Mom said everyone sort of got hush-hush about the whole deal."

"So, what finally happened between Mom and Ken?" asked AnnaBelle.

"Mom said Susan was really pissed at Ken for doing such a selfish thing, to run away to the Marine Corp, which is what she thought he wanted to do, instead of staying to finish college and get married to her. Mom said most of the reason she was mad was that she felt it was like her fault for getting drunk and punching Jerri instead of staying at the party with Ken. If she hadn't, none of this would have happened.

"So, how did Ken and Jerri finally get together?" Asked AnnaBelle.

"According to Mom, when Ken finished his basic training, he came home on his first leave. This was the first time they would have spoken about any of this. Mom was over at Susan's house when Ken came to talk to Susan and she heard the whole thing. I guess Susan laid it on him pretty heavy, you know she's got a temper. Anyway, she told him what a selfish so and so he was for doing whatever he damn well pleased. I guess she hurt him pretty good about that naked truck thing. Mom said when he walked away from the house he looked like a whipped pup." Debra stood up and looked at the time on her phone. "I've got a class this afternoon and I need to do a little shopping first, want to come?"

"Sure," AnnaBelle walked down the hallway toward her bedroom, "So, how did Ken and Jerri get together?"

"Mom said after he left Susan's he must have run into Jerri. She must have treated him better than your mom because he came back on emergency leave nine months later; and that's when Adam was born." Debra saved this last until she could see the look on AnnaBelle's face.

"No shit," said AnnaBelle.

"Guess she paid your mom back for that punch in the face?" Debra held the door open for AnnaBelle.

"So, Mom got Dad on the rebound." AnnaBelle sighed. "You suppose Jerri got herself knocked up on purpose?"

"Stranger things have happened." Debra locked the door behind them.

Chapter 6

Adam drove west on 21st Street and took the Canal Route south to the turnpike. What the heck was he doing, thoughts of worry filled his head. "What if she finds somebody else? What if I fail? Why didn't I sit down and talk with dad about this first?"

He checked his gas gauge and decided he could make it to Oklahoma City before he needed to fill up. He figured the few thousand dollars he had managed to squirrel away would tide him over until his first paycheck.

Traffic was light; the four-lane road was good. People think Kansas is flat, he thought to himself. It is kind of a dreary windy place in this time of year with winter coming, but every few miles there would be a spot that let you see for miles and miles, rolling farmland, boring to most but just the type of land he yearned for.

He took out AnnaBelle's phone and thought he better get off a text to Justin. He turned on the phone to expose the keyboard and thumbed through the contact list till he found the right number, he started to peck away.

HOLY SHIT! The horn of the semi brought his attention back to the road and he swerved back into his lane. A big eighteen-wheeler had sneaked up into his blind spot and his lack of concentration caused him to drift over into the left lane. He shut the phone and threw it into the seat. Maybe a lot of people get killed this way he thought. He vowed to never again try to text and drive. It could wait till Oklahoma City.

Gas was a few pennies cheaper down here, after the fill up he sent a text.

To: JUSTIN
Just leaving Oklahoma City, expect to be in Lake Charles around 8.
Annie let me have her phone. I agreed but she will let me pay her back.
Adam

Adam purchased a one pound hot dog baked in a roll. He went through a dozen little packets of mustard and had nearly decided to get back on the road, Justin must be busy.

Message (1/105)
Fr: Justin
Best way to get there will be to come into Lake Charles from the west, I10 I believe drive over the big bridge and take the first exit. Drive around the east side of the lake and find the Old Smugglers Inn. I'll make reservations for us. Keep your phone on

---

That was a relief, old buddy Justin would be there. What a guy.

He wondered about the weather; and he was able to pick up an AM station out of Oklahoma City, it was sort of farmer friendly and they bragged about the credentials of their weather man; "Lightning Tim" Stephens. Seems that old Tim, when he was a kid, was pulling a big disc through a field for his grandpa and a thunderstorm popped up out of the blue. Being a kid, he didn't pay attention to the fact that he was the tallest thing out there amongst about a hundred acres of bare dirt. So, lightning did what lightning does and blew a big hole in the front end of that John Deere, sending young Tim flying off the tractor. Everyone agreed he was lucky that those discs didn't turn him into something like ramen noodles before the tractors momentum stopped dragging that ton of shiny steel blades. Young Tim went running back to the house in a crouched position, leaving the smoking tractor in the field. He gained a whole new respect for the power of a storm and a weather hero was born.

Adam figured they must mention that story every day. It was a good story he remembered times when he too had been on a tractor when the weather got a little rough. In flat country you can see a long ways and if you can see lightning you stand a chance of being struck and lightning doesn't care who it kills.

The drive was uneventful, nearly boring. He added a few miles to the trip by driving around Dallas and Houston but he figured it saved a lot of brain damage. As he neared the southern part of Texas he was surprised to see all of the forests. He always thought of Texas as flat. This was actually a national forest. Texans like to get places in a hurry; small roads that would be 55 mph at home were 70 mph in Texas. As he approached Louisiana he tried to tune the radio in to get some Cajun music. He picked up a lot of

Spanish speaking stations, one station that was broadcast in Hindu or something, a lot of country stations but not one Cajun station, yet. He settled for a clear country station.

The sun had set and he was driving through a small rainstorm when he came to the bridge, and what a bridge. It seemed to go up and up forever; with the rain and the lights he felt a weakness in the pit of his stomach, sort of like a carnival ride. He found the hotel with no problems and there was a message from Justin at the check-in counter that he would meet him for breakfast.

Adam searched on the contact list of the phone, settled on "Deb"

To: Deb
Deb
Hope this is the right number. can't contact Annie because I have her phone. Tell her I made it. Have her call me when she can.
Adam

He stepped out into the muggy air. No need for a coat down here, at least not yet. The hotel offered free breakfast starting at 6. He stepped back into the lobby and smelled freshly made toast. There were also bagels and waffles, coffee and juice, cereals and milk. There were even two silver hot food servers that contained biscuits and gravy and sausage and bacon and eggs and fried potatoes with peppers. He was hungry.

A text message came through.

Message (1/106)
Fr: Justin
Got in late last night. Know you're
an early riser. What time do you
want to meet for breakfast in the
lobby?

Adam typed a quick response.

To: JUSTIN
I'm in the lobby right now. Should I
wait?
Adam

He laid the phone down on the table and
waited for it to ring. As he sipped his second cup
of coffee Justin walked into the big room. Adam
had forgotten how much he looked like his sister,
strange since they were really cousins. He was
dressed in jeans and a blue polo shirt with the
word "RICHMAN" embroidered above the pocket.

Adam stood from the table and the two men
shook hands.

"I see you've already eaten, I'll be right back."
Justin rose from the table and soon returned with
a modest plate of food.

Adam stood, "want some coffee?" He asked.

"Strong and black," was the reply as Justin
began to eat.

"So, how was your drive?" Justin began when
Adam was again seated.

"Long and rainy," Adam replied, "when did
you get in?"

"Early this morning," Justin rose and returned with a cup of milk.

"Had a chance to get hold of Tom yet?" Justin asked.

"Thought I'd wait for you," Adam replied as he stretched out in the chair.

"We'll talk awhile then we'll drive on down there." Justin also got comfortable. "How's Annie?"

"She seems fine, mean as ever; she said she'd call when she gets her new phone." Adam laid the phone on the table.

"Don't worry about the money, Adam. For now Dad's paying the bill and he can afford it."

"I think your dad doesn't even like me," Adam said with a little worry in his voice.

"Of course he does, if he didn't there would be no doubt in your mind," Justin said with a smile.

"What's your job anyway?" Adam pointed to the words on Justin's shirt.

"I have sort of become a go-to guy, the sort of person that can get it done, whatever it might be. The engineering degree sort of let me into the club and I like to travel and there is plenty of that."

"You think I'll be hired?" Adam asked with worry in his voice.

"You're hired already, sport. Tom and I go way back, well as far back as when I started here. He and I worked a lot of hours together as a matter of fact; he was responsible for my getting bumped up in management.

"Right now, oil is king. This company spends millions every day and good dependable help is hard to find. You're just what we're looking for. So, is your room to your liking?"

"Great, king-size bed, couch and table, sort of a kitchen area with a sink, microwave and refrigerator; I can look out the window and see the lake." Adam was enthusiastic.

"You can stay here till you can find a better place; I put it on my expense account. I can't say for sure, but you'll probably need to go through about two weeks of training before you start the real work. It's a pain in the neck but necessary. You get paid to sit in a chair."

"Can you give me an idea of what kind of training?" Adam asked.

"Asbestos, and Lead and Hazmat and safety, you'll learn about confined spaces and hazardous locations, mostly safety stuff," Justin replied.

"Is it dangerous? I know Annie was worried. Should I be?" Adam was serious.

Justin leaned back in the chair and crossed his hands on his chest and began to remember.

"A refinery is the nastiest most miserable place I have ever been in my life. It is composed of miles and miles of piping and vessels. Every pipe has something in it that will kill you, from six hundred pound steam to 800 degree oil. They try to fix the steam leaks but they are everywhere, the fumes are always present, the smell of tar and sulfur and other nasty things. They taught me that when you are in a refinery; always know which way the wind is blowing. There is a lot of hydrogen sulfide gas, H_2S. It is heavier than air, the first breath you take smells like rotten eggs and it kills your sense of smell. You won't smell the second breath because your sense of smell is gone and that breath will drop you to the ground. Now, your head is on the ground where the gas is and the third breath will kill you. So, if you smell rotten eggs, hold your breath and run as fast as you can cross wind and hopefully by the time you need to breathe again you will be out of the release."

"A steam leak can be strong enough to cut you in half. And if you're in a somewhat confined space, a steam leak will take all the oxygen and you will never make it out. Sailors on ships with steam leaks hold a broom in front of them and the invisible leak will shred the broom first. Some of the chemicals in the refinery burn with intense heat and produce no flame. You could walk into fire and not know it until you were burned up.

"One of the units produces phenol, which is the substance that they put in the throat spray bottles to stop your sore throat, this is a diluted form. If you get pure phenol on your skin, the amount it takes to cover a two square inch spot will kill you."

"Whenever you go into a refinery, they will make you wear a flame retardant coverall made from a fabric called Nomex. Nomex burns and turns to ash when there's fire and will no longer burn. One problem with these is that they are real bad about building up a static electric charge. We had a problem one time where some guys were climbing up to the top of the Cat unit and they would always get shocked at the top. I'm talking knock your dick in the dirt shocked. We thought it was a 277 line gone to ground or something, maybe 480 as bad as they were reporting the shock. Come to find out there was a steam leak and as they walked up the flight of stairs they would pass through the steam. The coveralls would build up this static charge and when they would get to the top they would touch a grounded surface and the static electric shock would hit them."

"I didn't think static electricity could hurt you," Adam said.

Justin explained, "Static is one of the biggest problems in the refining industry. Any fluid in motion creates a static charge. Any time fluid is transferred from one vessel to another there is a bonding wire that will keep the containers at the same potential. Static is so bad that even when they are fighting fires, the fire hoses have bonding wires on them. Many people have been burned when they were filling little lawn mower gas cans in the back of pickup trucks. If the pickup has a liner that is nonconductive, there can be a static charge built up in the can and a static spark can then ignite the gas. Static is a big deal, they will teach you about that."

"Have you ever been in a fire in a refinery?" Adam asked.

"Not me, but a friend of mine was, before we worked together. He and I were eating lunch together one day and I smelled hydrocarbon. I asked him if he did but he remembered that I have a pretty good nose for that sort of thing. We were in an office at the north end of the refinery, having a break from some training or whatever, and I looked out the door back toward the refinery. This office was probably a quarter of a mile north of the crude unit. First thing I saw was a bunch of people running toward us, away from the refinery. Behind them was a great billowing cloud of dark grey smoke. Now these people were really running. I asked John to have a look and he turned white as a sheet. 'Come on,' he screamed and beckoned for me to follow him. We ran to his truck and just as he was ready to start it a manager from the refinery ran up to his window and told him to not start the truck. He said they didn't know what that cloud was made of but that the starting of the truck might set it off. John was scared to death, because he had been in a refinery fire before. Me, I was too dumb to be scared."

"What happened?" Adam interrupted.

"We coveyed up like a bunch of quail in the office, all of us just waiting to meet our maker when the cloud exploded. Luckily it was noncombustible exchange oil and after a couple of hours they called the all clear. Course it could have gone the other way. When heavy materials flow through any kind of pipe, it wears the pipe thin. Pretty soon the pipe is so thin that it is a hazard and the refinery has what is called a turnaround. That is where all the units are brought back up to specs. It requires a lot of work and it is my belief that you will be involved in a partial turnaround so you should get as much overtime as your little body can stand." Justin smiled and patted Adam on the shoulder.

"Wahoo!" Adam laughed, "The sooner I can get done here and save enough money I can get back home and marry Annie. I'm already worried enough, but is there anything else I should keep in mind?"

Justin thought for a minute, "we had a guy one time that was using a spray nozzle from an air compressor to blow some filings from his arm and he had a cut on his arm and he inflated all the skin off his arm, like to killed him. I was told about another incident; they were doing some re-piping on one of the units and got the pipes crossed up and connected one of the feed lines to a water fountain. One of the operators went to the water fountain to get a drink and gulped down about three good swallows of goo before he knew what he was doing. They took him to the hospital, brought his family in, and he died. Another guy was in a hurry, too big of a hurry to hook up the angle worm bleeder cleaner and as has happened many times before he opened the valve and when it failed to flow he just took a welding rod and jammed it up into the valve. Well, the vessel was under pressure and the boiling oil flowed out on his arm. I was told that the skin on his arm and hand just flowed off onto the ground. Bad deal."

There are large aeration ponds that look like a pond but they are nasty and brown and have big ten horse aeration motors in them. The product is full of air bubbles and if you fall in, you sink to the bottom. This would not be my preferred way to go.

"I guess just remember that there is nothing good about oil. A refinery looks like what you would imagine Dante's inferno to look like. Miles and miles of pipe, steam leaks and dripping oil everywhere, everything covered with black goo. The ground has fumes rising from it and every

46

once in a while, something goes wrong and the operator needs to divert the flow to the flare. The flare is a sort of last resort, if you see that flame really burning it means something went wrong and the product is being burned instead of being sold. Those big storage tanks, the bottoms of many of them are rusted out and the product is leaching into the ground.

"A lot of what happens in a refinery is done on the basis of seniority. The older guys get the best deals like whatever vacations they want and whatever jobs they can bid into. Everyone supports this idea because that way they know that if they stick around one day they too will get to cut a fat hog. Since you are the new guy on the block, you will be getting all the shit jobs. You will be expected to do all the work while older guys often sort of don't get much done. Some of these operators, all they have to do is to watch gauges and respond to alarms sort of sit around with nothing to do. It can be quite boring and sometimes they fall asleep due to boredom and stuff doesn't get handled fast enough. There have been times when the operator of a unit leaves at the end of his shift without waiting to be relieved and the replacement operator is sick or late and wires get crossed and barrel after barrel of product get run through with no one at the controls. So, be careful out there and don't let them kill you."

"We are dealing with so much product that sometimes stuff gets missed. One time by accident, we lost 40,000 barrels of unleaded between one refinery and another. To this day we have no idea where it went. There are miles and miles of pipelines that crisscross this country. When we get out there I will show you a map and it looks more concentrated than a road map. There are pipes everywhere except in the mountains. These are not little pipes but really big pipes. Airplanes fly periodically along the route and report when there is a leak. This doesn't work so well for tar sands though, when tar sands leak they go down into the water table; not up where a leak can be detected."

"I know I can't stay with this company much longer, but I'm gaining experience. There are some companies out there that don't put the bottom line ahead of everything else. When I find the right one, I'm out of here." He complained.

"Sorry to hear about that, Justin. Maybe I shouldn't take the job?" Adam asked.

"Nonsense, this is good as any, Tom won't let them get you killed. You just take the money and run and don't risk your life for nobody, it's not worth it for a couple of barrels of oil. And, if I hear of anything that I think you should know about I'll let you know. Let's go see Tom and get you started." Justin threw a five dollar bill on the table and led the way out.

Chapter 7

Justin led the way into the parking lot and found the rental car. They drove back north around the little lake and turned west on I10.

"Are you and Annie still planning to tie the knot?" Justin asked as he settled in his seat. He plugged a GPS device into the power outlet and pushed a few buttons as he laid the device on the dash.

"We still plan on a wedding after she graduates. It might be as soon as the end of the next semester if she can catch a couple of classes in the intersession." Adam explained. "Those are short courses they give in between the full sessions."

"You still plan to get back into the farming game? I know we used to talk about it all the time." Justin asked.

"Still the plan, I had hoped to finish school and save a little money first but the economy sort of stopped those plans. I looked everywhere for work with no luck, finally I had to move back in with Dad and Mom to save money and I lost all my little toys like my computer and cell phone. Being poor is a bitch."

"This little gig should go a long way toward helping your money problems," Tom said, "you can probably start right away and he can authorize a hiring bonus that would mean some cash up front to help till your first check comes in." Justin was being really helpful.

"Are you sure it's alright? I didn't expect anything like that." He seemed worried.

"We do it all the time, no big deal, remember this company deals in millions and millions of dollars. I can spend upwards of 50 thousand without anyone batting an eye." Justin smiled.

"See this nasty looking place on the left?" Justin pointed. "This is the plant that Tom manages." Adam craned his neck to look past Justin. Smoke stacks billowed black smoke into the air.

They pulled up to the guard shack at the entrance to the refinery. A guard compared their driver's licenses with a list of names on a clipboard and gave them back. The guard returned to the shack and stood in the doorway speaking on the phone. A few moments later the yellow and black striped gate rose into the air and the guard saluted. A large white sign with black letters and a black arrow directed visitors to the office area. Justin looked down the long paved road that led into the refinery. There were several red brick buildings with tin roofs and other larger buildings made of steel. Several blocks in the distance were the large vessels and piping that comprised the refinery. As they turned and parked in front of a building he could see in the distance many large white storage containers with earthen dams built around them.

They entered the office area and were standing in front of the receptionist desk when a large gray headed man of perhaps fifty years; with a reddish beard approached from a hallway.

"Justin." The man exclaimed. "Damned good to see you boy, I hear you're doing quite well for yourself." He strode quickly toward Justin and they shook hands for a long time with both men smiling. He turned to look at Adam. "The son of a bitch learned everything he knows from me." He winked.

"Adam? I'm Tom." The older man held out his hand. His hand was massive and the grip firm. Adam wished he had gotten a little better grip.

"Good to meet you sir." Adam stammered.

"Come on back to the office." Tom led the way. He sat down behind a large desk and waved his hand toward a couple of chairs. "Sit, Sit."

"I've got a CQTI meeting I really need to go to in about five minutes. I'll be done around 11:30 and we can have lunch and catch up on old times and new ones. That sound alright?" He picked up the phone and spoke for a minute.

"Was everything like we agreed?" Justin asked.

"Just like we talked." Tom passed a manila envelope onto the desk in front of Adam. "There's a check in there and some papers to fill out, Adam, do you have a place to stay for a while?"

Adam nodded.

"Good, looking forward to working with you." He stood and again shook both men's hands. This time Adam got a more firm grip, looked Tom in the eye and he trusted the man.

A young man in his early thirties stepped into the room; he was wearing a white lab coat and a white hard hat. "I'm Bill Whitney, Tom said to help you any way I can."

"Good," said Justin. "We need some Nomax and PPE and a ride out to the Cat Unit.

"No problem," said Bill, he left for a moment and returned with coveralls, hardhats and safety glasses. "I'll be just outside this door. I'll need to get a cart; it'll take five minutes or so."

When the man had left, Adam asked a question. "Justin, what are CQTI and Nomax and PPE?"

"Nomax is fire retardant coveralls, PPE is personal protective equipment, like gloves and safety glasses and steel-toed shoes etc. CQTI means Continuous Quality Total Involvement; it's a term used here to improve quality."

They donned their PPE and stepped out the doorway into the waiting golf cart. They were driven through the maze of tanks and vessels and piping and catwalks and steam lines that were the refinery. The air was filled with new smells, most of them bad. It was just like Justin had described it, only he had failed to mention the people that kept the place running. They all wore hard hats that were covered with decals from all the manufacturers that supplied material for the plant. Most were wearing gloves and coveralls and almost all of them were covered with black oil in one form or another. The ground was smoking, the pipes were everywhere steaming, and the smells varied from bad to worse as they drove through the various units. They stopped in front of a massive array of steel piping and Bill led the way through the piping to a little platform. There was a massive belt perhaps two feet wide that passed through circular holes in the floor. The belt passed through every floor and onto the top deck over a big pulley and then returned to another pulley on the first floor. It had little steps for the feet and little hand holds four feet above the feet steps. There was a rope beside the belt that caused it to start and stop.

Bill pulled the cord and as the feet pad approached, he stepped onto it and took the other in his hands. He held his body close to the belt and passed through the floor. Justin was next, and then it was Adams turn. He had never seen anything like this before. He stepped onto the foot pad and grabbed the hand hold. It was like a little carnival ride as he passed through one floor after another until there was a sign that told him the top floor was coming, he looked up and Justin was just stepping off of the belt. He stepped lightly off the belt and Justin pointed toward the rope. Adam pulled the rope in the direction that the belt was turning and the belt quit moving. Bill led the way to the east side of the unit. It was very high in the air and there was a good view in all directions.

"I want to show you why I came here," Justin explained. "Look out this way, see the green trees? Pretty and green, right?"

Adam agreed that it was indeed pretty.

Justin led the way to the south side of the unit and they agreed that everything looked green and lush. They did the same on the west side of the unit.

Finally, Justin led the way to the north side of the unit. "Look out that direction, do you see anything unusual?"

Adam looked to the north, and sure enough, there was a path of brown foliage, as wide as the refinery and as far as the eye could see.

"Think we had a release?" Justin chuckled. "It's my job to convince all the nice locals that even though all their trees look dead, that this stuff, whatever it turns out to be, couldn't possibly harm them."

Justin turned to Bill, "Have they figured out exactly what did this?"

"Not yet sir, they think they have it narrowed down, but that's what the CQTI meeting is for."

"Very well," Justin turned to Adam. "Stuff like this happens all the time. We'll grease a few wheels, donate to a few charities, pay a few people and it will all go away. So far it always has."

"Could this have killed someone?" Adam asked.

"What do you think?" Justin looked at Bill.

"I moved my family fifty miles away," he apologized "Does that help answer your question?"

"Let's get back to the office, I've seen enough." Justin led the way back.

"Justin, Tom asked me to introduce Adam to Martha Wilkerson; she's in charge of training.

She'll take charge of his orientation. There a lot of films to watch and so forth." Bill said.

"That's good, when we get back, you can go see Martha and I'll go to the CQTI meeting." Justin followed Bill onto the belt.

Adam was sitting in Martha's office when the phone in his pocket rang. He quickly pulled it from its case and, not knowing which button to push, simply turned it off.

"Thank you," Ms. Wilkerson said. She finished her presentation and handed a file folder to Adam. "I know there is a lot here to digest, but training is a really big part of this whole process. You'll be two weeks in training before you will be allowed to enter the refinery. That's just the way it is. It's my understanding that you and Tom are friends and he has asked me to expedite this process, but there is only so much I can do. I'm sure you understand. We are looking forward to having you with us Mr. Thomas."

She rose and held out her hand. He grasped it gently and shook it. He was not used to shaking women's hands, except in church, but figured she wouldn't expect a good hearty handshake.

He stepped into the hallway and walked toward Tom's office. It was empty, so he stepped outside and turned on the phone. He saw that there was one missed call and a text message.

Message (1/106)
Adam
Got my new phone. Hope you're ok.
We have class today all afternoon.
LUL.
Annie

He typed:

To: 555-555-4203
Sorry I missed your call, I was in a
meeting with the training lady, I'm
with Justin. I'm fine. Call me when
you get out of class. Love you.
Adam

When he was done, he stepped back into the building. He didn't feel comfortable sitting in Tom's office alone, so he went back into the room with the receptionist, found a chair and began to fill out some of the paperwork he had been given.

Justin came into the room from the other hallway; he was in a hurry. "Come on, let's get out of here." He walked quickly past Adam and stormed out the door.

"What's wrong?" Adam asked as he hurried to the car.

"Those bastards couldn't figure their way out of a one hole outhouse."

Justin got into the car and unlocked the door for Adam.

"What about Tom?" Adam asked.

"He'll be in meetings the rest of the day and said we could get together this evening. Damn I'm pissed. It's the same everywhere; everybody tries to cover their own ass; it's always somebody else's fault. People make mistakes. If they would just own up to them, we could get on with business. I need to come up with an explanation of what happened and they don't know. How these dimwits keep their jobs is beyond me. Tom said you need to be here at six in the morning and to come to his office and he'll get you started." Justin drove quickly out of the plant.

"What kind of work will I be doing?" Adam asked.

"He said he's got openings in both the welding shop and the electric shop; sounds like you can take your pick or work two shifts and do both if you can take it." Justin smiled. He knew that Adam could easily handle two shifts for a short while.

"No problem." Adam thought he just might make that wedding date after all.

Chapter 8

AnnaBelle and Debra were returning home from their last class and AnnaBelle was swearing at the phone. "Stupid phone, why won't it make the stupid call?"

"Your phone is from up here, maybe your carrier doesn't get good reception down there. Try texting," suggested Debra, as she turned east on 21st street.

AnnaBelle typed out a message:

To: Adam
TRIED TO CALL stupid phone won't go through
If this text does I'm out of class now.
LUL
annie

Adam sent one in return:

Message (1/1)
Fr: 555-555-1963
Had interview..start tomorrow..in a meeting..justin says hi...talk to you this evening.
Love.
Adam

She slammed the phone shut. "Meeting my dying ass. He's drinking with my brother and they're probably shit faced drunk already."

"Is that all he said?" Deb asked, as she turned a corner on nearly two wheels. She drove entirely too fast, tailgated people, never came to a complete stop at stop signs. That's why AnnaBelle liked to drive so much; Deb scared her.

"What he said was, that he got the job, that he starts tomorrow and that he's in a meeting. I don't believe that for one minute. If Justin said hi, they both have a cold beer in their hand and one of them is patting some waitress's ass." She laughed. "But I love them both."

"Sounds like it." Deb said in disbelief. "It would be a bitch if they didn't like each other."

"Enough of them; I've got a History test tomorrow. Let's get some ice cream on the way home." AnnaBelle trusted Adam completely. "The sooner he gets to work, the sooner we can get married and start raising young 'uns."

Chapter 9

Edwin Meeker drove slowly past the old house in his new black pickup. He drove slowly, so that the brown gravel wouldn't mar the finish on the new paint. From the time he was old enough to drive, he traded trucks every year.

Might as well sell the place, he thought to himself, *the way it's beginning to fall apart, it would only be worth less.*

He owned several pieces of property just like this one and they were all in a state of disrepair. He saw no sense in putting hard earned money into buildings that ought to be torn down anyway. That Wichita Realtor said a corporation out of Texas was buying up property in Kansas for hunting and he really didn't give a damn who bought it.

He was the kind of man who left a dime tip at the restaurant and thought it was too damn much. He drove slowly up to the crest of the hill and looked over John Williams' property. He remembered John's father; they used to be classmates years before. He always sort of thought John would make him an offer. Never did. Good thing too, he thought. He would have doubled the price.

He remembered that time, years before, when John and that friend of his had stolen his truck and driven it into the pond. Boy had he raised hell about that, like it was some collector's item or something. Truth be told, he had been glad to get rid of the old thing and get another. John's dad had paid the insurance deductible and then taken it out of John's hide. Served the boy right. Spare the rod and spoil the child, now that was a good motto. He thought he just might drive past that property over on Burton road. It wasn't worth much for farming, only pasture and there was a lot of timber and a creek. Maybe that Texas outfit might want it too.

Chapter 10

Jerri Thomas put the finishing touches on the flower arrangement at the kitchen counter, wiped the bottom of the vase carefully, and carried it to the center of the new end table. She stood back and admired her work. The yellow flowers worked well with the new couch and loveseat; they would sell quickly. She heard the back door slam and knew that Ken was home. The slamming door meant that he was upset about something, so she'd better defuse the issue, whatever it might be. She hurried toward the kitchen.

Ken was already in the shower, so she spoke through the door.

"What's the matter hon?"

"Have you heard from that ungrateful son of ours? It's been three days and we don't know if he's alive or dead. I'm ready to call out the Mounties."

"Not a word so far, but he's alright or we would have heard otherwise." She yelled over the sound of running water. "I'll go set the table."

Ken liked to eat as soon as he got home after work.

Jerri knew that the reason Ken was in a bad mood was that he was worried. She was worried too, but it wouldn't help Ken any if she showed it. Adam was a smart kid and Ken was a good teacher. This mother knew that her boy would be just fine, but to Ken he would always be that little kid.

He came to the table in good jeans and a dress shirt. She smelled that cologne he always wore when he felt like he was dressing up.

"Going out?" She asked, knowing the answer. He would not have bothered to wash if he planned on doing chores.

"Union Meeting tonight. Did you feel that earthquake around two o'clock this afternoon?"

He noticed as she nodded her head that she hadn't.

"This is Kansas; we are not supposed to have earthquakes in Kansas. There are only a few spots in the state where we ever paid attention to the possibility of earthquakes. We have tons of wire hanging on poles out there in the wind and we don't need earthquakes shaking our substations and loosening our poles. We have enough to worry about with the weather; we don't need earthquakes. Those fracking guys are tearing this country up; the roads, the bridges, the buildings are all shaking apart. There's a crack in that new building out there that wasn't there yesterday that I could see daylight through. It's just not right that a few greedy companies can tear up the whole country so they can make a profit. We hope to do something about it."

"Good meatloaf." He ate heartily.

Jerri struggled with cooking and Ken never failed to comment one way or another. She knew she could never match Susan's cooking. He never mentioned it and she had long since quit trying.

"Why don't I try to call AnnaBelle? You know he's been in touch with her." Jerri asked.

"Those two are joined at the hip. Don't get me wrong, I like the girl a lot, but you think the boy would at least have the common courtesy to let us know if he was alive or dead." He started to rise to refill his water glass, but Jerri rose first and took the glass from his hand.

"Thanks," He said, as he continued to eat. "The only thing I've got against that girl is her worthless father."

Ken accepted the glass from her.

"You two were best friends for years, Ken, why can't you just kiss and make up? It's stupid for two grown men to hold a grudge for all these years. You better think about it, because when those kids get married there will be the grandkids to think about and we won't need the tension at all the family gatherings." She was firm on this issue, as she had been many times before. She never mentioned that there was a part of her that often wondered what it might have been like if she had stayed with John.

"He owes me an apology and I'll be damned if I make the first move." Ken grumbled. "He was driving that damn truck, not me."

"And how do you know that, you were both so drunk you both admit you couldn't remember what happened the next morning. You could have both been killed. Now, figure out a way to let bygones be bygones. It's been over twenty years."

He stood from the table and placed his dishes in the sink. "Good food, thanks."

"Don't forget to brush your teeth." She ordered.

"Yes, Mother." He replied as he hurried back down the hallway.

As he passed out the back door, he commented. "If you get ahold of the little bastard, see if he needs any money or anything. And tell him to be careful." The door slammed.

Jerri smiled to herself. Boys were supposed to have their moms wrapped around their little fingers, not their fathers. She thought for a moment, she didn't really like that word, "bastard." She would never admit to Ken that she had gotten pregnant more or less on purpose. He thought it was an accident. After he joined the Marines in such a hurry, she was afraid she might never see him again and figured it was the best way to seal the deal. When Ken came home from basic training, she knew it was the right time of the month for her. Maybe she should have taken precautions then, but she was young and stupid and now they wouldn't trade Adam for the world. Of course he arraigned for leave, hurried home and did the right thing. She made him just as happy as Susan would have. Of course she did. He was doing just as well, financially, as he would have if he had gone to that stupid college. Still, she thought, if she had stayed with John, she would be buying new furniture instead of trying to sell it.

She tried to call AnnaBelle's cell phone and there was no answer. He'd be alright, he was a big boy.

The food didn't look good right now, so she decided to eat later, after she dusted the front room, again.

Chapter 11

AnnaBelle was glad this day was over; she had two term papers due in one week, but she had gotten them done. She knew Debra was home because the cat was out. She left it out and decided she needed to remind Debra to keep the door locked, because it was the smart thing to do. Debra was at the table with her head in the laptop, there was a large glass of iced tea beside her.

"Is this sweet tea or regular?" AnnaBelle took an orange pitcher from the refrigerator and raised it in the air over the counter so that Debra could see it. "What's that in the oven?"

"Today, answers are one dollar each." Debra said. "Yes, that is sweet tea, and the smell is from chicken pot pies that will be ready in about 25 minutes. That will be two dollars you owe me; cash only, no checks."

AnnaBelle poured a glass of tea and set the container back into the refrigerator; then went to the sink and washed her hands.

"We really take this water for granted you know." She said as she turned the water on and off and on. "We talked about this just today in class. Many places in the world don't have any clean water and we have all this. What will happen someday, if the only clean water we have is what we have to pay a lot for? No more showers, no more long hot baths and no more swimming pools. You suppose it's true there are people who want to destroy our clean water, so they can make a profit by selling us water?"

"You sounded just like your brother, just then." Debra put her nose back in the laptop. "You're a lucky girl AnnaBelle."

Chapter 12

Tom raised his hand for the cute little bleach blond waitress. She saw the gesture and prepared to bring another round.

"Drink up boys, Richman Oil can afford it." He took the half smoked cigar from the ash tray and tried to draw smoke, but failed. He swore to himself and dug in his pocket for a lighter to fire up the end. A great cloud of smoke enveloped the table. Both Adam and Justin sort of leaned away from the table to avoid the aromatic smoke.

"Think you can handle the job?" Tom addressed Adam as he drained the last of his glass of beer.

"Yes sir, I do," Adam said.

"If you're half the man Justin is, you'll have no problems." Tom smiled toward Justin who raised his glass toward Tom, then drained it as well.

They were seated in the lounge attached to the hotel where Justin and Adam were staying. The bar could seat over a hundred, but in the late afternoon, the three men were the only patrons. The east wall of the bar was comprised of large glass panes that faced the lake. Ducks and geese were floating and landing on the lake that could be seen across the four-lane highway. Traffic was brisk.

"How did the meeting go?" Adam asked. "If it's any of my damn business."

"Hell, you're one of us now boy, of course it's your business. Wait till you get that fat production bonus check at the end of the quarter and you'll damn sure know that everything in this company is you're business." Tom pushed his empty glasses in the direction of the waitress as she approached the table with a tray. She set a tall glass of beer in front of each man and then followed that with small shot glasses filled with whiskey.

"Here Darcy," Tom addressed the little blond. He held up a five dollar bill folded lengthwise. Her hands were filled with empty glasses so she leaned closer to Tom who lovingly placed the bill in the top of her blouse between her ample bosoms.

"Thanks Darlin'." Darcy smiled and winked at Tom.

"Now there's why we fight wars." Tom said in a too loud voice, as he watched the girl walk back to the bar.

Adam wasn't used to this type of garish behavior, but then again he didn't spend much time in bars, nor did he spend much time with oil field workers. Tom seemed to be getting a kick out of this and so did the girl. No harm, no foul.

This was the second round of boilermakers they'd had since the men sat down. Adam was feeling hungry, but the beer was cold.

Tom raised the little shot glass in a salute, "confusion to the enemy." He toasted, he finished the shot glass of whiskey in one gulp then chased it with about half the glass of beer. Justin and Adam drank the toast.

Adam began to cough from the whiskey and could barely swallow the beer.

"Take a deep breath and hold it before you drink the whiskey boy; it'll keep you from drowning in your beer."

Tom thought that was funny and laughed so hard he nearly choked. Justin too found humor in the statement.

"About that bonus, Adam." Justin explained. "The bonus system is a lot of what is wrong with this company. It makes everyone from the top down sort of profit motivated. There a lot of dangerous things going on in the oil industry and if a man's mind is too much on production, he may let safety concerns slide."

"Damn right, Mr. Safety Man." Tom scolded. "You're turning into a whining suit, Justin. What you need is to get out of those clean clothes and get some oil under those fingernails." Tom presented his hands and they were stained with oil that looked like it would never come off.

"Keep your ears open, Tom. I'm looking to jump ship," Justin confided.

"Sure thing buddy, you keep yours open too. I'd like to get on one of those deep water rigs; fourteen days on, and fourteen days off. Some of those rigs have bars and bowling alleys and movie theatres. When you're going home after your shift, you make out a grocery list; whatever you want to eat when you return. I'll have a two inch thick T-bone steak every night. Two weeks off will give me time to fly up to Missouri and see my family before they all die off. This job's a good one, but it's the same old thing day after day;

we're always looking for the next better deal." He turned and smiled toward Adam as he said this.

"But, I thought you had the perfect job?" Adam asked Justin.

"Well, there is no doubting that this is the dream job for me. Good pay, travel, lots of responsibility, but I hadn't met the people that I work for until a couple of weeks ago. The bloom sort of faded from the rose after that." He sipped his beer.

"What happened?" Adam asked.

"I finally got a chance to meet the man that I ultimately work for. There was a meeting in Dallas a couple of weeks ago and I was invited as part of a team to meet with the great man himself, William Howard Bennett, Senior Vice President of Operations for Richman Oil. There were three of us that went to the meeting and it was held in his private office. Opulent beyond description; this guy must make a hundred million a year or so. His office was bigger than most businesses and the four of us were seated at a table that would hold thirty. There were leather reclining chairs and a secretary that brought us coffee and rolls and whatever else we might want. Mr. Bennett was a small man, sort of strange, but real smart. The meeting went quite well and the three of us were pleased that the great man was happy with our work. He sort of finished up the meeting and then gave us a little pep talk that didn't sit well with me. He made no bones about the fact that this was a business and as such, our goal was profit; to hell with everything else. It was all about the bottom line. Now, you know that I majored in engineering and minored in environmental studies. I took this job to learn about the oil industry and for the longest time, I felt that in their hearts, they wanted to do the right things with the environment. I found out differently." He sipped his beer.

"Don't confuse the issue boys." Tom warned. "We always talk about keeping the earth green in public, but the cold hard truth is that we get paid to bring the black stuff out of the ground and make it so it will burn in your Hummer.

Justin continued, "So, to prove his point, Bennett walked back into his office and, from a marble pedestal, he brought to the table a clear acrylic object with something inside. And he explained about how he picked up a nickname that he was proud of. It seems that several years ago one of our rigs had a minor blowout and fouled some beaches in a South American country. At that time, he wasn't the big man that he is today, so the company sent him to appease the natives, so to speak. As he was walking along the beach, one of the natives threw something at him and it fell to his feet. He looked down at it and it was something covered in black goo. He kicked it away with his shoe, and the man that had thrown it yelled at him, "Swart hart!" The goo ruined a thousand dollar pair of shoes.

He went on to his meetings and forgot the event until he had been back for a couple of weeks. One of the people that worked for him brought him a package and inside was this acrylic trophy thing. The object inside this acrylic trophy was this dead seabird. One of his staff had taken the bird, sort of opened it up, so you could see that it was a bird, and had the thing encased in a clear acrylic trophy. The man that had been screaming at him was screaming the words, "swart hart." That translates to "Black Heart." The acrylic encased bird had a brass plaque at the bottom with the words "BLACK HEART" written in bold letters. He passed the bird around for us to see, he was actually proud of the whole deal and told us that he didn't mind if his friends, and we three were now his friends, called him Black Heart, as long as no one else was listening. It was sort of a secret password or something.

The damn pair of shoes he ruined meant more to him than this dead bird. When the poor pathetic bird was passed to me, I wanted to throw it through the window and damn near threw up." Justin paused and finished his beer. "Old Black Heart Bennett, proud member of every environmental organization there is. Let's eat."

Tom raised his glass in the direction of Darcy. The room was beginning to fill up and finally the girl brought the tray.

"Can we order?" asked Justin.

"I'll get menus." The girl began to leave.

"I know what I want," Tom held his hands wide. "I want the biggest steak you've got, rare, with a baked potato."

"Word of advice," Justin whispered to Adam. "Don't order steak, you'll be disappointed. Get seafood."

Chapter 13

Justin left early in the next morning and Adam showed up for work early, beginning one of the most difficult periods of his working life.

Message (1 / 106)
Fr: 555-555-4203
Adam
Passed all my classes, finals are
over are you
coming home ever? I know you work
two shifts
but can't you call me?
Annie

Message (1 / 1)
Fr: 555-555-1963
Annie
Glad you passed, one more
semester, right?
Toms got me working double shifts.
Theres a job
trailer at the refinery that I'm
staying in. there are
no bars on the phone so it won't
work. Somehow
these texts get thru. Ill be here till
spring. Im

---

covered in oil and sleep as soon as
my head hits
the pillow. Dont worry about me. Ill
be in touch. Love.
adam

Message (1/106)
Fr: 555-555-4203
Adam
We all miss you here. You need to
stop working so hard.
You need to come home. LUL

Chapter 14

Richards stepped out of Bennett's office and closed the door quietly. He was carrying a large black briefcase. He stopped for a moment in his cubical to shut off the computer and as he did so, he raised his head over the half wall.

Jenny Houston was nearly the same age as Richards; they had built up a friendly working relationship in the years they occupied adjoining cubicles. "Hi James, what's up?"

"Can you meet me in the cafeteria? I'll be in the booth over in the corner, the one the camera can't see." He began to move toward the elevator without waiting for an answer.

"Sure." She spoke in a quiet tone in the direction of the retreating Richards. "I'll just stop right here." She began to save her work and gather her bag.

Richards was seated in the booth with the black briefcase on the table in front of him. He watched as the girl approached. He felt she was the prettiest girl in the building and certainly one of the sweetest. Too bad she was already taken. He wasn't the kind of guy to put the moves on a married woman. He raised his hand and stood as she approached.

"Sit here, I'll get us a soda. Do you want something to eat?" He stood back so she could sit in the booth. She laid her hands on the table on either side of the briefcase and looked up with a question in her eye. "Iced tea is good for me."

"While I'm gone, you might look in that briefcase. Don't let anyone see you looking though." He hurried off toward the vending machines.

She looked in all directions and wasn't surprised that the room was nearly empty; it was a good half hour before break. The prebreak people would be sliding in any minute though. When she was satisfied that there was no one looking she opened the case. She gasped and shut the lid and snapped the latches in place.

Richards set the two glasses of ice and two glass jars of tea on the table; he had a smile on his face. "What do you think?"

"This briefcase is full of hundred dollar bills." She exclaimed. "How much is it?"

"I thought you might get a kick out if it; and I have no idea how much is in there." He removed the case from the table and set it next to him on the seat.

"What's it for?" She asked as she began to sip her tea.

"Bennett calls this the, 'oil that greases the wheels of legislation'; it's bribe money but don't let anyone hear you call it that."

"What shall I call it?" She asked.

"Just say it's a campaign contribution."

"Who's it for?"

"That is entirely up to the lobbyists." He patted the case. "Notice this zipper pocket in the front?"

"That is kind cute, what's that for?"

"Here's my take on the whole situation. I've been tasked with delivering this briefcase to our lobby people. I assume the rest and I may be wrong.'

"Kansas has a legislature that only sits for a couple of months, this gives the farmer legislators a chance to get on back to the farm and harvest those beans. Once the session opens the senators and representatives scurry around trying to get reelected and they only have a couple of months to do it. They like their jobs and in order to get reelected they need to have more yard signs than that guy down the road. And they only have one thing to sell, their vote. So, rich guys like Bennett do what rich guys do, they trade votes for yard signs."

"While the legislature is in session these guys are all running around like chickens going to committee meetings, shaking hands, and getting reelected. As the session comes to a close they realize it's time to go and they haven't gotten a blessed thing done. There will be a lot of disagreement between the house and the senate; a lot of finger pointing, etc. Finally it will come down to the nut cutting. These guys are at their wits end as to what to do. Enter our lobby guys with this suitcase. Inside the zipper pocket will be a juicy piece of legislation that looks friendly. Our legislator will be given half a dozen reasons why this is vital and he will gladly put it on the pile with the others. Ever tried to read a piece of legislation? It is about half numbers, numbers that refer back to other legislation; it would take a good man a week just to decipher it. When it's gone into overtime everybody's so tired they are willing to vote on anything just to be able to go home. They get their yard signs and Bennett gets his fracking and his pipeline and his oil wells. There were several more just like this one heading different directions.

"Don't get mugged." Jenny warned as she headed back to the cubicle. She squeezed Richard's shoulder as she passed. He smelled good. She wondered why he never asked her out.

Chapter 15

AnnaBelle threw the little tab into the trash; she had waited four minutes, but only one line was showing. What a relief; she was a week late with her period, but she wasn't pregnant. Must be something else. She was trying to clean the apartment before she went home to visit the folks. Debra said she would help with the project when she returned from the store; she was taking her own sweet time.

She finished with the vacuuming in the front room, rolled up the cord on the vacuum and wheeled it down the hallway to put it back in the little utility closet in the bathroom. As she flipped off the light switch, she happened to glance down at the little strip lying on the top of the trash. She was shocked by the sight of two stripes, not one. The directions had told her to wait between four and ten minutes; clearly she hadn't waited long enough. She was pregnant.

Well, this was bad, she thought. Her parents would kill her, she wasn't done with school, and she didn't have a husband. She remembered there were two testers in the box; maybe this one had a false reading.

Ten minutes later, she was crying on the couch with a box of tissues in front of her, when Debra walked in.

"What's the matter, AnnaBelle?" Debra dropped her bags and hurried over to sit beside her friend.

"I'm pregnant!" AnnaBelle sobbed.

"Are you sure?" Debra questioned.

"I'm late and I checked it twice," AnnaBelle explained.

Debra leaned back on the couch for a minute, thinking. "You know of course that you have two options."

"No, I don't!" AnnaBelle said.

"Not the "A" word?" Debra asked.

"No!" AnnaBelle exclaimed.

"A for adoption?" Debra clarified.

"I'm having Adam's baby," she said.

"Have you told him yet?" Debra asked.

"I just found out." AnnaBelle started crying again.

"Let's get the tears out of your system and then decide what to do." Debra began to put cans and bottles into the cupboards.

"You can't tell Adam, that's the first thing." Debra insisted.

"Why not?" AnnaBelle began to gather the pile of tissues she had created.

"Because, he would leave his job and run home to do the right thing. And you guys are going to need the money." Debra insisted.

"I suppose you're right, but when he comes back I'll be all fat and stuff and he might not want me." AnnaBelle began to cry again.

"The question is, what will your parents do?" Debra folded the last paper sack and placed it under the sink.

"I'm going home this weekend and I won't be able to not tell them." You probably might just as well start making plans for the funeral, cause they'll both kill me." She slowly walked into the bedroom and started to pack.

Chapter 16

The little yellow pickup truck drove slowly past the Old Man Meeker's place and came to a stop in the middle of the road. The snowplows had already been through this morning, because the road was clear and heaps of snow lined the sides of the gravel road.

Something's different, AnnaBelle thought to herself as she took a closer look at the old place. Nothing had been done here for years, but now something was happening. A work trailer was parked in the driveway. She backed the little truck down the center of the road and looked closer. The driveway was filled with new fallen snow so she didn't dare pull in. She looked closely at the writing on the side of the trailer and recognized the last two words, "Dallas, Texas." Maybe Mom would have the answer to this puzzle; she drove up the hill and down to the house to take her medicine.

The driveway down to the house was cleared of snow; she could see her dad down by the barn. He was driving a big green tractor with a front loader and was pushing the snow from the driveway. She parked in front of the house, pulled her bag from the front seat and walked up the sidewalk to the house. Daddy must have been busy because the sidewalk was cleared.

She walked around to the back of the house and under a large carport, stamped her feet on the mat and entered. Front doors on farm houses are for occasional guests; she was family and wouldn't think of walking into the front room with muddy feet. The back door opened onto a little porch where boots and coats were left hanging. Another door opened into the kitchen and a large living room with a raging fire burning in a large fireplace. The smell of fresh baked bread was in the air. She looked toward the kitchen and her mother was just pulling the last of four loaves of bread from the oven.

"Hi Mom, I'm pregnant." She couldn't help herself.

"Hi Annie." Her mother continued to remove the bread from the loaf pans and place them just so on wire bread racks.

"How's school?" Her mother asked, she must not have heard the second part of AnnaBelle's greeting.

"I should graduate this semester." AnnaBelle set her bag down and walked over for the hug.

"Good, your father will be so pleased, I'm not so sure how pleased he'll be with the pregnancy thing but I guess we're going to find out." She took off her apron and hugged AnnaBelle. Then she stepped back to look at her figure.

Her mother walked over to the bag and began to carry it into the rear of the house.

"I can get that Mother." AnnaBelle followed her mother into the house.

"Your father's been expecting you since noon, I'm sure he saw you pull in, he'll be here in a minute. Why don't you pour him a cup of coffee while I unpack for you?" AnnaBelle figured that her mother didn't want to be in the room when she broke the news to her father. She returned to the kitchen and set a cup of steaming coffee on the table in front of her father's chair.

Soon there was the sound of heavy boots being cleaned at the rear door. A large burly bearded man stepped into the room and filled it with his presence.

"Hello daughter," he exclaimed in a loud voice. "Where's my hug?"

She ran to him and they shared a hug. AnnaBelle began to cry.

"What on Earth is the trouble daughter?" John held her at arms length and insisted, "What's the trouble?"

"I'm pregnant." She cried.

The man gave her another hug and patted her on the shoulder. "Adam's I hope?"

"I'm sure of it." She replied.

He sat down at the table and patted the place mat to his left. "Sit girl." He spoke as he shoveled three spoons of sugar into the cup and began to stir it.

She sat on the chair with her hands on her knees, "Are you mad?" She asked.

"Haven't decided yet. Too soon to tell." He sipped his coffee.

"How's school coming?" He asked.

"Good, I should graduate this semester." She replied.

"Where's the boy now, he still down in the oil patch?"

"Still down there." She replied

"He gonna marry you?" John asked.

"We talked about it." She lowered her head.

"So, what did he say when you told him he was going to be a daddy?" John pounded his fist on the table.

"What's all this racket?" Susan Williams entered the room. "Now don't you get too excited John, it's bad for your health.

"I simply asked the girl if the young man was going to marry her and she said they had talked about it." He raised his voice.

"I'm sure he'll do the right thing, John." Susan poured a cup of coffee and sat down at the table.

"He doesn't know." AnnaBelle said.

"Doesn't know if he's going to marry you or not?" John asked.

"Doesn't know I'm pregnant!" AnnaBelle said.

"See John, how can the boy make a decision like that if he doesn't even know the girl's pregnant?" Susan was relieved, but maybe a little worried.

"For crying in a bucket," John exclaimed. He finished his coffee in one gulp, walked to the counter and taking a knife from the drawer sawed one of the fresh loaves nearly in half and threw the knife back on the counter. Taking a bite of the loaf he spoke with his mouth half full, "You two hens figure this out; I'll be in for supper. Good bread." He raised the half loaf in salute to Susan and left the room.

Susan waited till he was gone and patted AnnaBelle on the knee. "Why haven't you told the boy?"

"He gets bad phone reception down there; it's the wrong service provider or too much steel or something. I don't want to text him and I'm afraid he'll change his mind." She began to cry.

"Now, Now." Susan slid her chair over and hugged AnnaBelle.

A moment later, AnnaBelle asked, "What's happening over at the Old Man Meeker place? I saw a trailer there."

"I heard that someone bought it, someone from Texas, looks like they started to do some work over there, you know how those people like to lease that land for hunting?"

"That means the place is sold?" AnnaBelle said in dismay. Adam had been working so hard down in that hellhole to save enough money to buy that place and marry me, AnnaBelle thought. He'd been crushed when he found out.

"Why not, that place has been a wreck for years, your father was going to buy the place just to tear it down and grow beans, but he said it would cost too much since he and Old Man Meeker had that falling out. Come help with dishes." Susan rose from the table.

"Tell me about what happened between Dad and Mr. Thomas, Mom?" AnnaBelle pleaded.

"That was a long time ago, Honey, but you're old enough now. You wash, I'll dry."

"Yes Mother," said AnnaBelle.

Before they could get a good start on the dishes, they heard a loud crash outside and the growl of a large diesel engine.

"What could that be so close to the house?" Susan exclaimed as she ran out the back door, through the lean to and around to the west side of the house.

John was now driving a large piece of earth moving equipment and was in the process of pushing down a tree, roots and all. The big machine had two steel tracks like a tank and a large blade on the front. He would back the machine up for a ways then the engine would race and large billows of black diesel smoke would rise from the big exhaust pipes. The machine hit the trunk of the tree again and again, each time a little more of the root system was exposed. Finally the tree fell to the ground and he used the machine to push the tree and root ball a good distance from the house.

He was driving the machine past the house and toward the barn. Susan and AnnaBelle ran out into the road to speak with him.

Susan yelled at the top of her lungs when he stopped and idled the engine so he could hear her. "What are you doing John?"

"You know that addition you've been pestering me to build for years? Now's the time, we'll need a room for the baby." He revved the big engine and drove out to the barns.

"Susan took AnnaBelle's arm and led her into the house. "Guess he's excited about the baby, who'd have guessed."

AnnaBelle followed Susan back into the kitchen and returned to the dishes. "Tell me about you and Ken, Mom."

Susan dropped the cup she had been washing and turned to face the girl. "I love your father, AnnaBelle, he's been real good to me and he loves you kids."

"That's not what I asked, Mother, but I guess you just answered part of my question." She resumed drying the plates.

A moment later, Susan spoke. "It was a long time ago dear, we were young and stupid and young people make mistakes."

"What mistake are you referring to Mother, getting drunk and hitting Jerri or marrying Daddy?" AnnaBelle was becoming confused and a little angry.

"Who have you been talking to girl?" Susan said sharply.

"I just got the story from Debra's mother. Is it true?" AnnaBelle asked.

"Peggy wouldn't lie, she might not remember everything the way it happened but you probably heard most of the truth."

"So, why didn't you ever tell me?" AnnaBelle was insistent.

"What would be the point, it's over and done with. All those things happened a long time ago. By the time I came to my senses it was too late, they were married with a little baby and it wasn't long before your father and I got married and you kids came along. We've been happy together, haven't we?" There was a pleading in her voice.

"I've tried to be a good wife and mother, I know I don't keep the house like your father would like, I'm not the fancy showpiece that he would have preferred, I sometimes feel like he wishes he had married Jerri instead of me." She began to cry.

AnnaBelle couldn't remember seeing her mother break down like this before. They stood in front of the sink, Susan weeping on AnnaBelle's shoulder; as AnnaBelle watched her father through the window dragging the big tree behind the tractor with a chain. The limbs of the tree carved a wider path through the snow and small branches littered the white roadway.

She noticed that he was singing, she wondered what song.

Chapter 17

Adam waited in Tom's office as he had been directed to do. It was early morning and the receptionist provided Adam with a steaming hot cup of coffee, black. It sure didn't seem like three and a half months had gone by since he started here. The work was hard but satisfying in that the paychecks that went directly into the bank were huge. He was truly exhausted but all this work would pay off when he was finally able to afford to go home. Frugality was his middle name, when all the other men went to town to buy liquor and party he stayed and worked when he could and otherwise he tried to catch up on his sleep. Tom sent the word for Adam to meet him here this morning as Adam was finishing up the evening shift; he had no idea what this meeting would be about. He wished he could be in bed asleep.

Tom finally strode down the hallway and into the office.

"Good to see you Adam, I wanted to talk to you in person to clear up any misunderstandings. I'm leaving." He took the seat behind the desk.

"We've been talking about this out in the plant for quite a while now. Most figured it was only a question of time before someone with your talents finds the job he wants." Adam had been expecting this but dreading it at the same time.

"I got a call yesterday. This will be a chance to go back to my roots; I came from the electric shop and now I'll go back, only this time it's to one of those floating drilling rigs. It's a small cut in pay, but it will be 21 days out and 21 days home; lots of overtime and plenty of time to see my family on the breaks." Tom paused. "Would you like to come along? You've done a real good job in the electric shop and I could use you. You'd get more money and plenty of overtime. You'll have three weeks off at a time to go see that sweetheart of yours. What do you say?"

"I think I ought to check with Justin before I jump ship. He might have stuck his neck out to get me this job. Can I let you know tomorrow?" Adam wasn't sure he really wanted to work way out there on the ocean, but he trusted Tom. If it meant more money well, that's why he was here.

Tom stood and extended his hand. "I gave them two weeks notice, not that they expected it.

Adam stepped out to the one spot where he knew he got good reception.

To: JUSTIN

Tom just told me he's leaving to take a job on one

of those off shore rigs. He wants me to go with

him. What do you think?

Adam

He stood around and waited for what he hoped would be a quick reply. As he stood there, his nose was assailed by a faint rotten egg smell. Christ, he hated this place. He wondered what it would be like to be trapped on a floating island miles and miles from shore. All these smells and dangers would be more up close and personal.

Message (1/106)

Fr: Justin

The safety record on those rigs is pretty good. It's hard work when you work but there's a lot of time off. I'd trust

Tom's judgment. Let me know what you decide.

It won't hurt my feelings one way or the other.

Adam stepped back into the building hoping to find Tom. He was seated behind his desk on the phone. He motioned for Adam to come in and take a seat. Adam couldn't help but eavesdrop and it was apparent that Tom was in the process of building a crew that would all jump ship together. Adam thought for a moment that if he stuck around there might be a better job for him when the others left, but put that thought from his mind.

Tom finished the call and turned to Adam with a questioning look on his face.

"I texted Justin and he said I should trust your judgment."

"That's good, I'll get the process started and I expect you will be able to get started in about three weeks; that will put you out there in good weather. I'll be in touch, you made the right decision." Tom stepped around the desk and again they shook hands.

Chapter 18

It was late Sunday afternoon and Debra was bringing a couple of sacks of groceries back from the store. As she neared the apartment she noticed the yellow pickup parked close, the bottom of the truck was covered with road dirt and great chunks of dirty snow were built up behind the tires. Whenever AnnaBelle retuned from home she always brought fresh made food from home, the thought of fresh bread made Debra's mouth water. It was a challenge to get the key in the door without dropping the sacks of groceries; she fought her way through the door and kicked it shut as she barely made it to the counter without dropping the bags.

When the bags were finally safely on the counter she turned her attention to the crying noises emanating from the living area.

"This is getting to be habit, AnnaBelle." She walked back to the door, kicked off her shoes and returned rubbing her hands together trying to get feelings back in her hands. "What on Earth is the problem now?"

AnnaBelle was seated on the couch with a pile of used tissues piled on the table in front of her. She turned as Debra entered the room.

"Adam's my brother!" She began to cry again in earnest.

Debra stopped in her tracks; the full impact of these words needed time to sink in. She changed direction and walked down the hallway toward the bedroom and threw her coat and scarf on the bed, she stopped in the bathroom long enough to blow her nose and wash her hands and returned to the refrigerator. Armed with a bottle of diet soda she seated herself on the couch beside AnnaBelle and began to speak.

"What on earth are you talking about Annie? What did find out when you were home?" She laid a hand on her friends shoulder.

"I had a heart-to-heart talk with Mom about Ken. She finally told me the story about how they dated in junior high and stuff while we were doing dishes and she sort of broke down and was crying, but that wasn't the whole story. Last night Dad went to bed early like he always does cause he gets up with the chickens and Mom and I had a little girl talk. She actually drank a beer which I have never seen her do; as a matter of fact she drank two beers." AnnaBelle paused a moment as she added to the pile of tissues. "After the second beer she wanted to make a clean breast of things. Ken and Dad were real good friends, growing up. Ken started dating Mom in junior high and Dad was too busy with the farm to waste time on girls until this new girl moves to town,"

"That would be Jerri, Adam's mom?" Debra interrupted.

"Exactly. This new cutie moves to town, she has no friends and Dad had the hots for her, so they started dating. Since Dad and Ken were best buddies, they did a lot of double dating and Mom and Jerri got to be best friends as well. So, all during their senior year Dad and Mom and Ken and Jerri are like joined at the hip, they sort of do everything as a foursome, and everything is going along just fine." AnnaBelle jumps up and gets a soda from the refrigerator.

"So, the boys are into camping and you know that piece of high ground at the south end of the east pasture, the one with the little pond?" AnnaBelle asks.

"That place with the good view, that one we rode the horses to?" Debra clarifies.

"That's the place. It's this high piece of ground with this great view for miles around and it's about completely surrounded by trees and there's this Artesian well thing that keeps this little pond filled with fresh water. This place is really isolated and it takes a good truck or horse to get up there and it's this perfect place to camp. So, its spring and a particularly warm year and they're all going to graduate in a couple of months and they've none of them ever done it before."

"It?" Debra interrupts.

"You know, "IT." They all decide it's high time they did it and decide to have a cherry busting party. In Sociology class this is what we learned to call an example of group think, like the Bay of Pigs, a bunch of otherwise intelligent people sit around in a group and come up with an idea that is really stupid and they sort of feed on each others stupidity. Anyway, they decide to have this cherry breaking party and they get a couple of bottles of cherry vodka for the occasion and the boys score some weed. They get this tent and some food and go on up to the top of this hill."

"Food, I'm starved," Debra steps up and runs into the kitchen area. "Don't stop talking; I need to put this food up."

AnnaBelle adjusts herself to sit cross-legged on the couch and proceeds. "So, they planned this big camping outing for the weekend and it's all about sex. Mom went into too much detail about how they planned to save themselves till they got married and all and how somehow they all decided to heck with that." She had to speak more loudly because of the noise Debra was making with the sacks and groceries. "So, it's real warm see and they get up to this really isolated spot and the boys are sitting up the campsite and they've got their shirts off and they're doing their manly thing and there's this clean little pond with the water nice and warm and the girls decide to break out the vodka and take a little swim."

"Is this fresh bread?" Debra has discovered the care package AnnaBelle brought from home.

"Fresh this morning, help yourself."

"Want some?" Debra is attacking the giant loaf with a large knife.

"No thanks, I ate till I'm stuffed." AnnaBelle continues. "So, here you have four young adults with no adult supervision, warm weather, crystal clear warm water and a few bottles of cherry vodka with sex on their collective minds. Mom painted this mental picture like it was happening yesterday. Mom said after the boys fired up a joint it all started getting a little fuzzy."

"Fuzzy, I guess," Debra returned with a heavy plate that held several thick slices of buttered

99

bread, a brown cloth napkin, and a large crystal glass filled with cold milk.

"Details," Debra insisted as she seated herself on the couch and attacked the fresh bread.

"According to Mom, the cherry thing turned out to be sort of an anticlimax to the whole deal, I guess the campout sort of became a blurry memory. But the bottom line is that they all had a great time; what they could remember of it. For the next several weeks camping was what they did. The weather stayed remarkably pleasant and unseasonably warm and dry for that time of year. The boys would go down in the four wheeler and knock out the chores and bring back vittles. The boys raided Grandpa's wine cellar and would bring back these big jugs of home-made wine. She said after a glass or two it wasn't bad at all. During this period of time she and Jerri became really close and they would just swim and sunbathe and cook and tend the camp."

"It was all sort of idyllic." Commented Debra.

"Exactly.' AnnaBelle continued. "Anyway, this sort of got to be a habit and the sex thing sort of became no big deal. Pretty soon, with the wine and the pot and the weather, the clothes thing sort of got to be no big deal either."

"Does that mean that they were all sort of running around naked?" Debra was finishing the last of the milk.

"Guess so, sort of turned into a clothing optional sort of deal. I suppose if you think about it, but maybe I don't want to." AnnaBelle thought for a minute.

"So, what's this deal about Adam?" Debra came back to the point.

"Mom was real apologetic about this whole thing. She said those weekends all sort of became a blur. They would stagger back home on Sunday afternoon and when they woke up on Monday to go back to school none of them had a real clear memory of what had happened the weekend before."

"But they kept doing it?" Debra insisted.

"Sure, Mom said it was like eating peanuts, you just can't quit. So, these weekends became this normal thing, filled with booze and sex and weed and they were sharing this tent and it got to the point where she honestly couldn't remember who she was having sex with but that it all felt so right that it didn't really matter."

"Holy shit," Debra commented. "You mean that their little camping trips turned into this sort of four way orgy sort of thing going on?"

"Yep." AnnaBelle now started to cry again. "My mother, the slut."

"But your mother was no more of a slut than was Jerri or your Dad or Ken." Debra clarified.

"It's different with guys." AnnaBelle insisted.

"How!" Debra stated. "They were all at fault."

"I guess if fault's the word. Anyway. Schools out and there's this big keg party not three quarters of a mile from this campsite. The four of them have sort of been in this otherworldly kissy feely drugged up sexual dream state on the weekends and now it's a weekend again but it's different, there's a lot of other people around.

They were all getting wasted as usual and in celebration Mom and Jerri give each other a big hug and celebratory kiss and they're drunk and Mom's tooth cuts Jerri's lip and now Jerri's bleeding and someone sees the blood and the rumor is out that Mom hit Jerri. Jerri leaves the party drunk and bleeding and Mom's gotten so drunk that your mom Peggy drags her out. After the party is over; neither one of them wants to admit what really happened."

"So, what about Ken and your dad?" Debra asked.

"They hear the story second hand, can't figure out why Mom hit Jerri, they're drunk and don't care so they take this big bottle of whiskey, steal Old Man Meeker's truck and drive up to the campsite. They take a swim, finish the bottle and by now they are shit hammered so in this drunken state they get back in the truck and drive back down the hill. They spent so much time running around all naked and stuff that they forget about the party and they end up in the pond with about a hundred party goers wondering what the heck."

"So, now the word is out that those two guys are a couple of perverts." Debra adds.

"Precisely." AnnaBelle concludes.

"So, what's this about Adam being your brother?" Debra insisted.

"Well, it sounds like my mother can't guarantee me whether my father is Dad or Ken." AnnaBelle started to cry again.

"Holy Shit!" Debra shook her head as she carried her plates to the sink.

Chapter 19

Bennett selected an envelope from the pile on his desk. He read it slowly.

"Hey Patrick," He spoke into the room as if someone were there; "I've been nominated to receive an award for my efforts on behalf of the environment. This suggests that if I contribute another ten grand I might actually win. Money well spent."

The phone rang and he answered and listened and hung up.

He then dialed some numbers. The phone was answered on the first ring. "Find the name of that company that makes that oil dispersant we use; yes, that nasty stuff that makes oil more toxic. However many shares I own, triple it; do it right now. I think we are going to be able to sell a few hundred million dollars' worth."

Chapter 20

AnnaBelle stood standing sideways in front of the full-length mirror with her blouse pulled up to her arm pits. She was showing ever so much she could tell it. "Deb, come in here." She commanded.

Debra came down the hallway and surveyed the tummy area. "Just the half gallon of chocolate chip you ate last night. This is your first baby, you wouldn't be showing yet."

AnnaBelle followed her into the living area.

"You talked to him on the phone last night, did you tell him?" Debra asked.

"No I didn't. He's going to change jobs and I didn't want him to get upset." She rationalized. She was afraid that if she didn't tell him about the baby in person that he might change his mind.

"So, when do you suppose you're going to tell him?" Debra scolded.

"I'll graduate this semester and he should be getting some time off, he promised he would come home when he could." AnnaBelle waltzed into the kitchen and dug through the refrigerator, something sounded good.

"You'll really be showing by then, you sure you want to wait that long? Don't you think he'll be mad?" Debra spoke louder to be heard over the sound of bottles and jars being moved in the refrigerator.

"I think I've gotten to the point where I'm sort of scared to tell him, to be quite honest. We seem to be drifting apart. He doesn't call very often and he seems to have his mind on other things." AnnaBelle was setting cheese and meats on the counter to make another sandwich.

"The poor man's been working two shifts for three months; I bet he's darn near dead from exhaustion." Debra stepped to the counter to help with the sandwich.

"You're probably right; I should call him tonight and tell him." She knew she wouldn't.

Chapter 21

Adam found out the hard way that he was not a seaman. He could have gone to the rig on one of the helicopters that made the trip quick and easy, but he had been given a choice and decided he might enjoy a boat ride.

From the moment that the little ship left the dock, Adam was seasick. The waves were small for the ocean but to a landsman they seemed to be enormous. The boat would rise to the top of the wave then fall back into the trough. He was feeling pretty sick so the first mate offered him a little yellow pill. He swallowed it and almost immediately, he needed to throw up. The boat had a small area in the bow, covered with black vinyl, where seasick people could lie down and heave their guts out. He was long past that point now. All he could do was sit there with his head in his hands, sick to his stomach, hoping to die or something.

Tom was true to his word and he'd gotten Adam a job with more pay and tons of overtime. Adam had convinced himself that this was the right decision and he was looking forward to his first three weeks off.

Soon, he'd have enough money saved up to convince Old Man Meeker to sell. Then he and AnnaBelle could begin their life together. Adam had been feeling alone and a little scared. He wanted to call Annabelle, but she seemed to be so distant lately. She was always short and seemed like she wanted to say something, but wouldn't. He didn't have much service way out here so he decided to text Justin.

To:
JUSTIN
Not much signal
Only have one bar here. Im on the
boat now going
to the rig. thanks
Adam

It was evening as they approached the giant drilling rig and Justin returned his text.

Message (1 / 106)
Fr: Justin
DO NOT BOARD DRILLING RIG.
Use whatever excuse u can use but
don't get on board. I'll explain later

To: JUSTIN
I don't understand but I'll stay on
the boat.
Adam

When they reached the rig, no one really cared if he got off the boat or not. As the boat was unloading, Adam found relief from the seasickness and napped.

As the boat got under way, he again took his position on the bench at the bow and resigned himself to the painful trip back. They weren't far from the rig when the air was rent with a small explosion. Adam hurried to the stern to see flames coming from the lower portion of the rig. Moments later, a massive explosion tore the rig apart and ignited the helicopter fuel.

Chapter 22

Adam lay in the front of the little boat, his seasickness forgotten as he helplessly watched the flames consume the massive structure. The pilot of the little boat was standing next to the wheel with a pair of binoculars watching the drama unfold. The little boat pitched and yawed with the waves. The massive rig was now beneath the waves but flames still burned on the top of the ocean.

He stumbled from his seat and worked his way aft to the pilot.

"Are we going to go back to see if there are any survivors?" He asked the pilot.

"Ain't none, Sonny," replied the weather beaten sailor. "I've been watchin' for some sign of life, but nobody could have survived that explosion. I suppose the least we could do is take a turn around the wreck. Take a seat." He pushed a lever forward and the little boat shot back toward the flames.

The massive flames were roaring high into the sky and a great billowing black smoke rose toward the heavens. Adam felt the intense heat long before they got close to the site. He stood on one leg with the other kneeling on the seat as he held his arm up to shield his face. The pilot took the little boat so close that the paint on the sides was beginning to bubble and Adam was afraid that if something happened to the motors the flames would consume them. When it seemed like it was almost too late, the pilot turned to starboard and began to slowly make way through the floating debris, large pieces of insulation, broken pieces of partially burned wood planking, plastic pieces of all colors and sizes with the occasional body part. The little boat made a complete circle around the flames.

"Wait!" Adam screamed at the pilot, "someone's alive over here."

Adam ran to the railing and released a life ring from its carrier; it was tied onto a long length of rope whose other end was secured to the railing. He tossed the ring into the water and it landed near a body floating with the aid of a yellow life jacket. The victim didn't notice.

Adam looked toward the pilot. "Can I go in?" He pleaded.

"Suit your own self, Sonny. Put on that life vest and go in feet first." The sailor commanded.

Adam fastened the life vest with the two plastic clips and lowered himself from the railing. The drop to the water was less than six feet once he let go. The water was cold and salty. It tasted of oil. He was a strong swimmer, but swimming with a life jacket was difficult. He made his way to the man in the water, but when he got close, he saw the deep gash in the man's head. The waves had washed away any blood but brain matter was visible and Adam immediately wished he had not been so impulsively brave. He looked around to see if there were any more bodies and he saw none. By pulling himself along using the rope, he made good progress back to the boat. The pilot had fastened a rope ladder onto the railing and stood waiting to help Adam crawl over the side.

"You did your part Sonny. I didn't figure there was any use in you getting wet, but we sailors got to stick together." He laid two towels on the seat and returned to the wheel. "Watch yourself Sonny, we're leavin' this wreck."

As the boat slowly got under way, the oily taste in Adam's mouth made him lean over the side and throw up, again, and again. The intense heat faded as the boat headed toward shore. The flames behind them seemed to grow and the black plume of smoke seemed to get worse.

Adam made his way to the rear of the boat where he could shield himself from the wind. He peeled off his jacket and shirt and then remembered his phone. "Shit!"

When the boat docked at the pier, the world was a nightmare of activity. Police and ambulance vehicles with sirens and flashing lights were everywhere. Several news trucks with big dish antennas were parked beside the road. The boat was tied to the shore and the sailor had left without saying a word. Adam just sat there in the sunshine, drying out so that is what he did for quite some time. He just sat in the sun and watched the black plume of smoke on the horizon get bigger and bigger.

Adam finally made his way back to the hotel and was able to phone Justin, who promised to pass the word back home that Adam was safe, for now.

Chapter 23

Adam and Justin sat at a window table in the bar. Adam told his story without bragging about his heroics.

"Had any word about Tom Hendrix?" He asked Justin.

"He should be back any time, he took one of those cheap two-week vacations to one of those islands with palm trees and fruity umbrella drinks. Looks like he planned it just right. He might have a better insight into what happened, but I talked to a few guys yesterday about it."

Justin was explaining what he knew. "What exactly failed that day will probably never be known, but my take on the whole thing is this. The well in question was a troubled one from the beginning. The rig that started the drilling process was damaged in a hurricane and a second, more expensive one was brought in to finish the hole. Any hole a mile deep in the ocean has greater risks than a hole drilled in shallow water. Divers can go down in shallow water, but deep water requires the use of submersibles and robotics that increase the cost of the well and increase the risks. At the top of the wellhead is placed a blow out preventer that is designed to seal the well in the event that the well casing fails. A drilling contracting company was hired by the oil company to supply a hole with a pipe inside that will tap into an underground reservoir. These contractors are often cutting corners to keep wells profitable. These cut corners increase the risk of blowouts."

"On this well, something failed and we'll probably never know exactly what it was. It might have been something in the wellbore, or it might have been a pipe collapse when the heavy drilling mud was replaced with light seawater. The men inside the control room detected the smell of methane and drilling fluid coming from the well and made an attempt to activate the blow out preventer. For some reason, the blow out preventer failed to seal the pipe. The methane gas rushed into the control room and was pulled into the intake of the generator. The generator began to rev out of control because of the methane which led to the first explosion."

"The first explosion tore through the rig and killed everyone in the control room. Without controls, the floating rig is at the mercy of the ocean and cannot remain over the wellhead. The methane gas and hydrocarbons, under tremendous pressure filled the rig until the entire structure was engulfed in flames. The flames burned and burned until the steel melted and the entire structure sank. At this point, the well is spewing gas and oil at a tremendous rate and might not stop until all of the pressure inside the oil pocket is gone. When those millions of barrels of oil are all finally released into the Gulf of Mexico, the Gulf will be as dead as the Dead Sea. All the sea life, all the birds, all the fish, and all of the phytoplankton; which is responsible for half of the earth's oxygen, will be dead, forever. This is all because one company drilled one hole into the earth."

Chapter 24

Adam raised his hand to order another round as Justin continued. "I downloaded some stuff, I expect most of it is wrong but you never know." He consulted his laptop.

"It had some interesting and entirely useless pieces of information regarding this Macondo well. According to this, the name of the prospect, Macondo, is the same name as a fictitious cursed town, in a novel by a Colombian prize winning author."

"The content of the oil reserve is a closely guarded secret; however, rumors have abounded that this particular pocket of oil could be the second largest on the planet. It has been suggested that if the cork is blown out of the bottle, so to speak, the well has the potential to dump an incredible amount of crude oil into the ocean. If the leak blows past the wellhead there is the potential to release a half million barrels of crude oil per day; and that this horrific leak could continue unchecked for ten years."

"Let's do the mental math; that would be 182.5 million barrels per year with a total outflow over a ten year period of 1.825 billion barrels. At forty-two gallons per barrel that equates to 76.65 billion gallons. Let's say this estimate is wrong by half and that there is only enough gas pressure to push half that amount against the pressure at the bottom of the ocean. That would still be *38 billion* gallons."

"Oil contains many toxic chemicals such as benzene, formaldehyde, and acetaldehyde; and when burned the emissions contain, carbon dioxide, carbon monoxide, sulfur dioxide, nitrogen oxides, lead, and others. These toxins kill wildlife and humans."

Chapter 25

Justin pecked away at his laptop. "Listen to this, Adam."

"The water in the oceans is not static, it moves. Surface currents are generally wind driven and account for perhaps ten percent of the ocean water. The surface currents are generally restricted to the upper 1,300 feet of the ocean. The other 80 percent of the ocean is moved by what are called deep ocean currents."

"The oil from the Gulf of Mexico will get entrained into the Gulf Stream. The Gulf Stream travels in a clockwise direction along the east coast of the United States, across the Atlantic, then turns south along the west coast of Africa and returns along the east coast of Cuba. The Equatorial Counter will carry the oil to the South Equatorial Current which will carry it along the east coast of Brazil in a counter clockwise rotation to the South Atlantic Current and along the east coast of Africa. At the Horn of Africa, the Antarctic Circumpolar Current will transport the oil to the South Indian Current in a counter clockwise rotation, along the west coast of Australia where the South Equatorial Current will carry it along the east coast of Africa. The Antarctic Circumpolar Current will carry the oil to the South Pacific Current which will take it to the west coast of South America; along Peru. It then will enter the South Equatorial Current that will carry it to the Equatorial Counter Current and the North Equatorial Current. This will poison the waters of East Asia and carry on to the North Pacific Current that will finally carry the pollution to the south coast of Alaska and the coast of California and the west coast of Mexico."

"A combination of density and salinity of sea water create what is known as the Great Ocean Conveyor. Cold dense salty water sinks to the bottom of the ocean and forces the deeper water to flow in a generally southern direction. This is called the meridional overturning circulation and this affects the climate of the earth. These currents are a delicate balancing act that keep Europe warm. Without them the temperature of Europe can drop by twenty degrees."

"The dispersants used in the Gulf oil spill have created oil plumes that will linger in the deep water, creating dead zones and affecting the density of the water which will in turn affect the Conveyor."

Chapter 26

Bennett pushed the button on the desk console that caused the great window blinds to close. Motors in the ceiling made a whirring noise and large drapes, from floor to ceiling, began to move across the room in front of the large windows. He disliked sunlight. He picked up the phone and speed dialed a number. The phone rang twice on the other end before it was picked up. "Hello."

"Bennett here, what have you got for me?" He listened for a few moments then hung the phone up without saying a word.

He pushed another set of buttons on the phone and the sound of a distant phone ringing filled the air. "Yes sir," a voice answered at the first ring.

"Go to Richmond. Leave now. We need more water; do whatever it takes to get rid of those tree hugging bastards." He removed a roll of mints from the top desk drawer, placed one in his mouth and trimmed the foil wrapping with a small pair of scissors. He carefully placed the scissors and mints back in the drawer and flipped the trimmings in the wastebasket.

"These folks hired a good environmental lawyer, sir," Pleaded the voice on the phone. "

"Come." He pushed the button on the phone and raised his feet to rest on the edge of the desk.

Less than a minute later, Richards hurried through the door where he stood catching his breath before the large desk.

"Do you really understand the problem, Richards?" The little man asked.

"I think I do sir." There was a tremble in his voice.

"The easy oil is gone, Richards. We sucked it out of the ground, refined it and sold it for huge profits. That was yesterday. We spent that money. Our jobs, yours and mine, Richards are only as good as what we do today. Since we have already picked all the low hanging fruit, so to speak, we are left with oil that costs a good deal to get out of the ground. We need to drill deeper and deeper and that costs money which means we need to charge more. One of these days that deep water drilling is going to come back and bite us in the butt. It is already too damn expensive, too risky and we might already be in trouble down there. It costs too damn much to drill that deep in the ocean. There is a price point at which Joe Consumer starts to look for an alternative. We know that will happen sooner or later and we need to hold that off as long as possible. We want natural gas to be the alternative to oil. We need to generate so much of it that the price is so low that Joe Consumer sees it as the natural replacement for oil. We do not want Joe to put a windmill or solar panel on his roof that would cut us completely out of the profit stream and that would be bad for us, right Richards?" The man waited for a reply.

"Yes sir, very bad for us sir." Richards stammered.

Bennett sat with his hands crossed on his chest and gazed at the young man without speaking.

"The problem with Fracking sir is that it is so bad for the planet." Richards began. "It destroys so much clean water and causes earthquakes."

"Fuck the planet, Richards." he replied. "The bottom line is that without this natural gas there will be no bottom line, do I make myself clear?"

"We cannot harvest the natural gas without contaminating the ground water, and any fool can see that. We can control the media and the politicians and convince Joe Consumer that everything is fine. Believe me; Joe Consumer wants to believe that everything is fine. Joe wants to drive home at night in his big gas guzzling SUV, pop the top on his six-pack of beer and watch reality TV. By the time Joe wakes up, we will have destroyed most of the ground water but we don't care because we are buying up all the water rights and we intend to make more money on water than we ever did on oil. Everybody needs water, even people with solar panels and windmills. Deep injection is a good thing, Richards, remember that. Get out there and convince Joe that his ground water is safe. Spread enough money around to convince that town council to let us pump water from that lake if we need to; we are the job creators. We are the good guys. Just get that gas to pumpin', Richards, can you handle that?"

"Yes sir."

"One more thing, make sure all our people down there know which politicians we like and explain how it is their civic duty to vote and support the democratic process. Then, pass out enough bonus money to get these tree huggers out of office. This is America, Richards. One man, one vote, so get out there and buy me some men."

"We're on that sir, we passed out enough money at the state and local level that each one of our people can contribute the legal maximum and we have padded our major supplier's invoices so their people can contribute as well."

"We can't take any chances, Richards, we need that water."

"The democratic process works, sir. It works for us." Richards left the room.

Bennett stood from his chair and walked to the pedestal with the acrylic trophy that contained the tar-covered bird.

"So, what do you think Patrick? Oil on the beaches ain't shit compared to the destruction of all the clean water. I hate the environment." As he walked out of the room to go to lunch he turned on all the lights.

"I hate this job." Richards was seated at a black metal table in the lunchroom of the office complex. He was speaking with Jenny Houston. They were each eating a ham and cheese sandwich bought from the vending machines and were drinking diet soda from aluminum cans.

"Not so loud," the girl cautioned.

"That son of a bitch is crazy, he won't be happy until we've destroyed the planet." He spoke in a quieter tone.

"He talks to that stupid bird like it's his best friend." He chewed another bite of sandwich and washed it down with soda.

"That bird is his only friend," Jenny replied.

"I've only been here three years," he spoke quietly, "How does a crazy person get to be so powerful?"

"Money, pure and simple. He does whatever it takes to get the product out of the ground and onto the market. Corporations reward people who increase the bottom line. Corporations have no souls, no hearts and shareholders only care about profits. Money is why we both work here, I would like to help the planet but I need to eat first."

"But how is it possible for someone to not care about the destruction of the planet?" He opened a bag of chips and offered her the bag. She looked in the opening of the bag and selected the largest one.

"Just one, thanks." She nibbled around the edge of the large chip. "I know it is hard to believe but there are some people who are so bent that they just can't be fixed. There is a small percentage of any population who are just plain broken. How is it so impossible to believe that a crazy person also can have marketable skills? Maybe he has a death wish? Maybe he wants to die and he wants to take us all down with him?"

"He's got us involved in those deep water wells that at any minute could spell the end of our existence. Now we're in the natural gas business. Do you have any idea how much fresh water we are taking from the surface of the planet and injecting deep into the earth, never to be seen again?" He finished his sandwich and opened the little towelette packet.

"How much?" she asked.

"Billions of gallons, every day. That is billion with a "B." There is a shortage of drinking water on the planet and we waste it like a drunken sailor. Over these wells' lifetime, they ruin 20 trillion gallons. Let me do a little math here." He took his phone and began to use the calculator function. "There are approximately 2.5 million fracking wells; each well is estimated to use 8 million gallons of water over its lifetime. That comes to 20,000,000,000,000 gallons of fresh water ruined. See how I have to turn the phone sideways just to get the numbers to fit?"

Jenny finished her sandwich and took the wrappers and empty cans to the recycle bins. "People think there is someone in the government looking after the planet. They don't realize that the whole kit and caboodle are bought and paid for by guys just like your boss. So, what do you think you can do about it, Jim?"

"Not a blessed thing." He took her arm as they walked back into the complex.

"Maybe something will come up. Maybe you need to be less good at what you do? Race you to the door." She sprinted ahead.

Chapter 27

Susan finished rolling the vacuum cord around the handle and set the blue machine in the hall closet. John had driven into town so the noise and dust and shaking of the house from the new addition had come to an end for a short time. She used that time to touch up the front end of the house. She would never be the housekeeper that Jerri was. Jerri kept a spotless house whereas Susan hated it, she consoled herself with the thought that Jerri hated to cook. She heard the oven timer beeping, just as she planned, cinnamon rolls would be ready in time for John's morning coffee break.

The rolls turned out perfect; the little brown rectangles of sugary goodness popped right out of the pan and were cooling on a wire rack. The air was filled with the homey smell of fresh baked rolls, gooey with cinnamon and sugar and raisins, with just a hint of coffee from the pot across the kitchen. She set the pan in the sink and filled it with water to soak the burned sugar off as the noise from the driveway caught her attention.

John must not have needed much in town he was back already. She thought back about how she used to feel at this time of the day. John would come in for coffee and compliment her on whatever little thing she served with the coffee. It made her feel special the way he appreciated her cooking. Often, in the past, after coffee he would lead her upstairs and they would make love but as they grew older those times were fewer. She thought about Ken until the noise from the back door caused her to turn in that direction.

John stomped his boots on the rug at the back door, dropped a stack of mail on the edge of the table and sat down as Susan brought a large cup of coffee with a spoon to set in front of him.

"Danged air hose for the nail gun sprung a leak," Susan bent down to receive a kiss and rubbed his shoulder with her left hand. "That hose ain't over twenty years old, they just don't make stuff like they used to."

He sat for a moment and watched the steam rise from the freshly cut cinnamon roll on the plate Susan placed near the coffee cup. "Sure looks good mother, I bet that hot sugar would take the skin right off my tongue."

"Let it cool a little," she cautioned.

"Heard any news from the girl?" He asked as he thumbed through the mail.

He selected an envelope, tapped the end on the table and using a pair of scissors cut off the other end. He blew into the opening to reveal the contents, pulled out a piece of paper and began to read it.

"She called this morning while you were in town," Susan sat at the table with a half-cup of coffee. "Everything seems to be going as good as can be expected."

"Those bastards," John flipped the sheet of paper onto the pile of unopened mail. "Five hundred dollars an acre, these guys are offering us to extract the natural gas from under the land here."

"Is that good?" She asked.

"It's terrible." He stood up and began to pace. "Remember the drought we've had for the last couple of years? Remember how hot the summer got and how we needed to haul water to those cattle over in that east pasture?"

"Yes," she remembered how difficult it had been, all of her summer days spent driving that big red hay truck with the white plastic water tanks on the back.

"We might be able to afford to do that for a couple of bad years but if we need to do that every year we won't be able to afford to keep the herd. We just simply won't have the water for the animals. We'll be forced to sell." He stood at the sink looking out the window. "It's taken years to develop that line."

"What has that got to do with that letter?" She asked.

"Pretty much everything." He began to pace again. "Since 2005, the gas companies have been given sort of free rein to do as they damn well please. They started out in the west where the only things they could pester would be a few antelopes and deer and now they have come east. They were allowed to drill on BLM land and I knew it was just a matter of time until they got here but I just hoped they wouldn't. The problem is that there are some people around here who will need the money and take it."

"Explain it for me a little, I don't get out much." She wished she could keep up with things a little better.

He walked back to the table, picked up the fork and began to eat the cinnamon roll. He took the time to blow on the bite so it would not burn his mouth. He washed it down with coffee and sat back with the cup in his hand.

"Years ago there were places on the earth where oil bubbled up on the surface. It was plentiful and fairly easy to get. It was nasty and gooey and black and nobody wanted the smelly stuff. Cars were designed to run on moonshine that people could make in their back yards out of any grain or plant. The oil companies hired scientists to figure out ways to use oil and the auto industry did their part by manufacturing inefficient gasoline engines to use more oil. Now we find ourselves at the end of the hundred-year oil age. We took it out of the ground, burned it up and polluted the atmosphere with it. It was a good run for them and they made zillions of dollars in profits. They used those profits to buy elections and put their people in many public offices. "

"The cheap oil is gone as is the cheap gas. Our dependence upon oil and gas is very like an ocean liner or a battle ship. It takes a long time to turn those babies around. We have gone for so long using oil and gas at such a rapid rate that it is hard to put on the brakes. The countries that used to be third world countries, like China and India are just now starting to use energy. They are the two most populous countries and their people have just started using oil and electricity.

Once a population gets a taste of modern life they will not be denied. China has bought up the coal mines in Wyoming and India has contracted with the Kentucky coal mines to feed their electricity needs. You know these countries won't put restrictions on pollution so it will just be a matter of time before the planet's air is unfit to breath." He took another bite of roll and swallowed.

"The oil companies have sucked all of the easy oil out of the ground and now they find themselves needing to drill deeper and deeper in the oceans to feed the massive monster they have created. One of these days, mark my words, those greedy people will drill down and find a pocket of something that has been buried since this earth was formed, something that is so nasty and powerful that we all will wish they had left it alone." He took another bite.

"Surely the government will step in before that happens?" She stood up to get the coffee pot and freshened the two cups.

"You would think so," he lamented, "as a group you would think that individuals who were elected would work for what is best for the country. The problem is that each elected official wants to be reelected. In order to get reelected, in order to win that next election that politician needs more money than his opponent. They have just one thing to sell and that is their vote. To get elected they must play ball with the people who have the money and right now it's the oil companies. Look at this fracking," he slapped the piece of paper with the back of his hand, "These people bribed legislators at all levels of government, had their corporate lawyers write legislation that was voted into law by these bribe takers; and have had their way all across the United States and the world. These corporations have taken fresh water from streams and rivers and shallow wells, contaminated it with chemicals and injected it deep into the earth to damage the rock formations and release natural gas."

"When we use fresh water we recycle it and it goes back into the air and streams and then someone else uses it. These big gas companies take it and contaminate it and finally inject it deep into the earth, never to be seen again. It's projected that the current natural gas drilling practices will destroy 50 trillion gallons of water, never to be used again. It explains the drought, it explains where the water went. And for what? So, some fat rich bastard can be a little fatter and a little richer? It makes me sick. The internal combustion engine is like 23 percent efficient. They are designed to burn up the benzene that is the carcinogenic byproduct of the refining industry. That means that nearly 80 percent of all of the oil that has ever been consumed has been wasted. It has been burned and has polluted the atmosphere so that some rich someone can be a little richer. Now the ice caps are melting."

"What about the letter?" She asked.

"They want to pay us $500 per acre so they can come here and take our ground water and inject it into the earth and extract some gas so they can burn it and pollute the atmosphere. This process will destroy our well water and pollute our streams and rivers. What will happen is they will spend enough money to fill our legislature with their puppets. They will write legislation that gives them special treatment so they can do whatever they damn well please and their puppets will sign it. We know they already own Washington by the way they have been able to have their way all over the country. They will destroy well water, sicken children, kill animals and buy up the press so everyone thinks they are good old boys. If anyone tries to sue them their legal team will hold things up in court as long as possible until most people just give up. After ten or fifteen years if anyone is left standing they will pay them off and then go on down the road to the next victims. They started out west and down south and pretty soon they will have destroyed the whole country." He finished the last of his roll in two bites.

"What can we do about this?" She pleaded.

"Nothing, not a blessed thing. As long as legislators are allowed to take bribes we don't stand a chance. The only solution would be if we could ever get lucky enough to get enough legislators who are tired of spending all their time fundraising to enforce existing laws on the taking of emoluments. Every one of these folks put their left hand on a bible and swear to not take bribes, its high time someone called them out. If we could get enough people to rail against the lobbyists we might stand a chance but it's probably too late." As he stood from his chair he walked to stand beside her chair and waited for her to stand to give her a bear hug. "Really good roll, thanks. I'll be done with the framing by tomorrow; we'll have it dried in by the end of the week. You hens need to get some paint chips and wallpaper samples picked out. Paint's on sale till the end of the month; we can save nearly ten bucks a gallon." As he walked to the door he turned. "We build that addition for that little baby and it won't stand a chance. We were supposed to leave this planet better than we found it. How in the hell did these evil people get so much power?"

"You should write a letter, people always say how much they enjoy reading them." She was clearing the dishes from the table.

She could hear him begin to whistle.

How in the world was she ever going to get him and Ken to kiss and make up? She didn't know about paint chips but Jerri would.

Chapter 28

AnnaBelle stood sideways looking into the mirror. She looked like she had a basketball under her shirt. She couldn't explain why she hadn't told Adam she was pregnant yet; perhaps she was still afraid that he might leave her.

I need to tell him in person, I have to go see him.

She scurried around the room, throwing various pieces of clothing onto the bed. She ran to the closet and selected a medium sized bag with airport wheels and a retractable handle and placed it on the bed. She concentrated on the bag for a moment and then hurried to the bathroom area to return with a towel that she used to wipe the dust from the top of the bag.

A few moments later, she hurried out the door of the bedroom dragging the overstuffed suitcase behind her, as she pulled it along it banged into the doorway and the walls of the hallway. She stopped before the hall closet and stood thinking for a moment. Finally, she dragged a raincoat from a coat hanger and left the closet door open as she locked the front door behind her.

The suitcase banged its way down the stairs and through the parking lot to the little yellow truck. She lowered the tailgate and forced the bag onto the bed, slamming the tailgate shut. She couldn't quite fit under the steering wheel with the raincoat so she tossed it into the back seat and adjusted the driver's seat to the last notch. As she sat in the seat she realized her feet wouldn't quite reach the pedals so she needed to raise the steering wheel and move the seat forward a little. Finally the truck was running and the tedious backing process was complete, she nailed the gas pedal but just as she was about to enter the street a small green car entered the lot and came to a stop, blocking the drive. AnnaBelle slammed the truck into park with just enough room between the two vehicles for the driver of the other car to come to her window and tap on it.

"Where in God's name do you think you're going, girl?" Debra was out of breath. "It's not even daylight yet, good thing I came straight home."

"You know where." AnnaBelle clenched the wheel with both hands.

"You can't go south, at least not alone, not with the mess down there." Debra was gripping the door of the truck equally hard. "Look, I'll go with. Give me those keys, I mean it." She insisted. "Pretty please."

"I'm not going to leave this seat," AnnaBelle handed the keys to Debra.

"Stay right there." Debra hurried back to her car, backed it up and parked it in the first available stall.

"Don't you need a bag or something?" AnnaBelle asked as Debra slid into the passenger seat, forced the keys in the ignition and started the truck.

"You know and I know you keep a spare set of keys for this truck because you're so scatterbrained that you lock your keys in here all the time. I know that as soon as I went back to the apartment you would use that set of keys to leave me here. Just call me Bilbo, leaving on an adventure without a handkerchief. Your credit cards can buy me anything I need, it will be fun. So, drive already!" Debra adjusted the seat to be more comfortable and crossed her arms across her chest. "Good thing you took that bitch cat home last time you went."

"She can have her litter in the barn just like her momma." AnnaBelle pulled onto the street.

"Got gas?" Debra finally broke the silence.

"Half tank." AnnaBelle forced a smile, "Thanks for coming."

"Let's hope we make it back alive, all the news from down there is very bad." Debra patted her friend on the knee.

"What's the latest poop, I stopped watching it was so bad."

"I can't believe that guy of yours hasn't got the good sense to get his butt back home." Debra thought for a moment. "Maybe if he knew you were preggers, he'd have a reason."

"So, it's my fault?"

"Sorry I said anything, have you tried his cell?"

"There hasn't been good cell service from down there for a week or better. As far as he knows we are still headed back to the folk's house for summer. Since you've kept up on the news why don't you get me up to speed?" AnnaBelle set the cruise on seventy-eight and settled back in the seat.

"This is the only thing that anyone is talking about on the radio. This big oil company that the men in your life went to work for drilled a hole in the bottom of the ocean. The Gulf of Mexico to be most specific." Debra was digging through every pocket of her purse. "Gum, I need gum, if you don't have any gum we need to stop somewhere because I'm having a fit"

"We need gas anyway, we can stop up here a ways, finish the story, please," AnnaBelle rummaged through the door pocket and came up with half a packet of gum. "This good enough?" She handed the packet over to Debra.

"Perfect, we still need to stop, thanks." Debra continued. "So, this oil company decided to drill a hole in the bottom of the ocean, couple of miles deep. As it turns out now, they had no idea what they were doing and no idea what they were getting into. Now, we find out, after it's too late; that guys on their team were warning them all along to not do it but the greedy SOB's, excuse my French, kept on. So, nobody ever did this before and they keep drilling in spite of everyone telling them to stop, but they won't. They drilled and drilled until they hit this giant pocket of boiling oil deep in the bowels of the earth. They knew there was a lot of oil down there, which is why they drilled the hole in the first place, but once they hit the pocket it was just too much."

"Too much oil?" AnnaBelle asked.

"Too much everything," Debra continued. "Too much oil, too much heat, too much pressure. They had no idea what they were drilling into because nobody ever had done this before. Once they hit the pocket, all hell broke loose. Literally, some people are saying now that these idiots drilled a hole right into the roof of Hell. This stuff was so hot and under so much pressure that it literally blew the drilling rig apart. Now, for months, there have been millions of gallons of oil spewing out of the earth into the bottom of the ocean and there's not a thing in the world we can do to stop it. That giant pool of oil has been trapped deep in the earth for millions of years without bothering these little ants that live on the surface and now it's all coming to the surface." Debra started to cry and it was a few minutes before she could continue.

"Now, to make matters worse yet, about a month after this rig exploded and while this oil is gushing out of the ground in an effort to relieve the pressure on this hole they drilled another and guess what the same thing happened again. These idiots tried to relieve the pressure of this one well by drilling another and now there are two big holes in the bottom of the Gulf of Mexico spewing boiling oil and they can't stop it."

"What are they saying is going to happen?" AnnaBelle was nervous.

"Some people think it will finally stop but others are saying that it will just keep spewing oil for years and years. Worst case scenario is that we all die." Debra let that sink in.

"The guy on the radio that seemed to know the most said the oil would cover the whole Gulf of Mexico. By the time the oil stops flowing it will kill everything in the Gulf of Mexico, destroy all of the beaches, kill all the birds and destroy much of the breathable air on the planet. The ocean temperatures will rise, storms will be worse and the ocean currents will be changed. When the ocean currents change, our climate will be affected and we will either be in for Arctic cold or blazing heat depending on whether you listen to AM or FM. We don't know for sure what will happen but everyone agrees it's going to be bad." Debra went silent and just stared out the window.

"That scares the hell out of me." AnnaBelle began to slow the truck. "Let's stop here for gas and gum. I could use a pee."

Debra and AnnaBelle took turns driving. The sun was rising in the east.

"Going to be a pretty day," Debra just opened her eyes; she rubbed her neck to get the kinks out. "Want me to drive?"

"In a little while, I'll pull over here in a minute. How did you sleep?"

"Not worth a darn, my neck aches. Look off to the west there, do those look like storm clouds? Debra pointed to the west.

"To the west and down to the south, that sky looks black." AnnaBelle checked the windshield wipers and the window washer fluid.

"Think I'll shut my eyes for a few more minutes if you don't mind." Debra drifted off to sleep again.

She awoke to the sound of squealing brakes and AnnaBelle swearing. The sky was black overhead, there was no sign of the rising sun and the windshield was being peppered with what looked like black hale.

"What the hell is that?" Debra set up in the seat.

"Just started," AnnaBelle explained. "The sky just kept getting darker and darker and all of a sudden it was like a hail storm except the hail stones are black and they leave a little black smudge wherever they hit."

The hail started to get worse.

"Pull over under that bridge behind that little truck." Debra commanded. "We need to sit this one out."

AnnaBelle parked the car behind a small pickup with a camper shell and the girls stepped out of the truck to stand beside a middle aged man and a woman and a little black dog.

"Never seen anything like this in all my born days," said the little man.

"Just like a scene from Hell." The woman made the sign of the cross.

They all watched as the black hail covered the highway and the ditches. The little hailstorm only lasted a few minutes and the sky parted and the sun shone through the dark sky.

"Let's drive while we can," AnnaBelle hurried back to the truck. "I want to find the next rest stop and go pee again."

She pulled the little truck out onto the highway. The yellow truck was now smeared with little black streaks. They drove for another five miles when the hole in the sky suddenly closed and the hail came down in a torrent.

"There's no bridge in sight, shall I just keep driving?" She asked.

"Might as well," Debra answered, "The last one didn't last long. Maybe if you go a little faster you can get through it quicker."

Suddenly the hail stopped and for a brief moment, nothing was coming from the sky. Then suddenly rain plunged from the sky, but not water, oil. The little yellow truck hit the spot of the highway where the oil had already fallen and lost all traction. The little yellow truck began to spin in the highway. As AnnaBelle applied the brakes the spinning seemed to get worse, the fender of the truck caught the edge of a guard rail and the truck spun onto the median and then began to roll and roll and roll.

Chapter 29

Adam felt fortunate, that rig might have sunk beneath the waves, but he still had a job. It was an even better job. There was to be a new rig and they were towing it toward the site right now, if this foul weather would cooperate they might have it in place in a month. They told him to go ahead and take four weeks, it would be paid because he had accumulated all of his leave time and sick time and he was to the point now that if he didn't use some of it he would lose it.

He decided to take this opportunity to go back home for a while and see AnnaBelle it had been a long time and they were out of touch.

All of his worldly possessions were packed into the red truck; he filled it up with gas, a case of bottled water, three jars of dry roasted peanuts and a sack of truck-stop beef jerky. He felt like a horse that has the barn in sight. The sun hadn't shined in days and the sky was a dirty grey color. The wind was starting to pick up and was blowing like a bitch. The way these trees were bending the wind was really fierce. Maybe he should try to catch the weather on the radio. All the FM stations were playing canned music, the same songs over and over; that meant that some months were better listening than others. This was a bad month for music. He turned the radio off, whatever bad weather was happening he was going to drive out of it. Christmas before last, AnnaBelle gave him a solar powered weather radio. By some lucky chance, Lightning Tim was the voice on the weather radio and whenever there was a report the little radio just crackled into life.

Weathermen love bad weather and Lightning Tim was no exception. The boiling oil was unchecked and was surging to the surface of the Gulf and killing all of the marine and plant life. Lightning Tim was a climate change denier and could wax poetic about the ice ages of the past and the temperature shifts caused by natural events. He could not deny this oil issue so he enthusiastically entered the climate change camp and was rooting for the good guys at every opportunity. The good guys being the human race and the bad guys being those large corporations hell bent on destroying the planet for profit.

The heated oil was warming the gulf waters and because of that Tim felt it explained this early hurricane season. "If you can remember back, folks, Hurricane Rita in 2005, Katrina, the Labor Day Hurricane of 1935 and the Galveston Hurricane of 1900 all came to us between Aug. 20 and Oct. 1."

"This one mimicked Hurricane Ida that formed on Nov. 3, 2009, in the southwestern Caribbean Sea. It possessed peak winds of 105 mph. and was classified as a category II hurricane. It struck the Nicaraguan coast, crossed the Yucatan Channel, passed over the massive oil spill and struck the southern coast of the United States."

"Holy Shit" Adam spoke out loud "There's a hurricane coming and I didn't pay attention." He turned up the radio.

Lightning Tim seemed to be getting more excited, "Hundred mile an hour winds are pounding the Gulf coast now and reports have come in that the hurricane is sucking the oil up inside it and raining it back down. We have black rain folks. This is an ecological disaster.

As if on cue, a single drop of something fell from the sky and landed in the middle of the windshield, Adam thought it was a bug. He was thankful that the window washer fluid tank in the truck was full. He turned on the wipers to get the bug off and the black spot smeared across the windshield leaving a black and yellow oily stain. He pressed the washer button and the mist covered the windshield but the oily streak remained. Maybe I didn't leave soon enough, he pressed down on the gas pedal.

Chapter 30

Bennett slammed the phone onto the receiver hard enough to shake the computer monitor. He removed a roll of mints from the top desk drawer, placed one in his mouth and trimmed the foil wrapping with a small pair of scissors. He carefully placed the scissors and mints back in the drawer and flipped the trimmings in the wastebasket.

He thought for a few moments then pushed a button on the phone.

The phone was answered after the first ring.

"Yes sir?"

"Come!"

Richards hurried into the room and closed the door behind him. He stood at attention at the front of the great man's desk.

"We have a problem with the pipeline and we need you to fix it," he looked at Richards closely. He liked it when he could see fear.

"What do I need to do sir?" Richards relaxed, thank God it wasn't something I did he thought.

"We opened that damned Trans America pipeline less than a month ago and we have a leak already. The tree huggers will have a field day with this if they find out. The problem is not the leak, we know it leaks; the problem is that somebody knows already."

"How do we know there is a leak, Sir, the pipeline is buried deep and the tar sands don't rise to the surface. They sink into the ground water; that is precisely why we buried the line so deep." Richards wanted to sit down but he hadn't been invited to, never was in fact; never would be.

"Remember the damned government required us to monitor the flow for the first 6 months as a concession to the tree huggers. We assured everyone that first there would be no leaks and second, that we would closely monitor the flow so that in the event of a leak we would shut the pumps down. We never had any intention of monitoring the flow and no way in hell are we going to shut down the pumps. Once that heavy shit stops flowing we might never get it to move again and we shore as hell aren't going to dig up 500 miles of 36" pipe." He slammed his fist down on the table. "What do you intend to do about this Richards you're the engineer?"

The young man tugged on his blue bow tie for a minute. "Those reports stack up for a week before they get processed and shipped out. The flow is monitored by two synchronized flow meters one in Canada and one at the Gulf. I can adjust the Gulf meter to match the one in Canada. The report from a week ago can show that our meters are in need of calibration and we can put new ones in and no one will be the wiser." He looked for a nod of approval. "Do we have the leak fixed? How much did we lose?"

"No you idiot we don't have the leak fixed. We aren't certain where it is, somewhere in Kansas. We are fairly certain that our fracking operations caused the earthquakes that caused the leaks; therefore we have decided that we like the leak just the way it is. We just need to push our time table up a little. Right now it is about 5 percent. We figure in 6 months' time we will have destroyed the Ogallala Aquifer. We thought it would take longer for a big leak to develop and we aren't really ready but what the hell. We will publicly fire the manager of the pipeline, privately give him a big bonus to go hide somewhere; apologize to the tree huggers, then make a killing on selling bottled water to the rubes. Just get down there and buy me a little time, we don't have the water processing patents all bought yet. I'll get the lawyers on that."

Richards wanted to object to this whole idea but held his tongue.

"You still here?" Bennett scolded after a short time, "Call me when you have those documents fixed. And I want a 50 percent increase in the fracking operations in the west."

"Do you have any kind of budget in mind for bribes sir?" Richards wanted to strangle this evil man. "We are going to need to grease the legislative wheels."

"Whatever it takes Richards. Everybody has a price." Bennett pointed toward the door and picked up the phone and began to dial.

"Yes sir." Richards spun on his heels and left the room. He hated the fact that he was treated like a slave. He was though, he knew it. The only thing that kept him going besides the fat paycheck was the fact that he knew he was going to get even. Like his daddy always said, "...don't get mad, get even."

Jenny would be the one who made travel arrangements he wanted to talk to her anyway.

He closed the door gently and walked briskly toward her cubicle. He looked over the top of the partition and she was on the phone. As she looked up at him he mouthed the words, "downstairs?" She understood, nodded, and held up her left hand to indicate 5 minutes.

When she entered the cafeteria he was already seated. The early lunch crowd was starting to dribble in and he had chosen a table with two chairs by the window the farthest point from the serving line. She was hungry and the food smelled delicious, as she passed the serving area, she checked out the daily special; liver and onions, mashed potatoes, green beans with bacon and onions, dinner roll, and medium iced tea for $2.50. Marjorie who ran the kitchen was a great cook and the food was the same as free but Richards seemed to be in a hurry so she would find out what he needed and then come back, there would be plenty.

She seated herself across from Richards and he slid a bottle of unsweetened tea and a glass of ice across the table to her, he was drinking a cup of black coffee, which he seldom did.

"Thanks. What's up?" She asked as she poured the tea into the glass.

"That criminal bastard needs to be put in jail." He was barely able to control his anger.

"You better stop drinking that coffee right now mister, you know how you get and you need this job." She was worried now. "What did he do this time?"

"I'm going to need it, the big man told me I need to get to the Control Center. We have an

146

ownership in that pipeline and there has been a major leak. I am supposed to get my butt down there and cover the whole thing up." He added more sugar to his coffee. "Can you get tickets for me please I need to leave right away."

"No problem on the tickets I can have them and your boarding pass sent to your phone before you can get to the airport. I thought there were monitors or something on that pipeline?"

"When we sold the plan to the activists who were opposed to it we told everyone that there were 16,000 data points that monitored the flow, we told them that they are refreshed every 5 seconds and that in the event of a spill we could shut down the pipeline in just 15 minutes. There is no way that pipeline is going to be shut down because of a little spill. Spills happen all the time for any number of reasons. We have 3000 miles of pipeline three foot or so in diameter flowing at a rate of about 400 barrels per minute. That is 16,000 gallons per minute or 280 gallons per second. Just imagine this whole room filled with tar sands oil in a matter of seconds. This stuff is heavy, even after it's diluted, which we have to do to get it to flow." He explained. "Even under the best conditions we gained approval to build this pipeline knowing that our safety system will allow 410 barrels per minute to flow for 15 minutes. That will be 258,000 gallons of tar sands at a minimum. We have a leak now, he said it is about 5 percent. That could be 30,000 gallons a day and nobody is going to notice that. In Alaska, we built the pipeline above ground with expansion joints; why would anyone bury a pipeline that carries those terrible dilbits."

"What will happen when it rises to the surface?" she asked.

"Won't happen, that's one of the big problems with tar sand oil, when it leaks it doesn't go up to float, it goes down into the ground water. This pipeline is buried around 4 feet deep, some places where it crosses that Ogallala Aquifer the water table is only a few feet deep, which means the pipe runs right through the ground water. The leak will go right into the water, sink down and no one will ever know until it starts coming out of peoples kitchen faucets. Remember the spill along the Kalamazoo River in Michigan? That was tar sands and it's still not cleaned up. The environmental crazies will have a field day with this one when they find out." He abruptly stood up to get another cup of coffee. When he returned he continued. "That pipeline has been a disaster since it started. That tar sand oil is just too nasty. It takes too much energy to get it out of the ground. It is too heavy to pump so we need to dilute it making it diluted bitumens or dilbits. The chemicals we add to it are especially toxic. Then it is still too heavy so we need to add pumping stations all along the route because we need hi pressure. This viscous product eats up the pipeline like crazy and then we have leaks. When they built the pipeline they stole peoples land using eminent domain which was just wrong and by making these kinds of enemies we have opened the door for trouble when we mess up. In your wildest dreams could you ever envision a U.S. legislator allowing a foreign entity to steal land from American citizens? Is that not what government is for, to protect citizens property from seizure by foreign interests? Does it matter whether a sword is used or a pen?"

"Did you know that there is a thirty year old law in the U.S. that the black stuff coming through this pipeline is not classified as oil, and that it is exempt from paying into the cleanup fund?"

"This pipeline is only designed to last 50 years anyway. We admitted that there would probably be 100 leaks during that period of time. These leaks were expected to amount to six to seven million gallons of tar sands. This pipeline only carries a small percentage of the oil that we use, automobiles are around 25 percent efficient so that means we waste 75 percent of the oil we burn anyway. Wouldn't it be better for our grandkids to just skip this pipeline and spend the five billion dollars on ways to be more efficient?"

"One branch of our company buried this pipeline deep in the earth, then another branch of our company starts fracking along the path of the pipeline. This fracking has caused earthquakes where there were almost none before and now we have a big leak. These people are fucking idiots. But, there is a little justice going on here, preliminary reports indicate that part of the leak is in Kansas. The greedy Kansas legislators allowed us a $50 million tax break and in exchange, previously earthquake-free Kansas gets the first earthquake induced leak. Karma's a bitch. Our fracking operations that Bennett is so proud of; those earthquakes are destroying the western part of the country. People in the know think that those earthquakes might even cause a volcanic eruption." He finished his coffee and took

149

his cup to the trashcan. "You know, they might be right."

"One more thing," he bent down to whisper in her ear; "I've decided to go to the EPA with this. I want to give you the chance to disassociate yourself from me."

"You better think twice about that," she cautioned, "the reason I was late was that the big man wanted me to look up a number for him and make a phone connection. Some guy with a funny name; sounds like Trillon; works for the EPA."

"Shit" said Richards.

"Corruption goes very deep in this country. You wouldn't believe the number of powerful guys Mr. Big talks to on a daily basis. You better not trust anybody and you better not think there is a thing we can do about this. Old Bennett might be planning to throw you under the bus and make you shoulder all the blame."

"You said 'we'?" He asked.

"Yeah, us, we and our grandkids. Now you be careful and don't talk to strangers if you know what I mean; I'll get those tickets to you before I eat." She squeezed his arm as she walked past him to the elevator. "Call me as soon as you get back, ya hear."

Chapter 31

Adam looked down at the speedometer, 30 mph. on this four-lane highway. The weather conditions were worse now than before. The wind pushed the truck around on the slick black roadway, the oily rain whatever that was smeared the windshield and the occasional bursts of clean rain didn't clear the black stuff from the glass. The wipers were on full and he was just able to see far enough ahead for the speed he was traveling. The other drivers felt the same way so the traffic was moving right along at a snail's pace. Middle of the damn afternoon and he was barely into Oklahoma the only good news was that Lightning Tim was still on the radio.

Ole Tim was in weatherman heaven, this was the "rootenist, tootenist, biggest, baddest storm in the history of mankind." All the stars aligned together, along with the tide, the hurricane and the great oil spill disaster to create the worst possible storm scenario. The hurricane had spawned over a dozen tornadoes already and these babies were big and wide and slow moving. He blamed the severity of the storms on the warm oil that was flooding the Gulf and warming the water. The winds were still pushing 100 mph and the eye was still at sea moving slowly toward Port Arthur, which was on the Texas Louisiana border.

Adam wished he had paid more attention to the weather and the effects of the spill he would have left two days ago. Since he knew he was coming home soon he didn't pay any attention to anything but work. He now wondered if he should have replaced that phone and kept in touch with home.

The nasty black stuff was no longer falling but the roadway was slick. His window was rolled down so that he could kind of stick his head out and see clearly instead of squinting through the occasional clear streak in the windshield. Since he was driving so slowly he had the opportunity to look around. Everything was covered with a layer of black goo. There were spots with no black but basically everything was covered. Many cars and trucks were in the ditch and the median, some abandoned, some wrecked. The thing that caught his eye was the tag on the front bumper that read, "Eat Beef," he could see that the truck was yellow and had rolled over several time coming to rest on its blown out wheels. His side rear view mirror showed him that there was no traffic coming up from behind so he slowed onto the left hand shoulder and backed up to take a closer look. The little truck was the right model and had four doors. What were the odds?

He hated to get out because he didn't want to drag the black goo back into the truck but he had to know. It had to be hers, the steering wheel was caved in and the windshield was broken and had blood stains where someone's head had obviously hit it. The seat belt was still clicked in place and was cut, most probably by someone dragging the driver out. It looked like the door had opened as the truck rolled and the seat belt had saved the driver from being ejected.

He recognized her overnight bag and suddenly burst into tears, this was all his fault. Had he called home and told them he was coming she would never have done this. Obviously, she was coming down south to find him. Maybe she wasn't dead. Somebody must have cut her out of the truck, he remembered seeing a little town about three miles back; maybe it had a hospital and maybe they took her there.

He pulled the overnight bag from what was left of the yellow truck and ran back to his pickup. He threw it into four wheel drive and left large ruts in the median strip as he headed back the other direction. About four miles later a sign beside the road was still readable, it was blue and held a big white H. Without paying attention to what the name of the town was he took the exit and followed the blue signs for several miles until he recognized a large building that must be the hospital. The parking lot was filled with cars and trucks and the driveway into the emergency room was filled with oil-covered cars. He drove through the small parking lot and couldn't find a place to park so he drove around the back and just pulled over the curb and onto the yard. The lawn guys would have a lot more to worry about than a couple of tire tracks.

The back door was unlocked so he worked his way down a long corridor to its intersection with another long corridor. There were many people down toward the emergency exit so he went the other way. He wanted to find the main entrance. He passed through a set of double doors and was surprised to see Debra standing in front of a vending machine pounding on one of the buttons.

Her left arm was in a sling and she was wearing an ill-fitting hospital gown. As he came close to her, she raised her head and smiled.

"Hello Cowboy, how did you know to come here?" She retrieved the soda from the machine.

"Is AnnaBelle OK?" He was out of breath and worried.

"Broke leg, unconscious, Doc thinks she'll recover, we don't know; baby's fine thank God."

"What baby?" He gasped.

"Ya'lls baby. She meant to tell you, but she was afraid you would leave her and then when she finally got up the courage she couldn't get hold of you, so she decided to come on down here and find you. I tagged along. That nasty oil rain or whatever that was caused us to wreck and we are lucky to be alive. So, how you been?" She smiled.

Chapter 32

John was seated in a solid oak chair just inside the large entry opening that led into the very large room. He had just completed cutting the opening into the existing structure. Two 55-gallon drums contained most of what was left of the wallboard and insulation. A large push broom was leaned against the siding of the existing house where the new stud wall was fastened to the old siding, and beside it was a large aluminum grain shovel. Beside him on the floor was an opened twelve pack of bottled beer and as he finished one he tossed the empty bottle toward the two drums and missed. The bottle bounced against the side of the plastic drum and fell to the floor unbroken. He opened another.

"Looks great," said Susan Williams as she forced her way through the plastic sheeting that protected the rest of the house from the construction mess. She was wearing jeans and a work shirt and well-worn cowboy boots.

She had left him to his own devices when it came to this room. He was the type of man that once he started something it was best to just stay out of the way. The farm possessed every imaginable type of equipment and it didn't take him long to dig the hole for the big basement and frame and roof the new attached structure. For John, bigger was better so he had sized the room based on the widest roof trusses he could get and built everything else around that. The walls were framed and sheeted but not finished either outside or inside and the floor was bare plywood with a stairs built down into the basement at one side. The hard and noisy part was when he blasted the hole from the new basement into the basement of the old house. He had actually hired a contractor for this work because he explained he didn't want to buy a concrete saw.

"Looks like a barn," John said miserably.

"What did you expect that it would look like when you started?" She asked.

"Not this, it was to be a sort of family room with space for the baby."

"Plenty of space here," she helped herself to a beer from the carton.

John didn't object but normally she didn't drink, hadn't in fact since her high school days. She was worried too.

She twisted the top from the bottle, tossed the cap into the barrel and took a good long pull at the bottle. "Why don't you call Jerri and let her help you with this? She does it for people all the time and if I tried to help this would still look like a barn." She patted him on the shoulder, leaned down and kissed him, and finished the beer. On her way out she picked up the empty bottle from the floor and placed both bottles in the barrel. "I'll call her because you're afraid Ken might answer; you boys need to get over it."

John thought about Jerri for a minute. That was a long time ago. She would know what to do with this big space. Susan really wouldn't care so long as it was attached to the kitchen. He tossed the empty toward the barrels, made it. He stepped through the plastic barrier into the old house. "How about if we invited them over for supper, you feel like cooking something? I'm done for the day."

Susan couldn't believe what she was hearing, for over twenty years John had refused to have anything to do with the man who used to be his best friend. She thought about Ken for a minute. "Seven all right?" She hollered.

"Perfect."

She dialed the number, "Jerri, hi it's Susan. Heard from Adam? Shoot. Listen, could you and Ken come over for supper around seven? I think John's ready to kiss and make up. Great. Not a word, it's been four days now since we heard anything from AnnaBelle I think John needs someone to talk to. OK, bye."

She started to hum a little tune. Ken's favorite was fried chicken, mashed potatoes and gravy, black eye peas with jalapenos, with homemade rolls and real butter. She cold thaw the chickens, start the bread, most of that apple pie was left from yesterday. Apple pie was his favorite, she felt like a schoolgirl, must have been that beer.

Chapter 33

Jerri Thomas laid her cell phone on the table. She thought about John for a minute. That was a long time ago. There was a lot of regret going on in her mind right now. Ken was out working in his industrial strength man cave as usual; many times in the past he had expressed a desire to apologize to John perhaps this was the time. He was worried about Adam, probably more than she. She knew how strong a man Adam had become due in large part to Ken's guidance. Ken couldn't see it; to him, Adam would always be the apprentice.

She walked out to the shop and heard the buzzing sound of a welding machine, she liked that smell. The bright blue light lit up the ground outside the double doors and sparks flew whenever the light flashed. She knew enough to never look directly at the arc and stood and waited for Ken to finish. He wouldn't be able to hear her with that welding hood on and she didn't want to cause him to hurt himself. It wasn't long before that part of the project was completed. He rose from the piece of metal, laid the welding rod down, removed the welding helmet and gloves and walked over to turn off the machine.

He was welding a hitch onto a trailer made from an old pickup truck bed. The shop was large and well-lit, not surprising since Ken worked with electricity. The shop was tidy but cluttered enough that one could tell that a lot of work got done here. A large truck was pulled into the other end of the building with the hood up and a large motor was suspended by chains ready to be installed.

"We still on for dinner out tonight?" She spoke as soon as the noise from the welding machine went away.

"Just finished this little job for Benny then I'm coming in to clean up." He walked over to a large stainless steel sink and began to wash his hands with dollops of heavy-duty industrial strength soap. It was in a big wall dispenser that read "BLOOP" or "BODO" or something like that. She had used it herself and it had a lot of grit in it and smelled of citrus. You used the soap without water then rinsed it off. "Bet you thought I forgot about dinner?"

"It never hurts to check, if you had your way you would work out here all night long. I changed our plans about where we are going to eat." She said as she turned to walk back to the house. "We're going to John and Susan's for supper and you boys are going to kiss and make up."

Ken thought about Susan for a minute. That had been a long time ago. Supper with Susan, what a treat, maybe she'd cook chicken. His mouth started to water just thinking about it. Thank goodness he wouldn't need to dress up now. Jerri liked him to wear a tie when they went out and he hated to dress up. He looked with regret at that motor, if Benny hadn't stopped him he would have had that motor in today.

As Jerri walked back in toward the house she thought about what to wear. Susan would be wearing a pair of jeans and a nice shirt, so jeans it would be, she had a new pair of boots with high heels, John liked high heels.

When she was ready to leave she looked at herself in the mirror. Heels, jeans, big belt buckle, and cowboy shirt. She unsnapped two buttons of the shirt to reveal a white low cut push up bra, if she bent down just this much, perfect. She snapped the buttons back; they would come loose by accident after the meal. As she left the room she dabbed on a little cologne here and here and a little there.

"You better drive," Ken walked to the refrigerator and chugged a can of beer, throwing the empty in the trash under the sink. "We need to stop at Johnnies on the way they may not drink anymore and I need all the help I can get."

She noticed he was wearing a tie and sport jacket. She felt slightly underdressed. She couldn't recall this happening before, must be Susan. Where were the feelings of jealousy? Why was it she couldn't stop thinking about John?

"Sort of a house warming present?" She asked as she locked the back door.

"We've both been to that house a thousand times back when we were kids, I thought maybe a little wine and beer." He sat in the passenger side of the SUV and looked straight forward. She thought he looked like someone going to a funeral, or lynching; their own.

Chapter 34

The radio crackled to life.

Lightning Tim here at this end of the mike folks; with some disturbing developments.

That black stuff you see on your lawn is oil from the Gulf. That little hole in the bottom of the ocean just keeps pumping hot oil to the surface. The hot oil is warming the surface water and the theory is that the warm water is helping to create these hurricanes. That first one that hit us was pretty close to Camille from back in 1969. It was the second most intense hurricane of record to hit the United States. The estimated wind gusts were nearly 200 miles per hour with sustained inland wind speeds of 120. A storm tide of 24.6 feet occurred at Pass Christian, Mississippi. There have been over a dozen tornadoes associated with this storm that have caused untold millions in property damage. It was responsible for over 250 deaths.

As that bad boy is pushing east another big one appears to be brewing. A tropical depression has developed near the southern Windward Islands. This one could mimic Hurricane Dennis from back in 2005. It became a Category 4 hurricane that pounded Cuba with 135 mph. winds and made landfall over the western Florida Panhandle. Ten tornadoes were reported in association with Dennis. It caused forty-two deaths and over $2 billion in property damage.

Chapter 35

Susan was wearing an apron when she opened the door, it was decorated with some sort of large red flowers with little yellow ones thrown in here and there, green vines and little green leaves connected the bunch. She held out both hands for Jerri, "Come in, come in; I'm just getting the bread." For just a brief moment her eyes met with Ken's and her face turned a beet red. "Long time no see stranger, welcome. Make yourselves at home. Those rolls are going to burn." She rushed off toward the kitchen.

Ken turned toward the noise before closing the door; John was taking a large four wheel drive tractor toward the barn. He smiled and waved from the cab.

Ken was overwhelmed with the smells, fried chicken and fresh made bread, his mouth began to water.

"Smell that?" He couldn't help himself.

Jerri smiled, and led the way into the house looking into each doorway as they went toward the family room. It was a large room with a fireplace in one corner, a high vaulted ceiling with a long stemmed paddle fan and lights hanging from the rafters. A large double sliding glass door faced the south and provided a spectacular view of the farm. The wet bar in the corner had five bar chairs and the back of the bar was stocked with all manner of bottles and empty glasses.

Jerri hung her little brown leather jacket on one of the pegs along the wall and sat on the first bar chair.

"This place hasn't changed since John's folks had it." Jerri spoke with amazement in a hushed tone. She tried not to sound catty; her place looked different almost weekly.

"Looks the same to me too," exclaimed Ken, "Except for that 72" flat screen on the wall. I remember watching cartoons every Saturday morning from right there. The couch has changed." He walked to the sliding door.

"The couch may be new but it's the spitting image of the old one." She turned with the sound of boots in the hallway and stood; her hand went up and unsnapped a snap.

John walked into the room, "Had to move some hay," he hung his hat on a peg. He took two steps forward and stood in front of Jerri, their eyes met then his eyes went south as she hoped they might. He smiled and hugged her with his left arm.

"Good to see you, welcome, welcome."

He walked across the room to where Ken was standing beside the door. He rubbed his right hand on his jeans then held it out. They looked each other in the eye and Ken took the extended hand and shook it. At the same time they both said, "I apologize." Then they embraced each other with their left arms.

Quietly Susan had entered the room and watched the two men bond.

"High time," she said. She had removed the apron and was wearing a low cut black dress. Jerri turned and they too embraced.

"It's been too long girl," Jerri spoke softly to Susan.

"Yes it has," Susan replied. They just held each other for a good long while.

"Sort of touching don't you think," John spoke. He and Ken stood and watched the girls. Just like old times, he thought.

"Want a beer?" Ken walked toward the sacks he had set on the counter.

"Is a pig's pussy pork? Does a bear shit in the woods?" John held out his hand for the beer that Ken offered. They each popped the top.

Ken held up his beer.

"To old friendships."

"Hear, hear." John held his beer up.

"The meal is ready anytime," Susan announced.

"I'd like a beer first. How about you?" Jerri asked.

Susan thought for a moment, "Sure."

Jerri took Susan by the hand and led her into the kitchen. "You're looking good, the years have treated you kindly," she stood back at arm's-length and gazed upon Susan. They sat at the kitchen table sipping their beers. "You know, I've been thinking a lot lately about how things were before."

"Before?" asked Susan.

"Before I turned into such a bitch, before I stole your man. I'm really sorry, I'd go back and change it if I could, but I wouldn't trade Adam for anything."

"I feel the same way about AnnaBelle," confided Susan.

"You didn't dress up like that for me?" Jerri asked in a whisper.

"No, not really. You might as well unsnap that next button; I've watched him look at you all evening." Susan confided.

"You could have saved that cute black dress, you had him with the apron," Jerri replied and they both laughed.

"You don't mind if I seduce your man?" Jerri finally got around to it.

"Turn about is fair play," Susan replied. She held up her can of beer and Jerri did the same.

John and Ken sat side by side at the bar.

"I didn't find out about how your dad made you join up until years later, why didn't you tell me at the time?" John asked.

"After Susan kicked me out I was sort of feeling sorry for myself. Then that deal with Jerri, look, I'm sorry about that." Ken apologized.

"That is all water under the bridge, we both did some stupid shit; now you guys have Adam and we have AnnaBelle. It all works out. Jerri hasn't changed a bit," John rose from the bar and set two more beers on the counter.

"Ever think about the way things used to be?" Ken confided.

"Lately I have." John admitted.

"Jerri didn't dress like that for me." Ken stated.

"I remember that smell, that food is your favorite, you used to con Mom into cooking it whenever you came over to spend the night." John said thoughtfully.

"We always had a rule that we would never go after the other guy's girl, and I broke the promise." Ken admitted.

"You weren't entirely to blame in that matter, as I recall she had a lot to do with it," John volunteered.

"So, where are we here?" Ken asked.

"Tell you what, let's you and me let the girls decide. You and I let bygones be bygones and agree that no matter what happens from now on we agree to uphold that pledge we made to each other when we were ten. Remember how we became blood brothers just like the Lone Ranger and Tonto. Hiyo Silver. Away. I like to bled to death over that deal; the knife was way to sharp." John rolled up his sleeve to look for that old scar.

"Still blood brothers." Ken stated and held out his hand. They shook heartily.

Chapter 36

"That was perfect, Honey," John pushed the empty pie plate toward the center of the table.

"Good choice," Jerri commented. She knew this was Ken's favorite meal.

Susan rose from the table with dishes in her hand. "I don't know if John mentioned it but we have a little project going on here that we could sure use some help with Jerri."

She returned and took the dishes that John offered. "I see you're both done, John why don't you take Jerri into the new addition and maybe when Ken's done with his second helping he can help me clear away the dishes and then we can join you.

"Sure, I'll help," said Ken after swallowing a mouthful; "You guys go on."

"Would you like another beer?" Jerri asked.

"If you don't mind." Ken stated.

"Me too." Susan volunteered.

John and Jerri looked at each other and smiled.

Jerri returned with four beers and John led the way down the hall to the hole in the wall where the new room was to be.

Susan noticed that now both of Jerri's snaps were unsnapped.

"Another piece of pie?" Susan asked as she rinsed the last of the dishes and placed them in the dishwasher.

"I'm stuffed, but thanks. You're the best cook I ever knew. I've sure missed it." He carried his pie dish to the sink and as he handed the plate to her their hands touched. It was like a lightning bolt for her and she dropped the little dish into the sink.

She rinsed it and placed it into the dishwasher. As she was tidying up the rest of the dinner mess Ken walked softly down the hallway and peered through the plastic sheeting into the new construction. He smiled and returned to the kitchen.

Susan was just removing her apron and Ken backed her up to where she was pushed against the sink. Her heart began to race.

"My wife and your husband are making out in a big empty room down that hallway. What do you think you and I should do about it?" He was slightly taller than Susan and their eyes were locked together.

She raised her lips to be kissed and he obliged.

Their passion was building at a rapid rate; they were locked in a heated embrace when they were interrupted by a ringing noise from down the hallway.

"It's my phone; I was cleaning that new room and left it in there. That ring means its AnnaBelle calling." Susan broke their embrace and listened toward the sound.

"Shall I answer it?" Jerri called from the other room.

"Please, go ahead," Susan said loudly as she adjusted her dress and kissed Ken one more time.

She quickly walked down the hallway and entered the room. She passed John on the way to the phone that Jerri was holding. He was in the process of tucking in his shirt. She stopped in front of John and kissed him. She could smell Jerri's perfume; it was like she remembered. "Where is she?" Susan was wondering about AnnaBelle.

"Just a minute," Jerri said to the phone.

Ken had just entered the room and walked toward the group.

Jerri turned to Ken and spoke. "It's Adam."

Chapter 37

Adam hated hospitals, hate was too strong a word he just never liked them very much. He didn't want to breathe the air or touch anything, it gave him the willies. Debra led him down the corridor of the small hospital to a hallway where the sign read, "Intensive Care." A big sliding glass door was opened part way and the large hanging drape was only partly closed. They were able to see into the room. A nurse dressed in a blue scrub top paused on her way out of the room.

"Can I help you?" she asked.

"How is she?" Adam asked in a halting voice.

"We think she is starting to wake up, there are certain signs that we look for. Would you like to go in?"

"Would it be alright?" Adam started to enter the room.

"Don't see what it would hurt." The nurse turned on her heel and walked toward the nurse station.

Debra followed Adam into the room and walked to the other side of the bed. AnnaBelle appeared to be asleep. There were tubes and wires attached from her body to various machines.

Adam pulled a chair up to the bed and held her hand through the silver railing. He turned toward Debra, "She been like this the whole time?"

"I guess," she held up her left arm with the cast on it, "I was sort of busy myself."

"Have you called her folks, they surely need to know." Sort of thought I'd wait till she woke up, my phone never made it here from the crash scene and she left hers in the bag in the truck which is God knows where by now." She sat down in the only other chair, opened her soda and took a sip.

"Did she have it in her overnight bag?" Adam asked hopefully.

"I think so; we left in such an all fired rush."

"I have her bag, I took it out of the truck. It was covered with pieces of glass so I left it in the bed of my truck, the phone is probably still there. Do you think I should go fetch it?" He started to rise.

"Let's wait a little bit, she might wake up. If I were a parent I would rather have no news than bad news, they can't do anything for her anyway. Damn, I'm hungry." She slumped down in the chair.

"Surely they have a little gift shop with food?" He asked.

"I didn't bring any extra money, this soda tapped me out." She lamented. "Don't worry about me I'll be fine.

"I've got jerky and peanuts in the truck, you're welcome to it."

"Maybe you better get that phone now, in case it starts to rain or something." She looked at Adam expectantly. "Don't forget the food when you come back."

"I'll be right back." He kissed AnnaBelle's hand and tucked the hand gently under the sheet.

"How sweet," Debra thought to herself, "where's my guy?"

Adam had a pretty good idea which direction to go as he followed the corridors back the way they had come. When he came to the intersection that led toward the emergency room he had his bearings. He decided to walk down through the emergency exit because it wasn't as busy right now. Back in the intensive care unit, the tiled walls and floors were shiny and clean like you would expect in a hospital. This entry to the emergency room was a mess. From high up on the walls, the area was covered in a layer of black oil. Handprints could be made out on the walls where people had leaned against them black shoe tracks were everywhere and led off down the corridor to the emergency room itself. He made an effort to keep from walking in the oily footprints because he didn't want to have to clean his shoes. When he'd gotten outside, he was shocked to see that everything was covered with a fresh layer of oil. There must have been a rainstorm when he was inside. But it wasn't just rain, it was black rain. He looked up at the sky and the dark clouds looked oily with kind of a yellow sheen. It wasn't that it was nearing sunset— those clouds had oil in them. He could smell it. Disgusting.

He tippy toed out to where the truck was parked on the grass and trying not to touch anything. He unzipped the travel bag and found the phone. He turned it on and checked the battery; it was good. It was tricky getting the door opened without getting oily but he managed. He wanted to just get in the truck and drive out of this nightmare, but he was a father now.

The noise caused him to look toward the east. It sounded like a big truck with the muffler torn off and that is exactly what it proved to be. Finally after what seemed like a long time a farm truck with a flatbed drove in to view. It was traveling at a high rate of speed and the noise was deafening. The truck was white with black streaks, streaks that ran horizontally; it had been traveling fast through that latest shower. It pulled up to the emergency entrance and a man in cowboy boots and a cowboy hat jumped from the drivers' seat and ran around to the back of the truck. He ran into the building and shortly thereafter returned followed by three hospital workers pushing a wheeled gurney. What he had thought was a pile of oily hay on the flatbed proved to be a person rolled into an oily blanket. As the attendants began to unroll the blanket and move the body to the gurney the driver finally ran to the ignition switch and turned the noisy machine off.

He listened to the driver now that he could hear, he was saying something about how it was all his fault, the oil, the slick roads, he apparently went sideways on the road, tore across the median strip and as he was coming up out of the ditch he had hit this ladies car right on the drivers side. That story would explain how he lost his muffler and exhaust system. There was no real sign of damage to the front of the truck but with the oil and all it was hard to tell, anyway a small car was no match for a big farm truck. He could see the lady move her arm so she wasn't dead. They wheeled her in and the door closed. The driver of the truck sat on the curb and wept.

He decided to say a prayer for the lady and the driver. It was all he could think to do. There was going to be a lot of this type of thing going on.

This really wasn't any of his business so he gathered his grocery bag from the cab and entered the hospital the way he had come in the first place. There was a mat inside the door that he wiped his shoes on before he went in.

Debra was nodding, half asleep. He set the bag of jerky and peanuts beside her chair without waking her. He resumed his position on the chair beside the bed and held AnnaBelle's hand. Then he too nodded off.

The nurse made several trips in and out to check various things, she noticed the two visitors sleeping she just smiled and tried to keep the noise down.

He was awakened when he felt AnnaBelle's previously limp hand, grasp his. He was suddenly awake. He concentrated his gaze on her face and it appeared that her eyes were trying to open. She blinked a few times, tried to focus and in a scratchy voice that was barely audible said; "Adam?" Her hand squeezed his tightly.

He rose quickly and went to the nurse station to tell the nurse. She summoned a doctor and suddenly the little room was filled with any number of people, each with their own piece of the medical puzzle.

The clatter woke Debra who sat up in the chair.

Adam placed the sack in her lap. "Help yourself."

Debra looked into the sack and smiled. She found the open sack of jerky and began to gnaw on a piece.

Meanwhile, AnnaBelle was responding to the ministrations of the attendants. The nurse was holding a glass of water to her lips as she drank.

"Where am I?" she questioned.

"No talking for a minute." The doctor ordered as he finished listening to her heart with the stethoscope. He placed the instrument around his neck and said, "Well young lady you gave us quite a scare, you've got some cuts and bruises but now that you are awake we can ask you if you feel any pain?"

AnnaBelle thought for a minute, "Not really."

He turned, spoke quietly to the nurse for a moment; and then left the room.

"You'll want to be seeing the baby," the nurse in the blue top adjusted the pillows. "I'll go get the child.'

"Baby?" AnnaBelle felt her abdomen. "How long have I been unconscious?"

"Long enough to become a mommy," Debra interjected. "Don't you remember the wreck?"

"I remember that terrible oil and the road was so slick, then nothing." She turned toward Adam. "How did you get here?"

"I was driving home and found your truck in the ditch and figured they took you to the nearest hospital. Why didn't you tell me you were pregnant, and who is the father?"

"You are, silly. Who else? You left me in a motherly way, remember how that could have happened?"

Adam thought for a moment and smiled. "Okay, is it a boy or girl? We better be getting married."

She smiled at that and held her arms up. They embraced as best they could amongst the wires and tubes. They kissed.

"Is that a proposal? You heard him Deb." She lay back against the pillows, she was obviously weak, but she had a smile on her face.

"Is now a good time to call?"

The nurse wheeled a little cart into the room. Inside was a tightly wrapped baby, sleeping.

The nurse carried the baby around to the other side of the bed and placed it in AnnaBelle's left arm. She smiled and the baby's eyes opened and smiled back.

"Do you feel up to this?" The nurse asked.

"I'm OK," AnnaBelle didn't sound too sure of herself. "What do I do?"

"Just do what feels natural," said the nurse as she pushed the cart to the side of the room. "Mamma's been feeding babies for thousands of years. You'll get the hang of it. Push the button when you want me to take him back."

"Him," thought Adam. Then it's a boy. He hadn't been able to figure a way to broach the subject.

"It's a boy, Adam." AnnaBelle spoke weakly. "What shall we name him?"

"I'd call him lucky," interjected Debra with a chuckle.

"We need to think on that for a while." Adam didn't want to make a rash choice. "For now let's just call him baby."

"OK Baby," AnnaBelle cuddled the little one.

The nurse came into the room. "I don't want to seem pushy or anything but we're starting to fill up with all these car wrecks. Would it be OK with you if we moved you two girls into a double room and expedited your release? You feelin' alright hon?" She checked AnnaBelle's vital signs. "Everything looks good here."

"How soon can they leave?" Adam asked the nurse.

"Under normal circumstances we would want to keep mother and baby for a couple of days just to be on the safe side, especially after the wreck and all. Today, Dr. Nelson said we could let them all go home tomorrow afternoon after his rounds, unless something unexpected comes up." She checked AnnaBelle's eyes with a flashlight.

"We're roommates." Debra volunteered. "Sharing won't be a problem."

"I'll get that room ready, and thank you." The nurse said as she walked from the room.

"I can drive us home tomorrow." Adam said.

"I don't think I can stand to ride in that old pickup for that far." AnnaBelle lamented. "Please call Mom and see if she and Dad could come down and get me."

"Your folks on speed dial?" Adam turned on the phone he retrieved from his pocket.

"Go to recent calls, it's the one called 'Susan.'"

He held the phone in his hand and did nothing. "Before I call, where are we?"

"I have no idea," AnnaBelle admitted.

He looked at Debra and she just shrugged her shoulders.

He stepped out of the room and returned a short time later. "We are in Grover's Corner, Oklahoma. We are around 80 miles south of Oklahoma City on Interstate 35. We're less than 300 miles from home. Want me to call?"

"Would you please, I feel like such a fool." AnnaBelle apologized.

"Lighten up sweetheart," Adam encouraged, "Things could have been a whole lot worse."

He dialed the number. "Mom? Is that you?"

Chapter 38

"This is a really bad connection Honey, speak up." Jerri listened into the phone.

"Something to write with." Jerri spoke to the room at large.

Susan left the room and returned with a little yellow note pad and a sharp pencil. She handed it to Jerri who placed the tablet on the table saw and wrote on the paper.

"Okay Honey, bye, love you." She turned the phone off.

"More beer," she emptied the can she had been drinking.

Ken returned with four beers dangling from the plastic six pack holder. He passed them around and they all stood looking at Jerri.

"That was Adam..." she began.

"But that was AnnaBelle's phone I could tell from the ringtone." Susan questioned.

"If I could finish," she stared at Susan who mouthed 'I'm sorry'.

"That was Adam, he is with AnnaBelle and Debra. Everyone is fine including the BABY!" She stared at both John and Susan.

"We meant to tell you but couldn't get around to it." Susan apologized.

"What's this about a baby?" Ken finally seemed to understand.

"AnnaBelle got knocked up, said it was Adam's; we have no reason to doubt her." John explained. "We've kept quiet about it because we were waiting for her to get up the courage to tell Adam."

"Anyway." Jerri continued, "Very pregnant AnnaBelle and Debra drove south to find Adam since they hadn't heard from him in several weeks. And neither have his parents I might add." She looked at Ken who nodded in agreement.

"There was a storm and she lost control and rolled the car in the ditch. Let me reiterate that both the girls are fine." She responded when Susan started to react in alarm.

"Adam came by the crash site later and seeing the truck in the ditch did some investigating and found them in a hospital in," she looked at the note pad, "Grover's Corner, Oklahoma, 253 miles south of here. She wants us all to come on down and get them tomorrow. John, do you think we could take the travel trailer? She wants to be able to lie down. Adam said they want to release them early because it's a small hospital and it's getting full because of all the traffic accidents."

"Sure." Answered John, "but what about the baby?"

"Adam didn't go into any great details only that baby and mother are fine but she is going to sleep now and that we could talk in the morning. He said to watch the weather channel about the weird weather going on down there and to bring rain suits." She opened her beer and took a drink.

180

John turned to Ken. "Have you got a 16' trailer with a wench that we could drag behind the travel trailer? It's got a 2" ball. We could use it to bring her truck back."

"I've got two that would work; no problem." Ken stated.

"That's settled, the RV is all ready to go. You guys spend the night here and we can pull out of here by eight or so in the morning, swing by Kens and pick up the trailer and be there shortly after noon. Been past that place a dozen times, never stopped, never needed to."

"Sounds fine to me, I've got lots of leave time built up." Ken answered.

There was a sort of uncomfortable silence building.

Jerri left the room and returned with four more beers, she passed them out.

"Okay folks; let's stop beating around this bush. We all know what's going on here. Are we ok with it?" Everyone nodded in agreement.

"Breakfast at 6:30, we're going to be in the basement in the room with the waterbed. You all do whatever. She walked over to John kissed him then took Ken by the hand. He ran over and kissed Jerri then followed Susan from the room.

"They get the waterbed eh?" Jerri commented.

He walked toward her and unsnapped the last of the snaps on her shirt. "We have the whole upstairs. Grandma.

Chapter 39

Bennett leaned back in his chair while he listened for the ringing phone to be answered.

"Is that you Peterson? He spoke before man on the other end could speak.

"Mr. Bennett, it is so good to hear from you. How can I help you today?"

"We're having a little problem down in the Gulf Peterson and it's going to be awfully expensive. We intend to hold the courts off as long as possible but it's only a question of time before we lose, big. What I want you to do is to sell my shares of Richman Oil as fast as you can without getting me thrown in jail. I'm sure the rest of the board of directors will feel the same. Start immediately, that's all.

"Yes sir;" the line went dead.

Chapter 40

Jenny carried her dinner tray to the farthest table, where they always sat. Richards had returned to the office this morning and she was anxious to hear how the trip went.

"I couldn't decide between soup or chili, so I got both," Richards took a seat opposite Jenny. His tray contained a soda, two large bowls and an obscene number of crackers in individual packages.

She was staring out the window in dismay. "We are responsible for all this oil."

A black oily mist was falling from the sky and the windows were streaked with rivulets of dark water.

"In a manner of speaking, I suppose we are;" Richards agreed, "It takes a bunch of little cogs to make a big machine and I suppose we need to take our share of the blame. If you can believe the spin doctors, this was a once in a lifetime event that happened because the moon and the stars were lined up just so. I think we know better. These greedy idiots drilled a couple of holes into the bottom of the ocean, hit a pocket of oil and pressure that no one ever imagined and now they can't get it to stop flowing.

"How long before it stops?" She asked.

"Best answer is that no one knows, when the pressure is gone I guess, could be weeks could be months.

"Is it safe? She began to eat her meat loaf.

"It can't be safe. The worst is probably over for now until another storm comes along. Just try not to breathe any more of it than you have to." He took a bite of chili. "Good Chili, spicy."

"How was your trip?" She wanted to get her mind off of the oil.

"Once again I pulled the big guy's titty out of the wringer." He smiled. "By reprograming those flow sensors we can make those little leaks just disappear, at least on paper. Just like they never happened."

"Aren't you talking about millions of gallons of oil?" She asked.

"Drop in the bucket. It will be an environmental catastrophe when the tree huggers find out. If they'd a had a little more money they might have stood a chance."

"Isn't that illegal?" She asked.

"Which side writes the laws? There are always tolerances built in to any contract. As long as our team writes the contracts and the laws we have enough wiggle room. That guy at the EPA that Bennett was talking to is the one who will impose any penalty. As long as we know what the fine will be we can plan for it and just put it in the budget. We will simply calculate how many people we will kill, put a settlement cost to that and compare that cost to the cost of saving the lives in the first place; whichever is cheapest."

"Let me get this straight, we know that there will be a substantial leak in that pipeline and we keep pumping anyway."

"Sure, we'll just cover it up till we get caught then we apologize and pay a fine; happens all the time. This soup is good too."

"Why are you not your usual combative self?" She inquired.

"I guess I'm just numb. You pretty much hit the nail on the head with that comment about us being responsible; I guess if we aren't actively opposed to the evil we condone it by inaction. Until individuals like Bennett are held accountable for their actions stuff like this will go on. As long as politicians are allowed to take money from people like Bennett stuff like this will go on." He looked out the window for a while, thinking; then turned his head toward the entrance.

A tall young man in a suit and tie was making his way through the serving line.

"I know him." Richards said in passing.

Jenny turned to look. "Who?"

"The guy in the suit with the red tie, his name's Justin Williams. Nice guy." Richards watched the man and waited a moment, then stood and waved his arm and nodded.

"You don't mind, do you Jenny?" He asked a little late.

"Not at all, he's quite good looking." She adjusted her shirt collar and dabbed her face with a napkin.

"You're welcome to sit with us if you like," Richards motioned to an empty chair. "This is Jenny Houston from our office."

"Glad for the company, James isn't it?" Justin shook hands with Richards. "Good to meet you Jenny," he nodded in her direction, waited for her to offer her hand then shook it gently.

"Vegetable soup looked good," he said as he took his seat.

"Plenty of crackers left if you want some," Richards pushed his tray in that direction.

"I just got back from the coast," Richards volunteered; "We blew a hole somewhere in the pipeline and Bennett sent me down to fix things."

"To fix the leak?" Justin clarified.

"No, I was sent to fix the evidence of a leak. Bennett wants to destroy all of the ground water so he can make more millions cleaning it up. His plan is that people will no longer have tap water, that they will have a big tank in their yard like they do with propane now and he'll make a killing selling clean water, it's the new oil." Richards gathered his bowls and empty cracker wrappers and carried them to a trash can.

"What brings you to town Justin?"

"The great man has sent me to disprove a nasty rumor." Justin flipped his tie over his shoulder and began to eat carefully.

"What rumor is that?" Richards asked. Jenny cocked an ear to listen.

"We won't be breathing a word of this to anyone else?" Justin looked expectantly at both of them. "I wasn't sworn to secrecy or anything but we all know there is no job security around here."

"No worries from this end," Richards and Jenny both nodded agreement.

Satisfied, Justin continued. "As you know," He spoke in a hushed voice. "Fracking activity began in 1947 with a hydraulic fracturing experiment at the Hugoton gas field in Grant County, Kansas. It really took off in 2005 when we were able to purchase enough of Congress to acquire the rights to all the federal land out west. In the last decade we have done a pretty good job of destroying the rock formations in the earth's crust."

Before he could continue Richards interjected a thought. "Before you go on let me tell you that I just got back from the pipeline project and most everyone agrees that our fracking is responsible for the breaks in the pipeline."

"I haven't heard about any breaks." Justin took this opportunity to eat a little more.

"We did a pretty good job of hushing it up. We are dumping a large amount of diluted bitumens into the aquifer. There are actually several bad spots but the worst seems to be in Kansas somewhere. In order to keep the tree huggers ignorant, we rewrote some of the software so that the readings changed slightly at the flow monitors. Now the leakage appears to be within specifications. I think I may have accidently left the old software on the backup processor; if it ever gets turned on there will be hell to pay for someone." He chuckled aloud.

"The fracking is causing earthquakes; which in turn is causing problems with the pipeline. Karma's a bitch." Justin pushed his tray away. "Good soup."

Justin leaned into the table. "There is a report out there. One that I have been tasked to disprove. That the increased earthquake activity has caused a shifting of the earth's plates and some of those heretofore dormant volcanoes along the west coast are beginning to wake up. There has been a call for the USGS to begin monitoring these bad boys and Bennett is afraid that somebody might point the finger at us."

"Should they be?" asked Jenny.

"I think yes." Justin answered.

"Me too." Richards piped in.

"It's like you bought a new laboratory with all the state of the art safety features. Then you found out you could bribe the inspector into letting stuff pass. Little things that ought to be fixed but weren't, after a while when the thing blows up you shouldn't be surprised. That's where we are in this country. Corporations with lots of money buy political favor and elections and get people in office who are friendly. A special favor here and there, what's the problem? The corporation uses its influence to get their buddies appointed to the watchdog agencies with a special favor here and there. The big corporation buys legislation that allows them to own the media. A special favor here and there, what's the problem? Each little minion does a little favor and it can add up "

"Let me get this straight," Jenny asked. "Do you think there is a direct connection between increased volcanic activity and fracking? They always promised me it was a harmless activity."

"I haven't read the reports yet but where there's smoke there's fire. Bennett thinks we need to '...put a lid on this before it erupts'. Those were his exact words. 'Put a lid on this before it erupts,' then he laughed and sent me out of the room. He said he wanted to talk to his bird in private."

"I feel all dirty, like that window glass," Jennifer moaned. "I don't want to be responsible for all this." She spread her hands in the direction of the windows.

"At least we're in a position to do something about it." Richards added. "Where's a tree hugger when you need one?"

Justin smiled.

Chapter 41

"Happy now?" Bennett was standing in his stocking feet speaking to his only friend in the world, an oily dead bird encased in acrylic. "I brought you a present Patrick, something most people wouldn't appreciate." He placed a grey pebble on the mantle beside the bird. "It's a piece of magma, Patrick, it came from a pocket of magma just a mile deep. One of our fracking operations drilled into this magma pocket Patrick, blew the drill to smithereens. They sent me this to show me that we have a problem. This ain't no problem. Being dead and covered in oil and encased in a glass block, now that's a problem. Having a volcano blow up your ass, now that's a problem." He walked into his private rest room. The face in the mirror was troubled. Those angry voices were screaming now. "She hates you, they hate you; they will always hate you." The cold water on his face wouldn't stop the noise.

As he left the office he turned the lights on. "I hate the environment."

Chapter 42

"How did that work out for ya'll last night and into this morning I heard?" Ken teased as they walked to the SUV.

"Kinda like old times." Jerri smiled. "How about you and Susan, we didn't hear a peep out of either one of you till breakfast."

"You know when you put on that old coat for the first time in the winter and it just fits right? That's the best I can describe it." He walked to the driver's side door.

Jerri handed him the keys and they embraced for a long time.

"We're still OK aren't we?" She asked.

"Same as ever, I guess." He kissed her then walked around to open the door for her.

"Always the gentleman," She was pleased.

"Try to be," He drove down the long driveway. "You two always made a good pair."

"We said the same about you two last night, well, probably this morning." She chuckled.

"How much time do we have?" He asked as they entered the house.

She checked her phone. "About an hour, you have something in mind?"

"We could save a little time if we showered together, it's going to be a long trip and since we got up so early I didn't have a chance to work all the kinks out of the system." He sounded hopeful.

"Can't have kinks in the system." She agreed.

Chapter 43

"He's going to want to drive, you know that?" Susan told John as they pulled around the back of the work building at Ken and Jerri's house.

"Fine with me, I hate to drive, wonder which one of these trailers he wants to use?" John always had trouble with the big RV. "We'll just wait here." He put the big rig in park.

Susan waved through the windshield. "Jerri just brought out two bags she says about ten minutes more."

She turned in her seat. "Now that we have a few uninterrupted minutes, I would like to know your take on last evening."

"I've been thinking about yesterday all morning. I think I want to say that yesterday was a great success as days go. In chronological order and not in order of importance, I finally got those big bales cleared out of that south pasture."

Susan made a noise in her throat and crossed her arms.

"Then there was that other thing," he continued. "A great meal followed by good friendship. I learned I'm a grandpa, that my daughter; who I was worried sick about, is safe and well. We had a great meal, thanks to you dear, followed by some mind blowing sex with my old high school sweetheart, thanks again to you dear. Part of the success of the evening was that I was with three other people who I care deeply about and it seemed like they were having a rather good time as well. Now we are going to pool our resources and get our babies home. Oh, and it seems our relationship is none the worse for the wear so, life is good. How about you?"

"I feel exactly the same. Here they come." She stood up between the two front chairs and kissed John, then stepped out onto the driveway.

John got down from the RV and shook Ken's hand. "Which trailer?" He asked.

"Sit tight, I'll get it." Ken disappeared into the big building and one of the overhead doors began to open.

A great rumbling noise came from the building as the diesel tractor engine started. Ken returned through the big doorway driving a green tractor with a front loader, great black smoke billowing from the black exhaust pipe sticking in the air above the tractor engine. The air was filled with the smell of diesel exhaust. Ken put on a pair of leather gloves and attached a chain between the loader and the front hitch of one of the empty trailers. He used the loader and chain to maneuver the trailer hitch over the ball at the back of the RV then lowered it in place. As he was putting the tractor up and closing the big door, John made the wiring connections and hooked up the safety chains.

"Want to drive?" John asked. He knew that Ken hated to ride with someone else unless he had been drinking.

"I can drive." He swung up into the driver's seat. He heard the passenger door shut and looked over. Susan was putting on the seat belt.

She smiled and winked. He looked in the mirror. Jerri was seated next to John on the couch behind the driver's seat; she and John were already busy with their laptops.

Once they were on the highway, Susan spoke. "AnnaBelle, and Adam too for that matter, caused us a lot of worry these last few months. John and I spoke about it and he agreed that we should have a little fun at their expense. You feel up to it?"

"Count me in." Ken chuckled.

Chapter 44

Bennett didn't care for public transportation he hated people, all people. Kids would pick on him when he was in school because he was small for his age and he didn't fight back. He didn't want to travel but he wanted to see how bad it was outside, maybe the weather reports didn't do it justice maybe it was worse than they let on, he hoped. He took his briefcase that contained the laptop and as he was leaving he spoke, "Bye Patrick, I'll be back but you won't know that I left because you're all dead and encased in plastic, sucks to be you." He turned on the lights as he left the room.

He pushed a set of numbers into a key pad on the wall of the elevator. It took him directly to the parking garage. He crossed the vestibule that separated the elevator from the parking garage and as he walked through the door he removed the trash can liner from the trash can and carried it with him to his large black car. He took the express path around the perimeter of the parking garage, it was reserved for VIP's and the chip in the windshield caused the gate to open as he entered the street.

The light rain still contained some droplets of oil. He could tell when he turned on the wipers, damn, he'd hoped it would be worse. A few blocks later he entered onto the interstate, traffic was light. He pulled up close behind an eighteen wheeler; that was better; the oil was quite intense here. He pulled into the left hand lane and drew up even with the rear end of the semi. He rolled down the passenger window and tossed the bag of trash out into the vortex created by the big truck. The bag exploded and the trash flew everywhere.

He cackled, "I hate the environment."

Chapter 45

Ken and Susan were enjoying catching up on old times. She was on the class reunion committee and kept up with everyone. Ken was interested, more or less, but never took the time to get involved.

He looked in the rear view mirror. "You all doin' all right?" He saw in the mirror that John and Jerri both had their noses buried in their laptops.

"Try to find us a smoother road sweetheart." Jerri pleaded.

"Yeah, try to find us a smoother road sweetheart." John couldn't resist.

Ken felt bad that he misjudged the road handling ability of the big rig and when he jerked the wheel in a playful gesture he was afraid for a minute that he might lose it.

"Sorry about that." He pleaded.

"Once John gets his nose in that machine you need to set off a bomb to get his attention." Susan volunteered.

"Same with Jerri," Ken offered, "say what ever happened to Herbie Meyers?"

"Now there's a long story," she began.

"Hey you guys," Jerri screamed over the road noise.

"What?" Susan screamed back.

"I just Googled John here, do you know what it says his net worth is?" She asked.

"I have no idea." Susan had no idea.

"Thirty million," Ken answered, probably more than that if he's as tight as he always was.

"It says here fifty million plus." She was shocked.

"Somebody's wild-ass guess," John replied.

"More?" She asked.

"We'd need to sell everything just right." He said.

"I'm impressed. I had no idea." She said.

"Those big tractors can cost a quarter of a million, easy." Ken stated.

"He has a lot of tractors." Susan volunteered. "Herbie Meyers is now Henrietta." She returned to the conversation.

"No shit." Ken answered.

"They may not be impressed, but I certainly am." Jerri patted John on the leg.

"We have had the help of three generations of work to build on. My great-grandpa is supposed to have said that wealth is passed down to your great-great-grandkids. So, I'm lucky. Is that field plowed or what?" He stuck his nose against the glass.

"Its oil," Ken answered, "We've been driving through oil for the last ten miles or so."

"This explains the wreck." Susan said, "AnnaBelle was always a very careful driver. This looks much worse than what we see on the news."

Traffic has slowed to 50 mph. All of the cars were creeping slowly in the right hand lane.

"Want me to drive?" John asked.

"I'm fine for now it'll be another couple of hours at this pace."

John lay back in the seat and closed his eyes. Jerri laid her head on his lap and they slept.

"Susan, Susan," Ken spoke more loudly. "Wake the sleeping beauties back there and tell them if they want to see the wreck it's coming up on the left."

Susan unbuckled her seat belt and stepped back to where John and Jerri were sleeping. John's arm was lying across Jerri's shoulders and her right hand was in his grasp. "That's sweet." Susan thought, and she meant it.

"I'm surprised anybody lived." John commented, as Ken drove slowly past the wreck, "How far to the turnoff. Has it been like this the whole way?"

"Two miles, and pretty much." Ken answered, "Seems like the oil sort of stopped for a while. It must have been quite heavy because everything is covered."

"What will that do to the crops and animals, John?" Susan asked.

"They are all dead, they won't know it yet but this goo is going to kill all the animals. It will have destroyed the crops. How far south of the Kansas line did it start Ken?" John walked back toward the rest room holding on to the overhead cabinets.

"About ten miles past the line it started to get noticeable." Ken answered. "Hold on to something, I'm turning here."

Susan read the directions from her phone to Ken. As they pulled up the street toward the hospital, the streets and parking lots were filled with cars. Ken turned right into a large parking lot.

"This rig is a mile long. We need to be able to get out of here." Ken said.

"Any sign of Justin?" John asked.

"You're Justin?" Ken asked.

"Our Justin, yes, he's supposed to meet us here." John was looking out all the windows.

"There they are," Jerri was pointing in the direction of the Hospital.

Justin and Adam were walking down the edge of the street, waving both arms in the air. Everyone poured from the RV and waited.

"How did you know Justin would be here?" Susan asked John.

"He works for us remember? We sort of communicate from time to time."

Ken and Jerri, welcomed Adam while John and Susan caught up on current events with Justin.

"They said she could leave any time, sooner the better." Adam stated. "They need the beds. At first the emergency room was filled with people from car wrecks. Now the place is starting to fill up with people hacking and coughing, and people sick to their stomachs and there seems to be a steady stream of people from car wrecks too. Did you see the truck on your way in? Some kind of mess isn't it?"

The air was split with the sound of the wail of a siren. It wasn't long before it came into view. The machine used to be red with a white top but now the top was covered in a layer of black oil. The lights on the top of the ambulance were flashing, red and white, and blue. It came down the road at too high a rate of speed and lost control as the traffic began to snarl at the emergency room. The big machine plowed into the back of a little blue jeep, which in turn smashed into the back of a yellow minivan. The people in both vehicles began to scream and moan. Attendants ran from the emergency room, one held a fire extinguisher and began to apply it to the engine compartment of the ambulance, which was beginning to smoke. The siren continued to wail.

"You guys wait here. Justin and I can bring the girls out here." He motioned for Justin to follow him and they ran toward the hospital.

"Don't forget the baby." Susan screamed.

"Come on Ken. You girls get back in the RV and get the bed ready for AnnaBelle." John ordered.

John and Ken ran toward the hospital following closely behind the two boys.

It wasn't long before they came out of the hospital. Justin was pushing a wheelchair that contained Debra. AnnaBelle was in the next chair being pushed by Adam and following behind was Ken carrying the baby. He had a smile from ear to ear.

"I'll take the chairs back," Justin volunteered as he helped Debra into the big rig. Adam would have carried AnnaBelle through the door if there had been room. The cast on her leg became the biggest hurdle but she was finally in the bed.

"Where's John?" Jerri asked.

"He wanted to make sure the bill was paid." Adam was helping Justin to return the wheelchairs.

Ken immediately lost control of the baby to the women so he went to the restroom before beginning the trip back.

"Justin and Adam are going to meet us back at the wreck," he took a seat in the passenger side.

"Buckle up." Ken yelled.

"Wagons Ho!" John yelled.

Justin was standing beside the road waving his arms back and forth. "Stop here, Ken, we'll unhitch the trailer then you guys can get on down the road. Adam and I can load the wreck. It'll take us a good hour to load it up and synch it down. We'll see you back at the house."

"What are you driving?" Ken asked.

"I've got a rental; they can pick it up later. Drive safe." He walked back to unhitch the trailer. Adam was already maneuvering his pickup to attach it to the trailer."

After they were back on the road Susan and Jerri were taking turns coddling the baby. "John, what did you mean before when you said they were all dead when I asked you about the oil?" Susan asked.

"Any animal that drinks that oil will be dead from it. Most of the people who breathed the oil will be dead from it. That wasn't just oil. Didn't you smell it when we stopped? There were other chemicals in it. They added millions of gallons of dispersant to the oil to try to contain it. That was a toxic mix that came down like rain. I doubt they will be able to get it all cleaned out and people will be drinking it too. There will be millions of deaths because of that oil, not to mention all the animal and plant life, you just wait. How is the baby? How is AnnaBelle?" He unbuckled the seat belt and walked back to the sleeping area to check on AnnaBelle.

"Cute and cuddly." Jerri was holding the baby.

Susan resumed her chair up front with Ken. She held out her hand in his direction and he squeezed it.

When John returned, satisfied that AnnaBelle was sleeping well, he sat on the couch next to Jerri and looked closely at the baby. Jerri placed her right hand in his lap and he held it.

Debra meanwhile, appearing to be asleep in a chair on the opposite side of the RV couldn't fail to notice the signs of intimacy going on. Nah, she was dreaming.

Chapter 46

The radio crackled to life

Lightning Tim here; my little girl was doing a class project last night and I happened to read it. The exercise was to imagine that you live fifty years from now and you were tasked with writing a report about our current condition. It made for something interesting to read. Listen;

"The third attempt to relieve the pressure in the Gulf resulted in a geyser of fire and oil that rose to a height of 40,000 feet before it ignited. The ensuing column of flame engulfed an airliner. There were no survivors. The flames destroyed the rig. As the rig sank beneath the waves the piping snapped off at the bottom of the ocean; the flames were extinguished but more boiling oil was now flowing into the Gulf.

The amount of oil on the Gulf of Mexico continued to increase. Every effort to stop the flow was met with failure. Some pockets of oil were 30 feet thick and a few brave adventurous fools put to sea and when they ran into these pockets, their vessels failed to float in the thin stuff because water was used for ballast in their hulls and the boat sank through the oil to the water below the oil layer and the oil then enveloped the ship. Usually some sort of fire onboard would ignite the pool and ship and crew would be incinerated in the ensuing inferno.

All manner of sea creatures died in the oil. Rotting corpses littered the black beaches. The smell of oil and rotting carcasses was overwhelming.

From time to time one of these deep pockets of oil would spontaneously ignite. In the evenings the Gulf was filled with the light of these burning patches.

Hurricane activity increased and one storm a week became common.

All schools were eventually closed, most businesses were closed. The smell of rotting dead animals was overpowering. Truck drivers refused to take their rigs into the affected areas. Martial law was declared.

The hospitals were filled with sick and dying people most all suffering some sort of ailment related to the oil.

As the oil traveled with the ocean currents around the globe; what had begun as one little hole in the earth's crust, became a global environmental catastrophe.

Remember folks, she's only eight."

Chapter 47

"Let's have that oil analyzed." John was standing beside the RV looking closely at the black streaks on the side of the machine.

"I'll have that done." Justin followed John into the house. "Can we talk?"

The strong aroma of freshly brewed coffee filled the air. "Coffee?" John poured two cups and handed one to Justin.

"What's on your mind?" John said as he sat at the table and motioned for Justin to take a chair.

"You need to read this report." Justin passed a manila envelope across the table.

"What is it going to say?" John asked as he sipped the hot brew.

"Mr. Bennett has directed me to compile a report. The evidence presented in that report is so overwhelming that it scares me." He added sugar to his cup.

"Is it a secret?" John hated to have to drag a story out.

"Several learned scientists have become concerned about the earthquakes being caused by our friends the frackers." He began.

"High time." John emphasized. Justin knew where John stood when it came to fracking.

"It appears that there has been a marked uptick in the seismic activity surrounding our fracking operations in the western portion of the United States. Unbeknownst to our company, a few hotshot frackers took it upon themselves to push the envelope." He drank.

"Which means what?" John pulled out the truth.

"A few of our crews went a little too deep in a few areas where our experts had warned them to stay shallow." He sipped.

"And?" John used both his hands in a come-hither motion.

"And now our scientists, several of them, have expressed a concern that the seismic activity is too near several sleeping volcanoes." He paused.

"And that means?" John asked.

"It means our experts fear that our fracking operations may be in the process of triggering a volcanic event."

"Fracking is going to cause a volcano to erupt?" John was aghast.

"Not a volcano, a whole chain of volcanoes." Justin finished. "At least that's the theory."

"Are these guys on crack?" John asked.

"Not at all, read the report; it scared the hell out of me."

"You think there could be a shred of truth in this hair brained theory?" John asked.

"These guys have always been right before, they are not crackpots. They are paid a whole lot of money because they have credentials a mile long. We hired them to make the case that fracking does not cause volcanic activity and they couldn't. On the contrary, they proved just the opposite." He took a long drink.

"The earth has this molten core that tries to boil up to the surface. These volcanoes sat there dormant for centuries. Science has been predicting for years that we are overdue for a seismic event and the fracking appears to have hastened the process."

"What is the bottom line here?" John rose and filled both cups.

"According to the report, and don't shoot the messenger; we are in eminent danger of experiencing the simultaneous eruption of up to six volcanoes, one of which is a sleeping super volcano."

"I never heard of a super volcano." John said. "Suppose all these do erupt and these guys feel confident that they will, what are the odds?"

"They feel that there is a 99 percent chance that these will erupt within the next 8 – 10 months." Justin sat back in his chair.

"And you concur?" John asked.

"After reading the report, I do."

"You're the engineer, I believe you. What will happen?" John was in deep thought.

"Volcanic Winter." Justin said. "You could Google it but basically it's like Nuclear Winter only caused by volcanic ash."

"These volcanoes plus this super volcano erupt. The sky is filled with pieces of glass and rock and smoke and the sun stops shining. For how long?

"Could be years."

"*Years*?"

"Who knows, this never happened before. One super volcano damn near extincted the human race about 70,000 years ago. This could be a whole lot worse. Theory has it that the earth will experience a major eruption every 100,000 years or so, give or take a few centuries. That means that we're due and this fracking has hastened the process.

"You just can't make this shit up." John put his head in his hands. He wanted to weep. "That's just great; those greedy self-serving SOB's are destroying the oceans; contaminating our drinking water with their unnecessary pipeline, destroying our atmosphere with their methane, and causing untold damage to the earth and all of our buildings and bridges with earthquakes caused by their fracking. And now you have a report that shows that this fracking is damaging the earth and is going to cause early volcanic eruptions. People just don't have a clue as to how fragile our environment is, even small changes can result in our extinction."

"I need to make a phone call," John took out his phone and entered a few numbers. "Ted? Look I changed my mind. Are you still interested? Good. You and I both know I could get another 5 percent without breaking a sweat so here's the deal. You up your offer by 1 percent; get the money into an escrow account in my bank by the close of business today and we can have all the paperwork cleaned up by the end of the week. Good. I thought so." He hung up.

"Remember that property up by Lincoln? I just sold it. $18 million plus 1 percent. How cold do you suppose it'll get?"

"Shouldn't be worse than eighty below." Justin was getting on board the John train and it was starting to pull out of the station.

"Fahrenheit or Celsius?" John asked.

"Fahrenheit I think, but who knows."

"How many years?" Take your time it's important.

"Those guys talked about it a lot, as I recall their best guess was two maybe three years tops."

"We can expect the temperature to drop to around 100 below zero and stay there for up to three years. Does anybody else know about this?" John asked.

"Whoever they told, we paid for the study; it was kept as proprietary so they know their jobs would be on the line if they spilled the beans. I haven't turned the report in yet I thought you ought to read it first. Another cup?" Justin rose and stretched and went to the coffee pot.

"No, thanks though. Look, don't tell anyone just yet, let me read this thing and get a handle on it. We've got some funding available, we can use that whole chunk of money from the Lincoln deal to do whatever we need to. Can you get hold of these guys and bring them up here for a meeting, have them bring their families but don't tell anyone else we don't want a panic. Find out how many people we are dealing with then get with Martha in town and buy a couple of houses. We can get Jerri to furnish them appropriately.

This is Tuesday; see if they can be here by Friday, no later than noon.

"What shall I tell Bennett?" Justin asked.

"Fuck Bennett, you're done with that outfit. If we start right now, we may not be able get ready in time for the freeze.

He took the report and carried it into where his reading chair was by the window. Two hours later he returned the envelope to the table. Beside the report he placed a yellow legal pad with hand written notes.

NUMBER OF ACTIVE VOLCANOES

NUMBER OF SLEEPING VOLCANOES

LAST VOLCANO EVENT

SUPER VOLCANO EVENT

SIZE OF EARTHQUAKE CAUSED BY FRACKING

DEPTH OF MAGMA NEAR VOLCANOES

DEPTH OF FRACKING ACTIVITY

DETAILS ABOUT FRACKING RIG THAT ENCOUNTERED MAGMA

VOLCANIC WINTER

PERCENTAGE OF OXYGEN IN AIR THAT IS SAFE

PERCENTAGE OF OXYGEN IN AIR NECESSARY TO SUSTAIN COMBUSTION

LOWEST RECORDED TEMPERATURE IN U.S.

LOWEST TEMPERATURE WHERE HUMANS SURVIVE

Chapter 48

"When do you intend to marry that girl, Adam? Your mother is asking the question." Jerri Thomas caught Adam's arm as he rushed out the door.

"We got married already, Mom. It's not a permanent thing but it was enough so that the hospital let me act as husband and father."

"In what church?" She asked.

"Wasn't a church, but it was legal with a marriage license and everything. Debra got online and for $25 she became the Reverend Debra of the Most Holy Tabernacle Church of the Apostles, legal in ten states. Happy?" He continued out the door.

"Where are you going in such a hurry if I need to ask?"

"I haven't held the baby today, he'll forget who I am."

Jerri smiled.

Ken came rushing in the room. "Ready to go? John just called and said we should come on over right away. He and Justin want to tell us something they found out through Justin's work."

"Adam just went that way; I want to hold the baby too." She was out the door before Ken.

Chapter 49

AnnaBelle was feeding the baby and sitting in the center of the big couch. Susan and Jerri were on either side of her waiting their turn. Everyone else was in the room including Clyde Richter and Thomas Preston, the two oldest and best foremen on the place.

"I am going to let Justin tell you his story. I just want you to know I agree and when he's done and the dust settles I'll talk." John sat down.

Justin rose. "You all know about fracking. It's where oil companies inject chemicals into the ground under high pressure to open up the earth and let out the last little bits of oil and gas that are still down there. It causes earthquakes that are damaging buildings and roads and bridges all over the world. About four months ago we started hearing rumors about how the earthquakes from fracking operations in the western U.S. have damaged the earth's crust so much that extinct volcanoes are threatening to erupt because of it. My boss commissioned me to generate a report based on data, supplied by trusted scientists that we employ, that would disprove those rumors. I approached the scientists and commissioned the report, they wrote it. The results of their findings proved that the fracking is causing earthquakes that are waking up dormant volcanoes." There was a gasp from the ladies. He continued.

"Their report contains conclusive evidence that there will be a major eruption of several volcanoes within the next several months."

"There are no volcanoes near here are there?" AnnaBelle asked.

"No, but the effects will come here. Most of the volcanoes are along the west coast. When they erupt, depending on the severity of the eruptions; the western portion of the U.S. will be covered in several feet of ash."

"When Mt. St. Helens erupted, people tried to drive their cars and the filters clogged with ash, when they removed the filters the ash then ruined the engines. This will hold true with all manner of engines. After that eruption the people out there found that the bearings in their wheels got ruined by the ash. The roadways will be clogged with broken down trucks and cars. These scientists estimate that the ash deposit will be several feet deep from the western coastline to this side of the Rockies. The ash will destroy the electrical grid and all the power plants in that area. What people don't die from the eruptions will die from the ash or the confusion created by the failed electrical grid."

Everyone in the room was too shocked to speak.

"The oil from the Gulf is destroying crops and animals from south of the Kansas border all the way to the Gulf coast. This volcanic activity is going to destroy crops and animals from just east of the Rockies all the way to the west coast, this is a few months from now but that's not the worst for us." He paused to let that seep in.

"How in the world could it be any worse?" Susan cried.

Justin continued. "When these volcanoes begin to erupt they will fill the atmosphere with dust and smoke and pieces of glass and vaporized pieces of lava. A lot of it will spill out on the ground but a lot of it will go into the sky. Until the rain washes the dust from the sky, the dust will block the sun."

"Nuclear Winter!" Adam volunteered.

"Close;" Justin added. "It's very much like nuclear winter but it will be what is known as volcanic winter. Same thing, different cause. In the history of the planet it has happened before.

A volcanic winter is a reduction in global temperatures caused by volcanic ash and other gases from the volcano obscuring the sun.

In 1991, the eruption of Mount Pinatubo cooled global temperatures for up to three years.

In 1883 the eruption of Krakatau caused record snowfalls worldwide and for four years after the winters were unusually cold.

In 1815 the eruption of Mr. Tambora was responsible for the "year without a summer" in 1816.

In 1783 the eruption of Laki caused the Northern Hemisphere temperatures to drop one degree C. It resulted in the death of much of Iceland's livestock and a famine that resulted in the death of a quarter of its population.

It is theorized that the eruption of super volcano Toba, about 70,000 years ago resulted in the near extinction of the human race. The sky will go dark one day and it will get very cold."

"How long will that last?" Asked Jerri

"It could be two to three years." John spoke.

"How cold?" Asked Ken.

"We hope it will peak at around minus75 degrees Fahrenheit." Justin answered.

"My babies going to die." AnnaBelle began crying uncontrollably.

Adam rose and helped her to leave the room with the baby.

"No he's not," Susan spoke. "Are we all going to die?"

"That is precisely why we are all here today," John stood "Anything else, Justin?"

Justin nodded his head and set on the loveseat next to Debra, who playfully used her hip to push him over, he pushed back then they got serious.

"Here is the problem as I see it." John began to pace. "We need to be able to survive minus 75 degree weather for a period of time. People in the north face this kind of challenge every winter. We will need to prepare to face the cold for an extended period of time. We will need shelter and food and water and heat."

"And electricity," Ken volunteered.

"What about our families?" Asked Clyde.

"What about Rita's mom?" Thomas asked, speaking of his mother-in-law.

"I have an idea that we might be able to save some of us if the cold doesn't last over a few years." This calmed them down. "Let me continue." John begged.

"Heat will be at the top of the list because if we're frozen nothing else will matter much. We have maybe six months to prepare, there will be plenty of wood to burn. We can take that big new multi-purpose building at the high school, triple insulate the walls, then build a smaller well insulated room inside the big building. If we heat the space between the outer shell and the new walls we ought to be able to keep the temperature to above freezing." Everyone nodded in agreement. "We can do that with any number of buildings, if we use two by fours on twenty-four-inch centers we could build secondary walls inside existing dwellings; pack a foot of insulation in the new void and staple plastic on the inside as a vapor barrier. Any homes we can't triple insulate we abandon."

"Clyde, why don't you and Thomas give this some thought and get back with me."

"John, we can't afford to fix up our homes." Clyde hated to say.

"I bought a warehouse full of insulation and two by fours this morning, you two need to find a place to put it."

"Thanks John." Clyde led Thomas out of the room.

John turned to Ken. "I think it would be best for all of us if you and Jerri and Adam moved in here till this crisis is over, there's plenty of room and we have a lot of work to do, I'm worried that this crisis will hit before we can get ready." He motioned for Ken to follow.

"Let me check with Jerri, I think you're right." Ken followed John into the new addition.

John stepped outside through a large framed sliding glass door. He turned to face the house. "I've ordered a steel building large enough to cover this house. We need to drill holes for footings for the beam bolts, the plans should be done in a day or two. I've ordered an excavator; it should be here in two days. I've also ordered a big track hoe. I've also ordered 300 fifty-six-foot empty intermodal shipping containers for $500 each that I want you to bury side-by-side right over there. I want you to take the track hoe and the excavator and dig a ditch that will connect this basement to the aisle way in front of the buried containers. So, you will need a ditch that starts here and is ten feet deep and as wide as a fifty-six foot shipping container plus a fifteen foot aisle way along their entire end to end length. At ten feet wide per container, that is 3000 feet long. That should take you to just about that elm tree out yonder. We will need to span across the aisle way from the fronts of the containers to the other side of the aisle way then cover the whole mess with dirt. Some units will be for living, some will be for bathing, some will be for cooking, and some will be for recreation. Don't think fancy, think fast. This won't have to last more than two years."

"Because after two years something else will have killed us." Ken agreed.

"Exactly."

"You are building an Ark." Ken stated.

"Two of each." John nodded.

"What about plumbing? Drainage? Electricity?" Ken asked.

"Experts will be here in two days. Can you do this for us Ken?"

Ken held out his hand and John took it. "Can Justin help me lay this out?"

"Thought you'd never ask." Justin had sneaked up behind them.

"Let's put that college to use, boy." Ken was at his best when faced with a challenge.

As John stepped up into the building Susan was waiting. "Is it going to be alright?" She was worried. He gave her a kiss and a bear hug.

"This needs to be our one and only focus, if we fail, we die. It is that simple. Can you figure a menu for a family of four on a starvation diet where we need to live off of canned food for enough meals for two years? Then put it in a spreadsheet so we can expand it to fit all the people and maybe we can get a handle on how much food we need to acquire?" He asked.

"I'll start right away, start thinking rice and beans." She said.

"Ken will expect a good meal for this work." John mentioned as he walked into the house.

"I know, I've got the bread rising now. Jerri's in the library, she said you might want to look at some swatches." She winked.

"Swatches? Sure thing." He winked back.

"You had a chance to talk with AnnaBelle about us?" He asked.

"You mean all four of us, right?" She answered.

"Yeah." He clarified as he turned toward the library.

"Waiting for the right moment." She added.

Chapter 50

Bennett entered his apartment. The walls contained no paintings and were painted a cheap brown color. He laid the sack on the table and turned on the national news. He liked it when there were stories about disasters, especially disasters he had helped to create. He shook the contents from the sack. Two TV dinners and a red aerosol spray can. He picked up the red can and shook it as he entered the spare bedroom. The walls here were lined with four inch deep shelves and the shelves were filled with many aerosol cans. He looked closely at the new one. On the front was a picture of a dead cockroach.

"Grr," he said out loud.

He shook the can again. He read the label that showed the contents out loud. He sprayed the can into the air and smelled the droplets as they filled the air. Satisfied, he placed the new can on an empty space on the shelf along with all the others.

He stopped for a moment as if in thought.

She hates you, they hate you; they will always hate you.

He paused on his way out the door. He looked lovingly at the first box on the shelves. It was filled with several rusty tin containers, with crystals still inside the containers. One of the few things he still possessed that belonged to his father. The label on the box was old but still legible. DEGESH ZYKLON. Few things survived the war years. He wouldn't be sniffing any of that.

As he left the room he turned out the light and relocked the door.

Chapter 51

Justin double checked the connection at the seat belt buckle. Good and secure. He didn't want John to see him checking. The two scientists in the back seat bounced along happily, oblivious to the danger. Justin lost his true parents in a car accident when he was small. All he remembered of the accident was the painful jarring of the crash, followed by the flashing lights of the rescue vehicles. He only vaguely remembered his real parents, John then wasted no time in adopting his brother's son and John and Susan had been like his parents ever since. Being strapped in a car seat always made him nervous.

"You've never liked riding in a car, ever since that crash." John commented.

"I don't really remember it but I remember it if that makes any sense." Justin apologized.

"It was a very tragic event." John thought for a moment then made the next right hand turn.

"I've never taken you to the exact spot of the wreck, have I?" John asked.

Justin thought back. "Not to my knowledge."

"This is the very road, my brother Jim, your father and mother left the farm and came into town that afternoon to buy groceries."

The SUV came to the top of a hill and John checked for traffic then stopped.

"Nice view from up here." He looked from side to side and took in the entire panoramic view.

"This is the highest point for miles and miles, this country road was a popular place for young couples to come and make out. Down this road to the stop sign is a pretty good incline. That's highway 58 down at the bottom and traffic is four-lane and goes about 70. Best anyone could figure is that your folks were stopped at that stop sign when one of those big water trucks from the fracking operation lost its brakes. All four tires left marks leading into the intersection which led all of us to believe that the tanker truck couldn't stop and plowed into the back of the car and pushed it slowly into the oncoming traffic. East bound traffic killed your folks and the west bound traffic killed the driver of the truck, you were the only survivor. And right here is the spot." John pulled to a stop at the stop sign.

The two men in the back paid no attention, their concentration was on their laptop computers.

"Thanks for that Dad. I'm sure that brings back painful memories." Justin added.

A left turn onto the highway and a few miles brought them to the high school, home of the Fort Pearson Huskies. Fort Pearson was a rural community; its population was around 2000 people and had remained at that number for the last 20 years. It was the county seat and the 150 year old courthouse dominated the town square. When the children graduated they knew there would only be enough jobs for a few of them and most gladly left as soon as they could. A few that wanted to be teachers were fortunate enough to be able to come back home and fill one of the few teaching jobs. One of these few was Jeremy

Whittman a recent graduate of Kansas State University and the new science and math teacher. Jeremy and Justin played on the football team together and Justin felt he could help them approach the school leaders.

The meeting was held at 4 pm in the science classroom. The scientists filled the whiteboard with charts and graphs and all manner of mathematical equations. They of course had little meaning for John but Jeremy seemed to be impressed.

"I'm convinced and I might add scared to death. How long do we have?" Jeremy asked the learned men.

The scientists conferred and the taller of the two replied. "The data we have been able to collect is leading us to believe that we must accelerate our timetable. We are of the opinion that eruptions will begin within six weeks.

One of the rules of geology is that if it happened in the past it will happen in the future.

A mere five miles deep below Yellowstone there is a pool of molten rock at 1800 degrees. The latest eruption occurred around 640,000 years ago, it began as a single eruption that turned into a series of eruptions. It is believed that it took less than two weeks to happen. Two thousand square miles of 12,000 feet tall mountain range settled three thousand feet into the earth and are now 9,000 feet tall. Thousands of square miles of mountains settled into the earth and two and a half trillion tons of ash were blown into the atmosphere. These particles remained in the atmosphere for over a year. This was the latest of a series of eruptions along the Snake River plane that extends into Idaho.

Our prediction of the near future based on historic data is as follows. There have already been numerous rumblings underfoot in large part due to the increased fracking activity in that region. The ground has begun to rise noticeably. There has been a 6 to 8 centimeter rise per year due to volcanic activity; now that has increased dramatically. The tremblors have increased in frequency and intensity.

Soon the park authorities will give in to logic and reason and begin to clear visitors from the park. Warnings will be issued to everyone within a hundred mile radius. Boseman, Montana and Cody, Wyoming will be told to expect the worst. New cracks will develop due to the increased earthquake activity and geysers of superheated water will occur.

Lava will begin to ooze out of the cracks in the earth. Magma contains a lot of gas. As the magma oozes from the cracks the pressure in the earth will be lowered and as the pressure lowers the magma will lose its gas explosively and we will have a large eruption. This will be followed in short order by other eruptions around the rim of the caldera. The pyroclastic flows will travel very quickly for fifty to one hundred miles.

Tourists and anyone with any sense will make an effort to get at least 100 miles away from the eruptions many will not make it and perish. Many citizens within the 100 mile radius will fail to heed the warnings, they will be engulfed within the pyroclastic flows and perish. There is a good chance that 100 miles may not be far enough.

Materials will be thrust into the air at supersonic velocities and will travel 80,000 feet into the air. A million tons of rock will be vaporized as several volcanoes erupt. Upwards of 400,000 people will perish with no warning. The immediate area will be covered with between ten and thirty feet of ash.

The states of Wyoming, Idaho, and Utah will be devastated; thousands will be killed when the roofs collapse from the weight of the ash.

Temperatures will drop 20 to 30 degrees C. Tropical vegetation has no adaptations for freezing temperatures.

Ash is basically glass, thousands of humans and most of the animals who breathe the ash will perish. It will kill the body from the inside by attacking the lungs and bones. After Toba, the last super volcano, volcanic ash was in the air for six years. Imagine six years without a growing season. It will be the most severe condition that humans will have ever experienced. Millions will die from starvation.

All of this is in the report."

Chapter 52

"I think that went well," Justin commented as they were driving back from the meeting.

"Jeremy seems like a nice kid," John helped the scientists into the rear of the SUV. "He thinks the school board has enough sense to get behind this idea. They need to make up their minds pretty quick it's going to take a week to close off that multi-purpose building and two weeks to insulate the whole thing and cut the firewood. The list is endless I just don't know if we can get it all done in time."

"They did suggest that it might not be as bad as we think and that maybe it won't last as long as we fear." Justin was hopeful.

"Yet, if we plan for the worst, we survive the worst. If we plan for the least case our family could die. You and I must protect the family. Mankind has never been here before. Did Jeremy say to come back tomorrow? My concentration sort of drifted near the end." John asked.

"Four o'clock, same room. They'll be damn fools if they don't take you up on that offer."

"How many people in this country would believe a hair brained scheme like the one we are suggesting?" John asked.

"Including us?" Justin quipped.

"Do you suppose there are half a hundred people who have even heard about this; much less, believe it?" John sounded worried.

"One third," came the answer from the back of the SUV. "We imagine that less than a third of the population, given all of the facts and data would choose to accept our conclusions. And of that third that believe us probably twenty percent or less will actually do anything proactive."

Justin did the mental math, "One fifth of one third of the population will be willing to actually prepare, that would be about six in a hundred; roughly six percent of the population. That would mean that out of a city of 2000, plus the surrounding population of 5000 we could expect between 3 and 4 hundred people who believe."

"Once the temperature starts to drop there will be a few more believers." John added.

John drove the SUV into the driveway to the house and surveyed the situation. He turned to speak with the scientists. "You fellows are done for now, if you don't mind we want to do this same thing again tomorrow, we'll have a bigger audience for sure. Justin, please come with me."

He led the way to the nearest grain silo. It was a massive cylinder that rose into the air and was filled with some kind of crop, this year it happened to be corn. There was a metal stairway with a railing that wound its way around the structure and ended at a landing at the top. They were both huffing and puffing by the time they reached the top, John only needed to stop one time to catch his breath and Justin was glad he did. The view from a couple of hundred feet was quite impressive. The landing and hand rail circled the entire bin so it was possible to see for a long way in every direction. The red iron framing for the building that was to encase the house was nearly complete with only one end remaining unfinished. The contractor had convinced John to wreck the old fireplace chimney and to connect to the new roof with triple wall stainless piping. The crane seemed to be setting that last truss now. The steel siding and insulation were about half done and it didn't look like rain. The extra insulation was being carried into the horse arena and should be installed within a few days.

"Ken's coming right along with those conex trailers," Justin mentioned and pointed toward two pieces of earth moving equipment.

"He wanted to change the layout a little because he encountered some rock and we didn't want to blast. Looks like about two thirds of the trailers are already set." John commented. "See how the excavation tends to veer over to the left; that was that rock."

"What's the little trackhoe doing down in the big dig?" Justin asked.

"Ken and some of his team thought plumbing would be a good idea so we dug the hole a bit wider and are adding drainage and sewage. I hadn't thought of it, I guess the slope of the hill is perfect for drainage. Looks like things are working like a well-oiled clock, craftsmen are a wonderful thing; show them what needs done give them what they need to do the job then get out of the way." John walked to the other side of the silo.

Justin caught up. "Reminds me of a thing I heard on the radio the other week, a leader:

"Knows the way, shows the way, then gets out of the way."

"Sounds like good advice." John pointed toward the next property over.

"See those greenhouses, those were going to be a surprise graduation slash wedding present for AnnaBelle and Adam. I hired an out of state company that specializes in greenhouses to come up here and fix them up. I was going to surprise them with the little house and the land and all new glass in those greenhouses; it was going to be a showpiece. Old Man Meeker wouldn't sell to me but he sold to one of my companies. I was sort of looking forward to seeing how they did with them. Too bad we won't be able to use them now." John spoke with regret.

"Why not?" Justin asked.

"No sun, remember?"

"Couldn't we insulate them and put in grow lights?" Justin asked again.

"We were planning to use the shipping containers, let's see if we have enough insulation and time. I'll check with Ken to see if we have enough watts for the lighting. That would free up those containers for more storage; good call. We done up here?" John started down the stairs.

"Looks like about two weeks." Justin thought to himself.

Chapter 53

Bennett pushed the chair back from the computer screen. The news was not good. Great swaths of the south were covered in oil, crude oil that his company had brought to the surface of the Gulf. The worst part was the internal memos that he couldn't delete. The emails would show that he knew about the dangers of drilling that deep in the ocean. The emails would show that he knew there should never have been a second well drilled to try and relieve the pressure from the first.

What had started as an accident with no one really to blame was now a major PR disaster and his head was on the chopping block. People were dead and dying and some court might want to point the finger at him. Just bad luck, bad luck that the oil pocket was bigger than anyone could have imagined. Bad luck that it seemed like the second well only made matters worse and triple bad luck that a pesky hurricane would march right through the area. The tree huggers were having a heyday. Literally thousands of endangered species were dead. Thousands of head of livestock were poisoned and thousands of people sick and dying. That stupid pipeline had to pick a time like now to rupture but Richards said he had that under control. One crisis at a time and things wouldn't get out of hand. This Gulf oil problem was only getting worse, there was no end in sight on that one until the pocket of oil petered out. The dead and dying in the south were going to be very expensive; he could not afford another hiccup. Those tree huggers out west were starting to put some pressure on him that he didn't need right now. They believed that his fracking operations were causing earthquakes that were going to cause some extinct volcanoes to erupt. So? He pushed a button on the phone.

"Richards," he spoke loudly into the phone.

"Sir?"

"Where is that report that Justin Williams was working on?"

"Haven't seen it, Sir," Richards replied.

"Have you seen Williams?

"Not for several days."

"Find him. And find that report, I need it Richards!" He was going to enjoy firing Justin Williams, he enjoyed firing anybody especially these college types that thought they knew it all.

A few moments later the phone rang.

"Well?"

"Payroll hasn't heard from him in weeks. Jenny Houston here in the office knows where he lives, she said his sister was in the hospital and he was using some medical leave."

"Have her make the arrangements, since she knows where to go tell her to come along. You and Me are going to get that report." He hung up. He was looking forward to the face-to-face confrontation with Williams. He loved to see people squirm. It wouldn't do the man any good but it would be fun to see.

Chapter 54

"That was one fine meal Susan," Ken placed his napkin on the table and rose to take his plate to the sink.

"You all just leave those dishes," Susan commanded. "I feel like I'm not carrying my weight around here, you all are so busy. You just do your thing and stand back and let me do mine."

"She's the boss," John rose and hugged Susan.

"At least let me help with the dishes, we can talk," Jerri began to take the plates to the sink.

"Where are the kids?" Ken asked.

"They'll be back late they took the baby out to show him off." Jerri added.

"Feel like a soak?" John asked Ken. "I turned the hot tub on this afternoon and it should be ready. I'll get us something to sip on."

Ken nodded and disappeared down the hall to the basement.

John was not one to spend money on frivolous things but a nice big hot tub was a God send on a cold evening. They installed it on the lower level due to the weight. It had its own tankless water heater so it was easy to fill with very hot water. John had built a separate room next to the basement bathroom. The entrance to the hot tub enclosure was a step through shower; he was anal about showering before entering the hot tub. White terry cloth bathrobes and matching towels were hanging on both sides of the shower. Ken was already in the tub when John got through the shower. Ken was praising the warm water.

"Damn, this feels fine. Why didn't you tell me you had one of these, we'd have gotten back together years ago."

"Wish I had," and he meant it.

"What ya got there pardner? Ken asked.

"Thought you might enjoy a little of granddad's blackberry wine. We used to steal it, remember, granddad knew we stole it and I think he was secretly pleased." He held up two magnum sized bottles.

"He was quite a character, I miss the old goat."

Ken set the green bottles of wine on a small table. He used a small hand towel to wipe the necks of the bottles and used a cork screw to open one. He smelled the cork, smelled the bottle then took a drink. Satisfied, he handed the bottle to Ken and stepped down into the tub. "Ahh, that's good."

Ken drank from the bottle. "I forgot how good this was." He took another long pull on the bottle and handed it back to John.

John drank and set the bottle where it would be easy for Ken to reach it.

"You've done a fine job on the project Ken, Justin agrees. You should be proud we couldn't have gotten this far without you."

"I think the end's in sight," Ken closed his eyes. "Another couple of days like the last two and we'll have it all backfilled. The contractor on the building that surrounds the house finished up the north end tonight so we can get in and finish the connection of the tunnel to the house basement tomorrow. Three days from now we'll be able to walk out that door down the hallway and three thousand feet later crawl out the other end. Pallets of food and supplies are being loaded as we sit here, but Justin thinks we need to add a couple more entry doors into the complex. It's probably not a bad idea and we should have enough time. What did you find out from the visit to the school?" Ken reached for the bottle and took a drink.

"The first meeting was all about getting Jeremy on board, I think Tweedle Dum and Tweedle Dee the scientists pretty much convinced him. When we left we were quite confident that at least one person was convinced. That next meeting was with the school board and the principal of the school and it was touch and go. I think we can swing most of them but some of them think it's a crackpot scheme that has no merit. We should know tomorrow if they will allow us to continue with the multi-purpose building. Since it will be a no cost item for them I think it will pass. I assured them that if we're wrong we'll pay to have the property put back just like it was and use the insulation material in a new building. I think that will sell the deal, they want a new building for the soccer team."

"Anybody else involved?" Ken asked.

"We've got the science teacher, the home economics teacher; Doc Means said he's in. We've got the vet and some weird guy I never met before that works at the vet clinic. Apparently this guys from Boston and works with the vet in the cryogenics part of the operation, sort of keeps track of the Bull and Horse sperm."

"What's this about Bull Sperm?" Jerri stepped into the room. She selected a robe, put it on, but left the front open.

Susan followed; she didn't bother with a robe. She walked to the small table and opened the bottle she had brought and filled two glasses handing one to Jerri. She stepped slowly into the tub.

"Feels good," she took a seat.

Jerri removed the robe and stepped into the tub being careful not to spill her glass, she offered it toward Susan who made the toast, "to old friends,"

"Amen, said Ken and took a drink from the bottle and passed it to John who drank as well.

"You girls are in better shape than twenty years ago, I'm impressed," John complemented them.

"Yoga classes three times a week," Susan sunk in to her chin.

"What's this about Bull Sperm?" Jerri asked.

"New guy that's been working with Doc Thatcher at the Vet Clinic came to the meeting we had with the school board. He's been working with the cryogenic stuff, like the Bull Sperm and

Horse Sperm and what not. He had a few ideas that made a lot of sense."

"For instance?" asked Susan.

"For instance, we think this Volcanic Winter is going to last up to two years and could kill most of the living things on the planet. Some things will survive because they live underground and it might not be as bad as we fear, stuff like that. Anyway," he took another drink "if it is as bad as Tweedle Dee and Tweedle Dum think; most of the warm blooded animals will perish. If we survive we will wish we had done something to preserve certain bloodlines. I hadn't thought about it but he is right. We should pick a type of dog, he suggested a beagle. Then he said we could save the eggs and sperm from some bigger breeds of dogs and use the beagle to slowly reestablish the bigger breeds. He was excited about doing this with many animals and plants. I told him to come on over tomorrow and get started."

"This is becoming a regular Noah's ark." Ken suggested.

"Let's all meet with him, he has some good ideas." John stated.

"What about medicine?" Ken asked.

"We're stocking up at the pharmacy and Dick has already made a list and placed a big order of pharmacy supplies. I told him to plan on 2000 people for two and a half years." John explained.

"Ken looks confused," Susan stepped out of the tub and brought back the bottle and refilled her glass and Jerri's. "A few years ago, after the brick plant folded this town was in danger of just going away. John and his parents have saved and saved and in his generosity he bought several of the businesses in town using shadow corporations so people wouldn't know it was him."

"What all businesses?" Jerri asked.

No one spoke. Finally John answered. "Most all of them."

"You mean to tell me you own all the businesses in town?" Ken was aghast.

"Pretty much." Susan answered. "He did a good job of keeping it a secret."

"That's why we haven't had trouble with the pharmacy or the groceries or the lumber yard." John volunteered. "Let's keep it among ourselves if we can."

"No problem." Ken took another drink.

"I have a question I want to ask the group." Susan began, "When and how are we going to break the news to AnnaBelle?"

"What news is that?" Ken asked.

"This!" She waved her hands in front of her. "This relationship we have going on here. Most of the population wouldn't exactly think this is normal. You all know how she is, sort of a stick in the mud."

"That's not a very nice thing to say about your own daughter." Jerri added.

"It's the truth," John added, "She was always like a grandmother. I wouldn't worry about it right now. Things have a way of working themselves out. I'm sure the right time will present itself and we can break the news to her, slowly I think.

"Well it needs to be sooner rather than later." Susan stated and filled their glasses.

No sooner did the words leave her mouth than there was a noise on the other side of the shower.

"Mother, are you down here, you said you might be." The words were followed immediately by AnnaBelle stepping through the shower into the room.

Her mouth dropped open, "Are you all naked? Together?"

"Calm down, AnnaBelle." Susan cautioned, "There's a reasonable explanation for this."

"Yes there is," Jerri piped in, "Your mother's a slut."

"Hussy!" Susan poured her glass of wine on Jerri's head. They both laughed.

Jerri used both hands to brush her hair back. "No, really, John and Ken were in here naked because they've been skinny dipping together since they were eight years old. Your mother is in here because she has been sleeping with both John and Ken. I'm in here because I've been sleeping with Ken and John. Pretty simple really."

AnnaBelle was in a state of shock. "Do marriage vows mean nothing?"

John began to speak.

Susan interrupted. "Let me dear. You see, Honey, marriage vows come in all shapes and sizes; it's not one size fits all. When you're father and I wrote our vows we sort of knew this day would come and we wrote in an exception. Isn't that about right John?" She looked toward John who nodded in agreement. "We just changed the wording in the vows to reflect the fact that we four have a special relationship, that's all."

Jerri chimed in, "You see Anny, except for that one exception we're just like normal people." Everyone agreed except AnnaBelle.

"Just like normal people; normal crazy people."

She began to scream for Adam and ran from the room. She could be heard screaming for Adam as she ran upstairs. A moment later she screamed down the stairs. "We're going out to eat."

"That went rather well, don't you think?" John commented.

"Seems so." Susan agreed. "She didn't throw anything."

Ken took another drink. "Remember how you girls used to do that floor show thing to get us all worked up?"

"We'll need some more wine for that." She held her glass out and Ken filled it. Jerri did the same.

Chapter 55

Susan pushed the start button on the dishwasher and looked around the kitchen. It was impossible to tell that an hour ago the place had been a mess, with pots and pans and dirty dishes. A sign of a good meal was that an hour after, one would never know what had been cooked.

AnnaBelle entered, carrying the baby. Grandma Susan hurried over to hold the little one. "How's the boy?" She spoke to him as if he would answer.

"Hungry, just like his momma." AnnaBelle went to the cupboard for a cup. She filled it from the pot.

"How about some cinnamon toast, it's got raisons just like you like it. I could cook a couple of eggs if you like; farm fresh free range, gathered them myself." She carried the baby toward the window and looked out.

"Toast would be fine, Mom; thanks. Better hand him over, he's starting to get fussy." She walked over and held out her hands.

"Look out there and tell me what you see." Susan stepped aside so AnnaBelle could see out the window.

"I see a big blue metal wall with some panels left out so we can see out. It is not normal to build a building over your house. Beyond that I see two grown men acting like a couple of school boys playing catch with a football. What's your point?" She took the baby back to one of the kitchen chairs and began to breastfeed.

"My point is that I've prayed for over twenty years that those two men would get back together as friends and my prayers have been answered." Susan began to slice the cinnamon bread.

"Mother, I'm not going to judge you. I will admit I was a little shocked last night and I apologize for maybe showing it but you and Dad are all grown up and what you two do is your business."

"I do want you to judge me. But I want you to understand. I have been on a guilt trip ever since Ken and Jerri got together. Rightly or wrongly I felt that it was on the rebound after I rejected him. I regretted it later and still do. Don't get me wrong, I love your father and wouldn't trade you or the time we've had for the world. When I see you and Adam together I think about how it was for Ken and me. We were high school sweethearts just like you two. And so were Jerri and John. They were a couple and we were a couple until I had that bitch moment and drove Ken into Jerri's arms. When she abandoned your father he blamed Ken and got me on the rebound. Your father is happier now than he has been in years, I can tell. Even after he has spent a third of his fortune and we're all afraid for our lives. Ken is happy too, I can tell. Jerri is happy and so am I."

"OK Mom, I sort of get it, but how does it work with two guys?"

"Well, last night was sort of a celebration, because Ken finally thinks he's ready with all that work," she spread her arms to include the whole place. "I'm pretty sore but it was worth it, it was Ken then John, then finally Ken. Ken likes to cuddle and so do I. John and Jerri are just alike, they like to bounce around like a pinball machine and they were up all night doing just that. Just imagine how you would feel if you were separated from Adam for twenty years then you got the chance to just hold on all night and it was alright with the rest of the world. I'll tell you the truth girl, I've never been happier and when you throw this little guy into the mix things are pretty good right now; except of course for the fact that we might all freeze to death." She took the toast from the toaster, buttered it, and set it in front of AnnaBelle with a napkin.

"Dad does seem happy," AnnaBelle admitted.

"He should be, he wore me out last night," Jerri dragged into the kitchen.

"We were just discussing you all's relationship." AnnaBelle commented.

"What's your take?" Jerri asked as she gave Susan a brief hug. Susan handed Jerri a cup of coffee.

"After giving it a lot of thought, I truly think it's great. Adam and I are doing the church wedding thing at 3 PM Sunday afternoon, followed immediately by a baptism. We expect all the grandparents to be in attendance. We don't care who is sleeping with whom."

"Great, we'll be there." Susan and Jerri nodded agreement.

They didn't know that by Sunday they would all be otherwise occupied.

Chapter 56

Bennett listened to the private detective on the other end of the phone connection. "You say he's building some sort of end-of-days survival compound up there? He's using information I paid for. We'll see about that." He hung up the phone.

"How about a little road trip Patrick?" He swept the oil covered bird statue off the mantle as he walked toward his desk. He opened the briefcase and removed a stack of file folders, he thumbed through them and stacked them in a neat pile on the edge of the desk. He was able to fit the statue into the briefcase, the width of the briefcase was just barely big enough. "You wouldn't have any trouble fitting in there if you weren't all dead and covered in oil and plastic. It sure sucks to be you." He carried the briefcase to the door, looked back into the room; thought a moment, turned on the lights and closed the door.

As he walked past the cubicles he looked into the one with Jenny Houston on the name tag.

"Do you have the tickets?" He asked.

"Yes sir." She replied.

"Have a car take you two to the airport. I'll have a car take me home and then to the airport. Have there been any cancellations?" He listened to the news regularly and these days it was not uncommon for flights to be cancelled due to oil mixed with rain.

"Not that I'm aware of." She replied. "Your car is waiting now."

"Good. See you in the terminal 15 minutes before the flight." He carried the briefcase out the door and downstairs to the waiting car.

"Did you hear all that?" She spoke over the partition. Richards had come to her cubicle and they had been talking when Bennett came by.

"You know we're going down there to fire Justin. He gets his rocks off by firing people, he likes to see them squirm. He told me so." Richards stood and wheeled his overnight bag past her cubicle.

"Should I try to get in touch with Justin?" She asked.

"I already did, he's either not picking up or he doesn't have any bars out in the sticks. Want me to take your bag?" He reached for the handle of her wheeled luggage.

"Mr. Bennett said one day, right?" She began to gather papers from her desk.

"Every other flight is cancelled now, from all the airports south of Oklahoma. This oily rain has become a nightmare to transportation." He started toward the elevator.

"Don't forget the health issues. This oil is starting to make people sick, I don't like to go outside anymore." She followed slowly, adjusting her bags on her shoulder.

'It's not just oil, there are a lot of other chemicals involved, millions of gallons of chemicals we used to help stop the flow, that is until we had to just give up. I'm still mystified at how so many trained experts could have been so wrong. Those guys have drilled thousands of wells without anything like this happening." She held the elevator doors open while he maneuvered the bags into the car.

"Didn't they drill a lot deeper than they ever had before?" She pushed the button for the first floor.

"This was a little deeper, but everyone was so sure of the data, we knew there was something down there and I guess we found out." He saw the car waiting by the curb. They fought their way through the revolving doors. He waited for her under the canopy. A gentle mist was falling.

"Pew." She said with disgust. "That stinks." She opened an umbrella. "The driver has the trunk open, better hurry."

He held his umbrella in his left hand and fought the bags with the other, helping the driver to load them into the car. "Try not to breathe it." He called to Jenny.

"I can't live like this." She told him after taking her seat.

"I can't either."

The driver turned in his seat. "We need to drive slow, if the oil gets much worse we'll need to shut the engine off until the weather breaks. It usually is only a half hour or so."

"How long is this sort of thing supposed to last?" She asked the driver.

"Till hurricane season is over, hope your plane gets off the ground we've got a bet going among us drivers in the agency; my bet is that by tomorrow one of those big birds will fly into a cloud of this stuff and just come right on down." He chuckled.

Bennett quickly packed an overnight bag. His briefcase still had enough room to fit three of the cans of crystals. He spoke aloud, "I'll show him he shouldn't steal from me. How about it Patrick, I've waited a long time for just the right opportunity to use this.

He stopped on his way to the door. The noise at his temples was intense. "She hates you, they hate you; they will always hate you."

He hurried to the airport.

Chapter 57

"Why do I feel like an idiot?" John asked Justin as they drove into town. "People treat me like I am crazy, I can just imagine fearful mothers hauling their children in from the streets as I pass."

"If the scientists are right, then you go from being the crazy guy to the savior guy, guess there's a thin line that separates the two."

"Who all did you invite to this meeting today?"

"I didn't really set it up, it sort of came about of its own accord. Once the school board approved the work on the multi-purpose building, word got over to the City Council and they feel they need to have a little input."

City Hall was just coming into view. John parked along the square and they walked up the sidewalk to the old building.

"The Mayor's office is on the second floor." Justin volunteered.

The room was nearly full of people and the noise level was high. The city council members were all in their regular seats at a raised table in the front of the room and the Mayor was speaking to a sheriff's officer who was leaning over his shoulder.

John led the way to a rear seat on the outside isle and let Justin in first so he could stretch out in the isle.

"John, it's good of you to come." The mayor was Roland Turner who managed the feed store that John owned. "We reviewed this report," he held up a manila envelope. "I must say that many here among us are a little skeptical of the findings. Meaning no disrespect here, but it does seem a bit far-fetched."

"I know it's hard to believe Roland, and I too was skeptical, but if we don't act and we're wrong, the consequences will be horrific." John wanted to tell the man that he felt like a fool and secretly wanted this all to go away.

"We took a vote a minute ago, just before you came and it was close but the City Council has voted to support your decision."

"That's no great surprise Dad, most of these folks work for you in one form or another." Justin whispered.

The Mayor continued, "Since there is no great risk on our part and you are willing to put up all the cash, what do you want us to do now, John?"

Before John could reply, the door burst open and a small dark haired man wearing black clothing burst into the room. He was accompanied by the sheriff's deputy who had been talking to the Mayor and a young man with a red bow tie and pretty young woman.

The short man pointed in the direction of Justin. "That's him; he has my property, make him give it up."

"Who is that little man?" John asked Justin.

"That is William Howard Bennett, my old boss." Justin stood and spoke. "If it's the report you came to get, it's up there in the Mayor's hands."

Bennett walked to the front tables and took the report from in front of the Mayor. "Is this the only copy?"

"There's probably a dozen or so running around, but it doesn't say what you want it to say. It confirms the volcano theory, read it for yourself." Justin sat down.

"If these idiots couldn't come to the right conclusion, I'll find someone else who will; someone with equally impressive credentials. By the way, you're fired Williams." He waved the report in Justin's direction and walked out of the room.

Jenny Houston remained standing by the door as Bennett stormed from the room. She waved at Justin and he waved back with a smile.

"Guess I won't be getting a Christmas turkey this year." He smiled

"I'll be in touch Roland. You've got another copy of the report; I suggest you do whatever you think is best." John rose and started for the door.

No one in the room would have felt it, but just as they were leaving, a great rumbling began just south of Yellowstone National Park. The rumbling would increase as the super volcano erupted.

Chapter 58

The large kitchen became noticeably darker when the workers completed the outer building skin. Sections of the building had been left out so that the windows still had a view. Now that the sections were complete, the entire house was encased in a second steel building. That outer building was insulated and there was a four foot gap between the house and the outer building.

"Part of me had hoped that those sections would never be completed. That would mean that the scientists were wrong." John held his cup up so that Susan could refill his cup. "Thank you Susan."

Everyone in the two families was seated at the large table. John wanted to have a meeting with everyone to discuss the latest change in plans. A mid-morning coffee break happened to be the best time for everyone. A television was on in the background with the sound turned low. Everyone was anxious and worried.

John spoke to the group, "Thank you all for coming, Ken and Jerri, Adam and AnnaBelle, Justin and Debra." They all nodded when their names were mentioned. "As I was saying, part of me hoped this day would never happen yet part of me never wanted to be seen as a lunatic. Justin and I have kept some of what we think to ourselves because we didn't want you to worry needlessly. With things the way they appear to be it is time for us to come clean and fill you all in so there won't be any misunderstandings."

"What's your take on the present situation, John?" Ken asked.

"Justin has kept a pretty close eye on the outside world for us while you and I have been tied up with the building process. He can answer specific questions better than I but for the time being it's enough to know that we are in some pretty deep shit. Everything the science guys predicted has come true so far and it appears to be even worse than they thought it might be. I felt it was time to batten down the hatches so to speak and that's why I'm having them close up the outer building. We put an airlock double door system in the north end; there is a man door airlock and an overhead double door if we need to bring in anything of any size. We don't have any idea at this time what that might be but we thought it might be necessary."

"We're going to be meeting like this every day and by the end of this, if we survive, we are probably going to hate one another."

"What do you mean IF we survive Dad?" AnnaBelle asked.

"As I stated, things are looking bad for the home team. The scientists predicted a volcanic winter that would begin with the eruption of the super Volcano at Yellowstone. According to Justin, that part of the prediction came true yesterday afternoon. For any of you who are unaware by now, fracking is the process whereby the oil companies inject vast amounts of ground water with other things added deep into the earth and destroy the rock formations thus freeing up trapped gases. We think fracking caused all this, now we're stuck. Justin and I have done everything in our power to stop fracking in our neighborhood and we have kept them away from here. Other parts of the country weren't so lucky."

"These idiots, in their search for more profits, came a little too close to the sleeping giants along the west coast. Our scientists predicted that this would happen and they apparently were right. The big one, the bad one, the worst one has started to blow it's top. I'm sketchy on the exact details, you can look it up, but the last super volcano was Toba around 70,000 years ago that caused a six to ten year global winter and nearly caused the extinction of the human race."

"Can you tell us what to expect here and now? Warm up anyone?" Susan carried the pot around.

"In a nutshell we expect the western portion of the United States to be covered in volcanic ash. The depth will range from a few inches to hundreds of feet. In much of that area, all life will cease. The ash will destroy all the plant life and the ash in the air will suck out the oxygen. No engines can run because of the ash so there will be no escape. The scientists also predicted that other volcanoes in the area would erupt and that the resulting ash cloud would circle the earth and shut out the sun. Since we are in the winter in this hemisphere the results will be even worse for us. We expect a full blown volcanic winter kind of like the old nuclear winter that scared people so bad it stopped the Cold War. The theory was that a nuclear war with its ensuing fires would fill the atmosphere with smoke and dust and block out the sun. The resulting cold spell would doom mankind." He sipped his coffee and ate a bite of cinnamon roll. "Great rolls Susan."

There was a murmur of agreement from the crowd.

"This volcanic activity will have the same results as a nuclear storm. The atmosphere will be filled with ash and smoke. When the volcanoes erupt, they will set fire to all the forests in the west and many of the cities. The resulting smoke cloud will cover the earth and block the sun. Once the sun is blocked the temperature will drop quite rapidly and we will be in the middle of a volcanic winter."

"How cold do you suppose it will get here John?" Adam asked.

"Let me get this one John, and you can rest your voice and finish that roll." Justin volunteered. "International Falls, Minnesota regularly gets down to something like fifty-five below zero. In the last winter we had a period where every state in the union experienced freezing temperatures. Our best guess is that worst case it will dip down to seventy-five below zero. We don't know how long it will stay there but we hope it doesn't get as low as a hundred below because at that temperature carbon dioxide will precipitate out of the air and we won't even be able to breathe."

"If it dips down even to fifty below people below the Mason Dixon line will surely perish. Most of the people south of Oklahoma are already in a bad way because of the Hurricanes. That was another mess caused by the oil industry, and we can't say for certain that this drilling in the Gulf didn't have something to do with the problems we have with these volcanoes. The Earth is a complicated thing and we haven't even touched the surface as far as understanding it."

"By touching the surface I mean that I learned that man has been able to get down about ten miles. The Earth is around 7913 miles in diameter, so that means that we can know for sure what is down there at a couple of spots where we were able to drill down one eight hundredth of the way."

"You think it might dip below fifty below here?" Adam wanted Justin to refocus.

Justin took a sip of coffee and continued. "We are fairly certain that the last super volcano triggered a global winter. It makes perfect sense to conclude that all that ash and smoke will rise and cover the planet. We can only guess at the magnitude of the problem. Humans can survive temperatures down to sixty below, they do it all the time but not for a long period, and not the whole planet."

"Just imagine for a moment all the possible temperatures in the universe, from the heat of the sun, 27 million degrees Fahrenheit to zero degrees Kelvin, minus 459.67 degrees Fahrenheit.

Now imagine the human animal, we can exist from about 145 degrees to about minus 50. That is a range of a whopping 200 degrees Fahrenheit. It has taken millions of years for this planet to evolve itself into an environment that can sustain human life. We have evolved from single cell organisms and thrived here. It has taken eons for this planet to get to this point and we can find none like it throughout the solar system. We are very fragile creatures and so is our ecosystem. We have the ability to change our climate. How these bastards were ever allowed to bribe their way through is a mystery.

"How long will this cold temperature last?" Adam asked.

"We think it could be a couple of weeks up to a couple of years, we just don't know." There was a gasp from the ladies.

"We hope it's no longer than that but we know it's going to be bad."

John began to speak, "Even if the temperature drops that low for a few days we're in bad shape. The people who live up north will probably survive because they deal with low temperatures every year. The people in the Midwest and down south won't stand a chance. Even in the best years there are times when cold weather dips way south. Now take the sun out of the equation for months, these people don't have furnaces. None of the vegetation can tolerate even a small cold snap. Man can live for three minutes without oxygen and three days without water. When all the water freezes for even a few days many of the animals will perish."

"What about our water, John? Do we have plenty?" Jerri asked.

"Most of the ground water in this country has been ruined by frackers. We think it was all part of a plan to sell bottled water."

"I thought fracking was all about jobs? We were told that fracking would create jobs and make us less dependent on foreign oil?" Debra spoke up.

"There was a time when you could build a little house in the country and drill a well and bring up fresh clean drinking water for you and your animals and your crops. Not any more, what you get is some nasty poisonous crap that the oil companies put in the ground. These big companies saw the inevitable, that the oil was running out and so they decided that the next market was going to be in clean water. They decided to corner the market on clean water and helped the process along by contaminating all the ground water. Many of these land owners bought into their line of lies and sold the water rights from under their property. Some people became quite wealthy from it but at what price? Justin and I have been working for years to keep the frackers out of this area so for the time being we have plenty of water. We have three fairly deep wells and so far the water is good; so we should be alright as far as the water issue goes."

"With temperatures dipping that low, shelter becomes critical. We built this outer building with a dead air space between it and the house. That space will be heated using ground water, and wood. It will be the same for the livestock building. All this stuff underground we expect to keep above freezing but some of it just barely. Solar will not be an option. We have tanks and tanks of propane just in case but we won't tap into those until we need to."

"As far as food, we have built up quite a store in the time we had. We don't know how many of us there will be to feed though. We expect that once the word about the volcanoes gets out people will start dragging in here. A lot of people will just try to ride it out in their homes and that will work for a little while but few people keep enough food to last more than a few days."

Ken began to speak. "Can I interrupt here a minute John?"

"Sure," John rose and left the room, "be right back."

"Most people have no idea how dependent we have become on electricity. When the power fails people are going to die in large numbers, think about it. We use electricity for lighting, when the power fails and the sun is blotted out by the ash cloud everyone will be in the dark. The power will fail. In some places the ash will take out the power lines. Ash buildup on transformers will cause them to fail. None of the overhead power lines are insulated; we use free air as an insulator. Dry air is the best insulator you can get, and the cheapest. When this open wiring gets all caked up with ash there will be failure after failure due to phase to phase faults across the ash buildup."

"We use electricity to refrigerate our food, when the power fails all of that food will spoil, tons and tons of it. Almost every conventional heating system uses electricity to run fan motors and valves and thermostats, no power no heat. If the weather gets down like we're talking about, no heat is a killer."

"But the ash might not be bad this far east?" Adam asked.

"True, Adam, but it's not only the ash that will kill the power here, it's the cold. The nuke plants have ponds next to them that are used as cooling water. When the temperature dips down to fifty below, the ponds will freeze. There are flow switches in the water lines that will shut the system down in the event of no flow, and frozen water doesn't flow very well. The coal plants have great heaping stacks of coal all outside and exposed. That coal has moisture in it and this extreme cold will make it impossible to dig the coal out of the pile. When the temperature gets as cold as that; machines stop running. Some specially designed machines will run in that cold weather but no machine around here or south of here would be designed for weather that cold. There are a few natural gas generators out there; we expect that there will be multiple problems with the natural gas. The first is that we are already seeing problems with the natural gas pumps down south. The oil from the Gulf hurricanes has damaged them and they sometimes work and lately sometimes not. There is a good deal of natural gas stored in salt mines west of here but the problem with natural gas is that there is a lot of moisture in with the gas. Temperatures this cold will cause that water to freeze up." Ken stopped for a breath.

Adam spoke, "Sounds like we lose nuclear, natural gas and coal power generation is that right? What's left?"

Ken continued. "Those are the three big ones, that leaves solar and wind. Solar is out with the sun blocked. Since the sun heating the earth's surface to different temperatures causes the wind I guess that means that wind is out too."

Adam spoke again, "No nukes, no natural gas, no coal, no solar, and no wind. What does that mean?"

"It means many people who have become dependent upon electricity for their daily lives will die from lack of water, lack of food and lack of heat." Ken stated without emotion.

"What will we do?" Adam asked.

"We have three generators all with multiple fuel sources. We only need one at a time. We have a great battery bank that will hold us if one of them goes down. John said to spare no expense when it came to that and we didn't."

"That account is about wiped clean by the way," John had returned to the room.

"Perfect timing, I'd say," Jerri spoke.

John resumed. "We should have the basics under control; we have electricity, water, shelter, and food. What we must all do is to realize that this condition may go on for quite some time. We must make this place self-sustainable. We have livestock and gardens that must be tended. We need to learn to consume only as much as we need and assure that what we produce is enough or slightly more than we need. Let's end these meetings with a little prayer. We are going to need all the help we can get."

What John didn't know was that Bennett was on his way here.

Chapter 59

Bennett left City Hall in a rage. People simply did not disregard him in this manner. He climbed into the back seat of the luxury rental car. "Drive us back to the airport, what time is our flight out of this flea-bitten backwoods?"

"Let me check." Jenny slid into the passenger side of the car while Richards took the driver's seat and started the engine.

"Drive Richards!" Richards did as he was told. Bennett was in a rare foul mood. It was rare that anyone was allowed to get on that man's nerves.

"Where do we go Jenny?" He asked quietly.

"Go toward Wichita, the airport is just south of West Kellogg on the west side of town I think that's highway 54. I'll see if I can download the flight information. Give me your phone." He passed her his phone as he was driving slowly toward the west. Before he had gone far at all she handed him the phone back, it was set to the GPS app., and the step by step directions were on the screen.

"Thank you Jenny." He whispered.

"You are welcome," she patted him on the knee.

Bennett was deeply immersed in the multi-page report. "What do we know about these two fellows Richards; these so-called scientists that wrote this report." Bennett waved the report in the rear view mirror.

"Best there is sir, just like you requested."

"Shit," Bennett spoke with unexpected candor.

"Flights are cancelled across the board sir. Seems there was an eruption of a volcano at Yellowstone. Until further notice all flights are grounded." She said worriedly.

"Make reservations for the first flight out, we'll need rooms while we wait." He had only read the first part of the report and it was all coming true, the report suggested that the first eruption would be at Yellowstone, followed by a string of others. He turned on his laptop to get the news.

A moment later, Jenny spoke, "Sir, we've got the penthouse suite." She checked closer, Bennett was asleep. She turned to Richards. "Go ahead and take us to the airport, I can show you where to go once we turn off Kellogg Drive." She opened her laptop and began to scroll down through the latest news stories.

"I don't think we are going to get a plane out of Wichita for the next several days, can you drive a little faster?"

Bennett was waking up as the big car pulled into the valet parking area. "Has there been any news about the plane?" He asked Jenny.

"They are all still grounded until further notice." She knew it was not the answer he wanted.

He stormed out of the car carrying the report in one hand and his briefcase in the other. He walked into the lobby and spoke with the manager. Richards and Jenny followed him in.

"The manager will see me to my suite. I won't need either one of you until tomorrow. Meet me here at 8 o'clock AM unless we can catch a plane. I'll have breakfast in the suite. Keep in touch with the airline and if something becomes available call me." He motioned for the manager to lead the way. He turned to Richards. "I don't know how it is with you two; get two rooms or one I couldn't care less. After reading that report and hearing the news if I were you two I would get a big bottle of Champaign and screw like bunnies. You may not get another chance."

Chapter 60

The radio crackled into life;

You folks got Lightning Tim here. Don't try to fly south. Another one of those nasty hurricanes popped up over the Gulf and brought another dose of oil to the mid-southern states. Those folks down there have just been hammered. All the airports from Wichita south to the Gulf have been closed until the storm lets up and the oil has dissipated.

Chapter 61

Jenny and Richards were having a drink at the bar their luggage resting on a luggage cart.

"What shall we do about a room?" Jenny asked as she sipped her gin and tonic.

"What would your husband say?" Richards asked in return as he sipped his Seven & Seven.

"What husband are you referring to?" She was puzzled.

"I thought you were married," he pointed to her left hand, "that ring."

She held up her left hand. "This ring? It belonged to my mother. I started wearing it when she passed; she wore it from the time she was about my age she said it brought her luck."

"You're saying we've known each other for over three years and all this time you thought I was married?" She chuckled. In her mind she had always thought Richards was gay and that was the reason he had never hit on her. She certainly didn't think she should tell him that.

"I don't know where I got that idea but it seemed to fit, you never seemed to flirt with me so I just assumed." He went back to his drink.

"Will it be OK with you if we change the nature of our relationship?" She asked expectantly.

"You have no other emotional involvements? He asked.

"None what so ever, and you?" She finished her drink.

He finished his drink in one final gulp, took her hand and led her to the front counter.

Before he got to the counter, he stopped and turned to her. "You heard what Bennett said, he might have been right. If it's the end of the world we need to speed things up. Would you like to be my wife?"

"Just for tonight?" She asked.

"For sure tonight, we can see how it fits in the next couple of days."

She thought for a moment. "Are you seeing anybody?"

"Not for a long long time," he answered.

"All right." She agreed. She felt a flush of excitement.

He walked to the counter, Jenny followed behind pushing the cart with the luggage. He spoke with the desk clerk. "My name is James Richards, we are traveling with Mr. Bennett. Do you have a nice room with a single king? This is our wedding day."

"Shall I register you as Mr. and Mrs. Richards then?" The clerk asked.

"That would be fine." Richards replied.

Richards unlocked the door with the electronic key, he held up his hand for Jenny to wait while he pushed the cart into the room. Once the cart was out of the way, he turned to Jenny.

"I believe in Kansas, in order to be legally married all you need to do is introduce a lady as your wife and that is binding." He unexpectedly swept her off her feet and carried her through the door, shutting it with his foot. "Welcome home, Mrs. Richards." He kissed her for the first time as he held her in his arms.

He finally let her stand. "You're the prettiest girl in the whole office complex." He said as he kissed her again and again.

"And you're the handsomest man."

Their marriage was consummated between the doorway and the king-size bed.

Chapter 62

The radio crackled into life;

You folks got Lightning Tim here; bad news for you air travelers trying to get out of the Great North West. Since Mt. Rainier blew its top, all flights have been cancelled coming from or going to the Washington area. Mt. Rainier used to be over 14,000 feet tall. The last time it erupted was in 1854.

We were lucky in 2008 when Mt. St. Helens erupted. We learned that planes and volcanic ash don't mix. If you need to go that direction you will need to go by land.

Chapter 63

At precisely 8 a.m., Bennett arrived where he said he would be.

"Planes?" He asked.

"No sir, they are all still grounded." She hated to deliver the bad news.

"Have them bring the car and load the bags." Then he seemed to be speaking to himself.

"If I had had that report in a timely manner I sure as hell wouldn't be stranded here in Wichita, Kansas. I can make that son of a bitch pay." He turned to Richards. "Tell me about John Williams and his project."

"Well, sir," Richards recalled a memory, "We started to pay attention to him and his little lunacy about the time that report went missing. He liquidated a lot of assets and then began to spend money on unusual items."

"Details, Richards," Bennett demanded.

"He bought a large number of intermodal shipping containers, tons of food, thousands of gallons of diesel and tank cars of natural gas and propane. He purchased three large generators, medical supplies, enough for a small army, oxygen generators and a list of other things that make very little sense." Richards wished he had brought that list.

The car was brought to the front of the building and the bags were loaded.

"Drive Richards," Bennett ordered.

"Where to sir?"

"The William's place, and drive fast."

Chapter 64

The radio crackled into life;

You folks got Lightning Tim here with all bad news. This indiscriminate fracking activity in the Northwest finally was the straw that broke the camel's back. The Cascades have long possessed volcanoes that have been given a very high threat level by The United States Geological Survey. There were nine volcanoes in the Cascade Range at that threat level and two of them have just erupted. Mr. Rainier, which hasn't erupted since the last century and Mt. St. Helens, which has had two eruptive episodes in the past several decades. Mt. Rainier has been listed as the most threatening volcano in that region because it is such a danger to Seattle and Tacoma.

To make matters worse and to add insult to injury; the super volcano at Yellowstone has decided to erupt again. It has been over 70,000 years since the last one but these manmade earthquakes have taken their toll. It is expected that this eruption will have an enormous impact on the weather and other human activities for quite some time.

Ash accumulation at the site is expected to be several feet deep and could cover the continental United States with ash that could amount to up to an inch all the way to the east coast. It is predicted to be nearly a foot deep in the Denver area. This will have a devastating impact on agriculture and all other forms of human activity. The death toll will surely be in the thousands.

We will keep you posted.

Chapter 65

Justin was tearing through the house looking for John. He found him in the library with his nose buried in a book. John was talking to himself. "We are so screwed." John looked up. "Hi Justin, having as good a day as I am having?"

"Sounds like it, what's the matter?" Justin was catching his breath.

"You first, you seem to be in the biggest hurry." John dropped his reading glasses on the desk next to the book.

"Remember we talked to a guy after the town hall meeting, named Chuck?" Justin asked.

"Charles Foster? Tall guy, crew cut, no nonsense, sort of a paramilitary type?" John remembered; the guy seemed OK.

"He's here. He brought his family and a couple of his relatives. They are sort of survivalist types, he wants to be head of security, and he wants to use his relatives as deputies."

"We don't have any security, but we could probably use some. What do you think?" John asked.

"I agree we probably could use some with all the people starting to filter in. What shall I tell him?"

"Do you trust him?" John asked.

"I think so, good handshake, good references. He was a colonel in the Marine Corp. He's retired.

Family seems nice, friendly, well kept, smart."
Justin wondered if he had forgotten anything.

"Turn him loose; tell him he's got my blessing
till he disappoints us. Better tell Jerri how we feel
first and make sure we don't get any negative
feedback from her. I kind of want her to be in full
charge of all the people down there. I don't want
to step on her toes since she's doing such a fine
job."

"Can I go and come back?" he asked.

"Go. Bring Ken with you if you can find him."
John put his glasses back on and continued to
thumb through the big book.

It wasn't long before Justin returned he was
still out of breath. "Jerri said fine with her. She
took them by the hand and was leading them into
the complex; they seemed to be getting along just
fine. I feel a little better already. Ken was in the
kitchen with Mom finishing a piece of apple pie. I
asked him to come when he was finished."

"Security is a good thing, wish I had thought
of it, oh well, the good Lord will provide." John
leaned back in his chair and motioned for Justin
to sit. "Slow down son."

Ken stepped into the room with two cups of
coffee. He set one in front of John. John took a
deep breath of the coffee before he drank any.

"Thanks buddy." John motioned for Ken to
take a seat as well.

After he had given Justin a moment to catch
his breath, John began. "We are so screwed. In
about two days the sky is going to turn black.
There is going to be a storm that seems like a

blizzard with lightning and thunder but it will be an ash cloud."

"So soon!" Ken exclaimed.

"I've been studying up on past eruptions and it's going to be very bad. Since this is January, this is the worst time for people who live to the east. The ash from those volcanoes will travel most of the way to the east coast. There could be a half-inch of accumulation well past Chicago. We are expected to get an accumulation of from three to twelve inches. The heaviest particles will fall nearest the volcanoes while the lighter ones will be carried higher into the air and fall farthest away."

"We won't be able to breathe outside without dust masks. The ash probably won't hurt but it will cause lung infections and long-term problems for humans, like silicosis. We just don't want to breathe it. It will cause severe eye irritation, so we need goggles. The animals are screwed. The ash will get packed in their fur and weigh them down. The ash in the water will cause them to stop drinking. The ash on the grass will cause them to have stomach and digestive issues and can kill them. Their eyes will become irritated just like humans. Any livestock at pasture that we can't bring into the compound need to be slaughtered and preserved. We knew we'd have to, now it's time."

"Ash fall a few millimeters thick won't have a lasting impact on the soil. Since its winter now and everything's dormant, it's the thickness we need to worry about. Thicker accumulations will kill small soil organisms and prevent the entry of oxygen and water. This can change the PH of the soil and lead to soil sterilization. We need to keep our fingers crossed about the thickness of the ash because if it gets too deep, even if we survive we won't be able to grow crops again around here. This prediction that I was reading suggests that the ash thickness near the eruptions could be up to a full meter, which would be around four feet of ash. All of the land west of the western Kansas boarder is going to be destroyed for sure. Depending on the rain and the wind and the severity of the ash cloud, land might be destroyed east as far as Chicago." John let that little piece of bad news sink in.

"Once the ash starts to fall it will disrupt communications, Radios, GPS systems, telephones, and anything used to send and receive messages will be affected. Ken, you better talk to our Ham Radio guys and get that word out." Ken nodded agreement. "Another big thing on your plate Ken is going to be the effects of ash on the electrical system. Apparently, ash becomes conductive when it gets wet. Even a half inch of ash will pack itself onto insulators and gather moisture and cause arcing across the insulators of the high voltage lines."

"We call that 'flashover,'" Ken volunteered. "That will cause a direct phase to phase fault and either blow the lines apart or just trip the overcurrent protective device."

"Same can be said for transformers." John continued. "The utilities will probably choose to shut down their systems to keep from losing them."

"Ash is heavy, wet ash can have the density twenty times that of a wet snow. We need to keep an eye on these new buildings, we beefed them up but we may need some better bracing. With a twenty to one ratio we better start to panic if the ash goes much over a half inch. There is going to be a tremendous loss of life just due to collapsing buildings."

"Any motor is not going to want to run, for long at least, in this ash. The ash will clog the air filter if there is one or the cooling coils will clog up. That will be true of all the condensing units for air handlers and refrigeration equipment. Even if the motors are sealed units the cooling apparatus will clog and the unit will shut down from overheating."

"We have a lot of transformers and capacitors that depend on fans to keep them cool. If the ash doesn't take out the lines from tracking it'll take them out from overheating." Ken volunteered. "Don't forget all the trees and vegetation that hangs over the power lines. Heavy ash accumulations on the plants will cause them to fall onto the lines as well. All of our stuff here is underground and protected from the ash and trees at least, we will have to constantly keep the filters clean on the air intakes. I think everyone will be fully employed during the worst of it."

John continued. "Any type of travel during the ash storm is going to be out of the question. Airplanes can't fly in it because the engines foul. Land vehicles can travel in it for a short while until the filters all clog up and the engine overheats and the pistons and bearings seize up. Even if you can figure a way to keep the engine running, the grit from the ash will get between the wipers and the glass and make it to where you can't see through the glass. If anyone could figure a way around all these obstacles, it would be like driving in a blizzard, even a little ash will cover the roads and a great pile of it will stop anything but a big truck. Any ash buildup in the sewer systems will set up like concrete." John waited for comment then continued.

"All government services at all levels will cease, no sewer, no water, no road crews, no communication, no nothing."

"Now this is just during the ash storm, right?" Justin asked. "How long do you expect the ash storm to last?"

"Since we've never encountered anything of this magnitude in Earth's history we can only make a wild-ass guess. I'm hoping only two to four weeks. Based on the stuff I've read, we'll be lucky if it only lasts four weeks. Nobody has seen anything of this magnitude before. The volume of ash is unprecedented, so the effects are completely unpredictable. The way I see it, in a couple of days the sky is going to go dark. We won't be able to go outside without goggles and respirators. We won't be able to drive or fly anywhere. Everything that is left alive outside now; will be dead or dying. All the animals, most of the fish and many of the plants will die. Some plants will survive since its winter and they are dormant. In a month or so we will be able to come back out and breathe unless the wind is blowing the ash around. If we're lucky and it rains two things will happen. The first is that the rain will knock a lot of the ash out of the sky and the second is that wet ash will be easier to get rid of."

"But wait," John continued, "When the ash covers the sky it will block out the sun and its winter now. If the sun is blocked the temperature will fall. I was reading here that it is speculated that the last super volcano called Toba lowered the temperature by something like 30 degrees Fahrenheit. We've been having bad winters around here lately with the global climate change caused by the hydrocarbons so if we add another 30 degrees to that we could be looking at a low of 40 to 50 below. Here is our volcanic winter we prepared for, let's hope we're ready."

"Oh, and one last thing; I saved the best for last." John held his head in his hands. "Half of the world's oxygen comes from organisms called phytoplankton in the water. When the water freezes they can no longer get sunlight and they die. When the plants and trees get frozen they no longer generate oxygen. When a volcano blows its top, thousands upon thousands of cubic feet of gas escape, much of that combines with the oxygen in the atmosphere and lowers the oxygen level. Humans can survive in an atmosphere that contains between 19.5 and 21 percent oxygen, if the percentage drops below 19.5 percent we struggle to breathe. And we die."

The room was silent.

Chapter 66

Bennett surveyed the bleak countryside. "What a terrible barren place."

"In the spring it will all be green with wildflowers and cattle grazing." Jenny said hopefully; she was raised on a farming community.

"Not this spring; nor any other for that matter." Bennett secretly enjoyed the thought that he had been somewhat responsible for all this. "After the ash fall nothing much will grow here. How well do you know Justin Williams?" He was speaking to Richards.

"We've eaten lunch a few times, he seems like an alright guy."

"Think you'll have any luck getting us into their compound?" Bennett hated to be dependent upon anyone.

"I have no idea, but under the circumstances and based on what you've told us about that report we either get in or we die." He placed his hand on the seat and Jenny grasped it.

Richards took his eyes off the road and looked toward Jenny, she blew him a kiss and squeezed his hand.

Bennett saw the gesture. "So, did you two get some Champaign and make the beast with two backs last night? You don't have to answer if you don't want to."

"We decided to get married, Mr. Bennett. And you're to blame." Jenny volunteered. "And yes we made mad passionate love all night long and into the morning." She became embarrassed and stopped talking.

"That was a little more information than I needed." He patted his briefcase and looked out the window. "Is that line of traffic the Williams' compound?"

"It must be, the GPS doesn't seem to be working right now but this is about where I think it should be." Richards pulled into line behind a minivan with a family of four and many bags.

The line moved slowly but steadily. Two men dressed in black and wearing pistols at their belts were letting people into the gate one by one.

"Are they checking papers or something?" Bennett asked.

"It looks like they are directing people where to park just like an amusement park." Jenny said.

When they stopped at the gate the man in black lowered his head as Richards rolled down the window. "Morning folks, follow that green van and park beside it. Looks like you're the last ones for a while. You won't need to lock your car, it's safe in here. You can leave your bags in the car for now, just walk over to the double doors and get signed in. Jerri will get you situated and we can help you with your bags later," he looked up at the sky. "We've still got a little time."

"Have you heard any more news?" Richards asked.

"I'm out of the loop out here, but the sky is starting to darken and that's got to be a bad sign." He pointed toward the west.

"Maybe we should hurry and get in?" Jenny pleaded.

Richards followed the green van and parked beside it. The parking lot was just a flat piece of pasture. The ground was dry with the occasional rock and cow patty, most of the grass was brown and dead looking, but occasionally there was a green plant that survived the cold. The pasture was on kind of a hill to the north of the main buildings. There were two large metal buildings and several grain silos. Freshly dug earth connected both metal buildings and extended all the way from the buildings up the hill to about where they were standing. People were carrying belongings from vehicles toward what looked like the entrance to a tunnel. Richards and Jenny led the way while Bennett followed behind clutching his brief case and mumbling to himself.

The entrance to the tunnel was a large overhead door and a small mandoor to the right of the larger one. Twenty foot or so beyond the first set of doors was another set of identical doors. This created what amounted to an airlock. Since the weather was mild and the traffic in and out of the tunnel was rather heavy, both overhead doors were open. From the second set of doors, the tunnel appeared to be 15 feet or so wide and extended gently down the hill toward the main buildings. A string of lights illuminated the tunnel, which went straight for a long way until it jogged. The left side of the tunnel was comprised of rectangular metal openings these were the open ends of the intermodal trailers that were buried side by side. Some were open, some had curtain like doorways and some were closed with wood framing.

A dark haired lady approached them and asked them to take a seat and asked them a series of questions.

Jerri didn't recognize the three people who had just entered the complex. The group consisted of a young couple, holding hands and a short nervous looking dark haired gentleman carrying a briefcase. The briefcase must be important to him she thought because of the way that he was holding it.

She was satisfied when she learned that they were not locals, were just passing through and were trapped by the storm.

"So, how long have you two been married?" She asked them after filling out the questionnaire.

"Just yesterday," answered Richards.

"This weather sort of messed up your honeymoon then?" Jerri asked.

"You might say this weather was the reason for our honeymoon." She grasped the young man's arm.

"Excuse me ma'am, but do you by chance know a Justin Williams?" Richards asked.

"Why do you ask?" Jerri was cautious.

"He and we, that is, Jenny and I worked with Justin. We used to eat lunch together from time to time.

"I'm sure he'll be pleased to hear you're here, I'll let him know when I see him." She held out her hand. "Please call me Jerri." She led them down the hallway to an open trailer door.

"You all can make yourselves at home here for the time being. We don't know how many people are going to be staying. We kind of figured there would be more than this by now." She was apologetic.

"Most people don't know what is coming." Richards volunteered. "If they did you'd be full."

"I don't know if that would be a blessing or a curse." She chuckled.

"Each of these units is equipped with beds, dressers, tables and lamps and chairs. There are comfortable recliner chairs as well. Sort of like a motel only without the sinks and toilets. Every fourth unit or so has been set up with showers and sinks and toilets. At this time, we seem to have plenty of water but that might change. Every tenth unit or so is set up like a kitchen with tables and chairs and refrigeration. We have some laundry facilities; we have some units set up for entertainment. We don't know how long we are likely to be down here but it could be quite a while. We are telling everyone right up front that we need to conserve on everything. If we do, we may survive this. If we don't we perish; it is that simple."

"We have been told to expect an ash storm, once that starts the doors will be shut and there will be no going outside. If you need anything out of your car, you better get it now. If you need help just ask someone. Once we get set up and know who all is down here we will put people in charge just like the old floor monitors in the dorms in college but that will be later. There is a lot of work to be done and everybody will have at least one job."

"What kind of jobs?" Jenny burst in.

"We have greenhouses and livestock and laundry and cooking and cleaning, all kinds of jobs. Is there something special you'd like to do?" Jerri asked.

"Are there chickens? I had chickens when I was a little girl and I loved to gather the eggs." Her eyes lit up like a child at Christmas. "Can we go see the chickens?"

"I would like to see the chickens too, if I may?" Bennett asked.

Richards and Jenny looked at each other with surprise.

Jerri thought for a minute. "Why not?" She led the way down the long corridor. As she passed a young girl in the isle way she spoke with her for a moment, pointed back toward the big double doors and handed her a clipboard. "I think you're the last for the day but we won't know for sure."

Bennett walked close beside Jerri. "You know, I'm an engineer by trade, I think I could be most useful helping with the facilities. Would you know is there a central air handling system for this complex?"

"I'll let Ken know you're interested in helping with that sort of thing. I think the air filter system is about half way down here where the two big corridors intersect.

"Thank you," Bennett dropped back a little. "I want to carry my weight. I don't want to be a bother."

Jerri led them to a wide corridor that intersected the first at a right angle. It too was illuminated with a string of lights high up along one wall. "This is the isle way that takes us to the big barn. Ken made it wide enough for a tractor.

"Mr. Bennett, that door right there is where the fans are." Jerri pointed toward a door.

"Please, call me Bill; I know we're going to be good friends." Bennett smiled.

Richards and Jenny looked at each other with a wide-eyed look of disbelief. They had neither one of them ever heard anyone address Bennett as "Bill."

They passed through a large set of double doors.

"This is in case we want to separate the people from the animals for some reason I've never seen these doors closed, but then we haven't been here that long."

Soon they were walking up an incline that led them into the big arena. She pointed in different directions as she described the different animals. "We plan to keep this area just above freezing because the animals won't mind. We have chickens, ducks, and rabbits over in this corner. Over there, we have a small breed of cattle. Over there, we have pigs, goats, and sheep. Inside that partition over there, we have some aquaponic tanks. John funded a senior class project at the high school and they used this building. The concept is that they can grow fish in a big tank, then use the fish water to fertilize plants and the plants clean the water for the fish. It is an amazing process that produces both plants and fish. It is a good thing they had it going already because it takes time to balance the system."

They walked past the chicken pens. "Usually Mary Southard is around here working, she's the chicken lady. After you folks have your stuff inside the complex just come on down any time and she will put you to work. Do you think you can find your way back? I've got some other things to take care of."

"Not a problem," answered Bennett, "Thank you for the tour, it has been most enlightening." He had made up his mind to do nothing until after the ash storm. He looked out of the big open doors and watched as the men hurriedly slaughtered the cattle before the ash came. He recognized John outside and determined to speak with him if the opportunity arose.

Chapter 67

The radio crackled into life;

You folks got Lightning Tim here; I guess we better talk a little bit about volcanic ash since it's going to be a big part of our lives from now on. Volcanic ash comes about when a volcano explodes. The magma is in the ground under high pressure and as it is blown out of the volcano, it decompresses. Exploding gas bubbles tear the magma into fragments, which solidify in the atmosphere as ash particles. This ash is composed of silica and iron and magnesium; pulverized rocks, minerals, and volcanic glass. When this ash mixes with water, it becomes corrosive and electrically conductive. Gases given off during an eruption include; sulfur dioxide, hydrogen, hydrogen sulfide, carbon monoxide and hydrogen chloride.

Volcanic ash can be very dense and heavy, especially when it becomes moist. It can cling to power lines and trees and cause roof collapses due to weight. It is extremely abrasive to the eyes and moving machine parts and should not be breathed. It looks like we might get a few inches of it down here so prepare for the worst.

Chapter 68

Mitch Michelson and his wife Sara were retired from the postal service. They both enjoyed good pensions but several years ago decided they were bored and volunteered to drive busses for the school district. Her bus covered the northwest quadrant and his bus the northeast. He and Sara both agreed that John Williams seemed to have lost his mind. He had every right to spend his fortune any way he saw fit and the building they were standing in was just a good example. Nobody believed there was going to be a mini ice age like he was predicting, so when he gave the school board the money no one batted an eye when they diverted it to new soccer goals and bleachers. The contracts for the soccer field had been signed for a long time everyone was just waiting for some funding. After all, didn't the team place third at state this year? The money was to have been spent to strengthen the community building and triple insulate it. When the ice age didn't happen, and everyone agreed that it wouldn't, he would be thankful that they had spent the money more wisely.

The multi-purpose building was less than five years old. John no doubt had a hand in having it built in the first place. He seemed to have his hand in most everything around here. The north part of the building held a stage in the center of the building. To the right of the north end was a kitchen where food was cooked for fundraising activities and for the children's lunches. The long tables were stored to the left of the stage when the stage was being used, like tonight. All the chairs were lined up in neat rows and the parents of the grade school children were seated in eager anticipation of the school's presentation of The Music Man.

Mitch was one of those individuals, and everybody knows one, who always carried a cup of coffee in his hand. Today was no exception. He stood in the doorway of the kitchen looking north toward his big yellow bus, number one. He was proud of that number. Sara didn't mind that she was number two. The school board thought long and hard about cancelling this production, but in light of the fact that it had been scheduled for months and involved the high school band, cancelling was simply out of the question. So, what if a volcano a thousand miles away was doing its thing? This was Kansas and people here worried about tornadoes, not volcanoes.

Still, Mitch was watching that ash build up deeper and deeper. Here it was only four in the afternoon and it was dark as night outside. The wind wasn't blowing, which was rare in Kansas. Heck, the word Kansas means wind in the Indian tongue. The ash was falling like a gentle snowstorm and where the bus was parked under the street light, he could see that the ash build up was two, maybe three inches deep. He wished he were home so he could shovel it off of his driveway, but that would have to wait until this play was over. They were just ready to finish up with intermission, he heard the band starting to warm up. Soon it would be the beginning of act three.

Sara walked into the room and poured herself a cup of coffee from the forty-two-cup coffeemaker. "I haven't been paying much attention to the weather lately what with all the to-do about this play. How much of this are we supposed to get?"

"I thought they said a half an inch tops." Mitch continued to stare toward the bus. "I've never had anything to do with volcanic ash, but it can't be good for you, can't be good for engines. It feels gritty if you rub it between your fingers and it gets in your eyes and throat. These kids should be home. They shouldn't be out in this. Who knows about the long term adverse health effects of breathing this? We should all have been issued those paper filters to breathe through."

"How about a coffee filter?" Sara walked to the counter and placed one of the big white filters over her nose and mouth. "This ought to get us out of the building. There's three or four packages of these filters in the cupboard." She rummaged through the cabinets. "That's enough for everyone that wants one. They should shut this thing down and send everyone home, this is ridiculous."

"You know how these theatre folk are Sara, the show must go on." Mitch was holding a coffee filter over his nose and mouth. "There might be four inches in places. How tall do you suppose a curb is? It's almost to the top of the curb in some places."

A large crash was heard from the stage area. It was the drums; they were announcing the beginning of the next act. Then there was another louder crash and the screams of many people in terror.

Mitch and Sara rushed to the other side of the kitchen and looked through the doorway that led out to the open seating area.

"My God, Mitch the roof has collapsed!" She began to cry. "My eyes, I can't see, it's in my eyes."

He directed her into the kitchen and to the sink. "This building's on a well, the water should still work." The water did work and she was able to wash out her eyes.

"That was the flat roof part, the roof over the stage and the kitchen is a slanted roof. We must get those children out of the building before the whole thing collapses. It must have been the weight of the ash. I never thought about the weight of the ash."

There was a kitchen entrance that led up a small flight of stairs to the stage. Mitch ran to that door and up the little stairway.

"You kids!" he yelled at the top of his lungs. "Don't breathe that ash and don't let it get in your eyes. Come this way. Come this way!"

The children worked their way through the dropped instruments and turned over chairs to the little stairway. Many of the children were crying, some from fear, some from choking and sore eyes.

"We need to get out of what's left of this building." Mitch commanded. Two teachers were on the stage at the time of the collapse. Miss

Warren, the drama coach and Mr. Simon the band teacher.

He drew the two teachers aside and spoke to them. "We need to get these kids out of this building. That ash must be real heavy and this part is going to collapse soon. Have them run out and get in the bus. Tell them to keep their eyes almost closed and put one of these filters over their nose and mouth. I'll run out and get the doors open."

"I'll get the bus door open, Mitch. You help to get the kids headed that way then check and see if anyone's still alive. Just don't dawdle and let this roof collapse on you, ya hear."

"Yes, Mother." He handed her the keys to Number One.

With the help of the two teachers, it wasn't long before all of the students were making their way to the bus. Many of them tried to stay and help their loved ones in the audience, but the teachers were firm and soon the two teachers followed the students to the bus.

Mitch crawled around the top of the wreckage. He called at the top of his lungs and got no response. There was still a dial tone on the wall phone and he dialed 911. Someone in the sheriff's office answered the phone. He explained about the collapsed roof and was told that there were many collapsed roofs including the sheriff's office, where the Sheriff and both deputies had been killed. The lady said she would get in touch with the fire department, but she didn't think it would do much good. He asked her what she thought he ought to do with the children and she said it looked like old John wasn't such a fool after all and maybe he ought to try to get out there before it got much worse. Mitch didn't think it could get much worse. He stuffed the rest of the coffee filters inside his shirt, placed one over his nose and mouth and walked slowly with his eyes only open a slit to the bus.

"Shall I start it?" Sara asked from the driver's seat.

"Not just yet, Sara." He stepped out to a little compartment on the side of the bus and removed a roll of material. He took it to the front of the bus and attached it to the hooks it was designed to hang from. It was a large American Flag. "Old Number One is always the first in the parade; maybe old glory will get us a few extra miles before the engine overheats from the ash."

"What about survivors?" Sara asked.

"Nobody could have lived through that, Sara." He whispered close to her ear. "There was blood and brains everywhere, those people were two times dead." He resumed normal speech so everyone could hear. "I called the sheriff's department and they were going to get hold of the fire department."

He turned to face the children. "Calm down, calm down. You've all been through a lot, but your alive that's the main thing. I want you all to just calm down take a few deep breaths and help the person next to you to not panic. We are going to take you out in the country where it's going to be safe."

"Is it?" Sara asked quietly.

"Beats me, I'm scared to death." Mitch was trembling.

Chapter 69

John and Ken watched the killing from the cab of the pickup. The men in the outdoor arena were working in two crews of four men each. There must have been at least a hundred head of cattle milling about the arena, seemingly unaware of what was happening around them. One of the men was dragging a large silver bottle on a red cart with wheels, he would approach one of the cattle and place a device that was attached to the bottle with a hose, on the cow's forehead; the cow would fall to the ground. Two other men would attach a set of chains to the rear legs of the animal and a third man in a tractor would use the front loader to raise the animal above the ground with its head down. The first man would then slit the cow's throat and the bleeding carcass would be transported into the building where other crews were removing the skin and entrails.

"Damn shame," John admitted. "Years of breeding have gone into raising that herd. See how gentle they are, and the best eating in the state."

"You've still got the genes John. Old Doc Nubury, he's got the genes cryogenically frozen."

"He seems kind of like a crackpot to me." John admitted.

"He's got credentials a mile long, these local farmers swear by him. He's the Spermmeister."

"Right now the million dollar question is will it get cold enough soon enough to keep all that swinging beef from spoiling." John asked.

"Don't we hang beef above freezing for twenty-eight days to let it cure?" Ken asked. "It's close to freezing every day now."

"Usually that or longer. An old butcher once told me to hang the meat until it turned green and you could poke your finger through it; then just cook the moo out." He chuckled at the memory. "Best meat I ever ate came from that butcher, inch and an eighth sirloin and you could cut it with a fork, I shit you not."

"Is that ash?" Ken pointed to a spot on the hood of the truck.

"Might be a leaf." John said hopefully.

"Look off to the west, its dark as night over there.

"Looks like we won't have time to finish, we need to get everything under cover." He drove around the fenced area and let Ken off at the corral, then drove the truck into the building.

Ken told the men to drive what cattle were left into the building and begin to take cover. By the time he was finished the ash was beginning to fall quite heavily, he was trying to breathe through his shirtsleeve and his eyes were beginning to sting. He ran into the entrance of the large building just as the last of the cattle were being driven into an area surrounded by five-foot tall metal fence panels. The cattle were upset and making a continuous noise with their mooing. Ken had his head lowered and his hands on his knees and was trying to catch his breath.

"Are the hoses in place for the roofs?" John approached Ken and the two stood looking out the open roll up door.

"Here and the house, how deep do you suppose we ought to let it get?" Ken asked.

"I wouldn't think we should let it get over an inch. Just to be on the safe side let's start washing it off the roofs now." As John finished speaking, the metal halide high bay fixtures went out. He looked across the arena and could see that the tunnel lights were still on. "Must have had a dip, enough to cause the HID lights to go out but we still have power because the tunnel lights are still on."

"I better get us off the grid, as soon as this stuff starts to build up on the transformers they'll start to blow, then that'll take out the fuses and the breakers will trip at the substation and that will be the end." Ken hurried off toward the middle of the complex.

"Well you were right Mr. Williams."

John turned to see Bennett standing beside him. "You're the man from the oil company. I remember you from the city council meeting the other day. How do you happen to be here?"

"Instead of being able to ride this out in a warmer climate, I foolishly let myself get stranded at the Wichita airport. You're not the type to turn a fellow human out in the cold, so to speak."

"Sometimes I wish I were. You and your greedy type are responsible for this ruination." John had to contain himself he knew he would get angry and say something he might regret.

"You can't blame the oil companies for seeking to be profitable. You can't blame me for doing my job well. Corporations exist to increase shareholder profit, which is why they exist. Individuals who are hired to manage those corporations do what they are paid to do, which is to maximize shareholder equity. If you feel you must blame someone, you must blame those who are paid to protect the planet, those who are paid to protect us. You should blame individuals who are paid to do a job and then through greed and corruption, choose to fail. Surely, you can't blame a corporation for supporting, and installing in power, individuals who will work for the betterment of the corporation? That is the corporation's duty to the stockholders.

John was beginning to get angry. "Is it the duty of the corporation to murder the stockholders? Seems sort of counterproductive."

"Unintended consequences, Mr. Williams. In retrospect and off the record and to you only, I will admit that had I known of the devastation that we were about to create, I may have rethought our position on hydraulic fracking." Bennett would not admit that had he known the results, he would have redoubled his companies' fracking efforts. "Is it always this calm here in Kansas?" He was looking at the ash fall straight down. He must not create such a powerful enemy this soon.

No sun, no wind. Most all of the wind is caused by the sun's uneven warming of the earth.

"You are seeing the fruit of the seeds you planted, Mr. Bennett. Smell that burning smell?

That's from the fires of hell that you unleashed on Earth. You better never let these people know who you are or you may be lynched, and I would supply the rope. I won't turn you out, but I suspect that I will wish that I had. Now, I need to wash some of your ash off of my roofs."

"Foolish man." Bennett thought to himself as he watched John walk toward the center of the complex. "I would have turned me out. It is the smart thing to do."

Chapter 70

The children were no longer crying, they were scared; just like everyone on the bus. The ash was spread in an even layer over everything, had it been white it would be a winter wonderland. As it was, the ash was grey and the sky was black when it should be the middle of the day. Mitch had tried the windshield wipers early on but the grit from the ash had scratched the windows and now he was having trouble seeing through the glass. A snowplow was parked at the outer edge of the other lane, the ash must have fouled the engine, and there it sat right where it had stopped. There would be no snowplows to clear the streets.

He drove slowly because he couldn't see the road and he wanted to avoid creating a dust cloud. The darkness was illuminated as transformers on poles would explode and the fuses would blow. The streetlights created little islands of brightness in the blackness, until suddenly they all went out at the same time.

"That must be the power plant." Mitch spoke softly to Sara, not wanting to alarm the children any further.

"How much longer to the William's place?" She asked worriedly.

"A long time, if we make it at all." The bus was leaving the city limits now and there were no curbs to guide them. "Keep a close eye on the ditch on that side, I'll try to stay in the middle of the road.

"Do you smell something burning Mitch?" She sniffed the air.

"Must be the ash, after all it did come from the fires of a couple of volcanoes. I don't see any red lights on the dashboard. With the headlights on bright I bet we can't see twenty feet ahead."

"Stop here. This is the road that we turn on to go north," Sara warned.

"Are you sure?" He questioned.

"Only stop sign on this road for miles, it'll be right up the road another mile on the right.

Mitch turned onto the wide road and drove slowly north. Eventually they could see a makeshift sign nailed to a fencepost. The sign read "WILLIAMS COMPOUND" with an arrow pointing to the right.

"This must be it Mitch, pull into the field through the opening in the fence." Sara pointed. "You've got four feet over on this side."

Mitch drove the bus slowly he swerved a couple of times to avoid a parked car but this seemed to be a road. He turned left at another homemade sign with a large yellow arrow pointing to the left. A man with goggles, a white dust mask and a flashlight ran to a spot in front of the bus and held up his arms. Mitch stopped the bus and waited until the man was beside the door before he opened it.

"Welcome," Adam said as he stepped onto the bus. "We didn't think anybody else was going to make it. My name is Adam." He held out his hand.

Mitch shook the hand heartily. "You have no idea how glad I am to park this thing. My name's Mitch."

"We didn't think we would make it." Sara admitted with relief in her voice as she took Adam's hand.

Adam looked toward the back of the bus. "You've got a load here, let's get you inside."

He turned toward the children. "Listen up kids; you shouldn't be breathing this ash. I'm going to run back in and get some masks for everyone.

He returned a moment later with a full box of white masks with little blue rubber bands to hold them in place.

He stood at the front of the bus. "Just leave it here with the keys in it, Mitch. That way if we need to move it we can." He turned toward the kids. "We don't have enough goggles for everyone so when you step off the bus I want you to close your eyes and take hold of the person's hand in front of you and we are going to walk slowly into that big door over there. Here we go." He led the way from the bus and the children followed in turn with the two teachers and Mitch and Sara right behind.

One or two of the children had not been able to keep their eyes closed and they were whimpering about their eyes being sore but otherwise the big airlock was filled with shivering children who had, most of them that is, left their coats at the school.

The word about the bus quickly made the rounds and several men and ladies were busy with vacuums getting the ash from the children's hair and clothing.

"Let's get you all in and situated." Jerri led the children through the second set of doors.

"What are we going to do with all these children, Mom?" AnnaBelle asked Susan as they followed the group into the compound.

"We will just have to put them to work," Susan said. "That can be your job, keeping the children occupied." Susan chuckled.

Chapter 71

The radio crackled into life.

"Lightning Tim here, I'm back on the air with another bit of weatherman wisdom to brighten your day. No, that isn't snow falling, it is volcanic ash and you don't wanna breathe it. That ash is composed of pulverized rock and glass particles that occur when magma is blown into the atmosphere by gases escaping from a volcano. This ash is composed of silica and iron and magnesium; pulverized rocks, minerals, and volcanic glass. When this ash mixes with water it becomes corrosive and electrically conductive. Gases given off during an eruption include sulfur dioxide, hydrogen, hydrogen sulfide, carbon monoxide and hydrogen chloride.

The heavier stuff will fall closer to the eruption while the smaller, lighter particles can travel for miles. The predictions are that most of the country will be covered in some ash; from a half inch all the way over to the east coast to several feet near the eruption site. My personal prediction is that if you are thinking of going there, don't and if your there get the heck out now.

All air traffic has been grounded. This ash will have a negative impact on all social services; automobile traffic, sewer, water, and electricity. Since moist ash is conductive, you can expect the electricity to fail throughout the country. Drinking water will be affected. The storm sewer systems will be clogged. There are all manner and ways that ash will find its way into the sewage treatment system; screens and filters will be clogged, the ash will settle in the system and reduce its capacity and motors will be destroyed. Don't try to breathe it and don't let it get in your eyes.

Ash is heavy, especially wet ash; it can weigh up to twenty times more than snow. It will not melt like snow and will become like concrete in down spouts and gutters. Depending on the structure of the roof it can cause the roof to collapse. This has been the cause of many deaths after volcanic eruptions. People will try to use water to wash it away and this will result in the overloading of the water supply.

Ash will cover the plants and animals that try to eat it will suffer damage to their teeth and internal organs. The ash will damage the soil and in many cases make it sterile. The ash will fall into bodies of water and increase the turbidity of the water decreasing the amount of light that gets to aquatic vegetation. Fish and other species that depend on these plants will be affected. The ability of the fish to absorb the oxygen in the water will be affected.

Finally and most important to yours truly; ash will have a negative impact on telecommunication. The towers and cabling and dishes will be destroyed by the weight of the ash. Most of our equipment requires constant cooling and this is accomplished by condensing units which will be destroyed by the ash.

Chapter 72

The compound settled into a routine. The boring days seemed to drag on. Everyone did their jobs as best they could. Most everyone cried from time to time, thinking about how things had been and about lost loved ones. The air was cold, the food was meager; everyone knew that if the ash didn't let up they would all perish. Most everyone was kept very busy and sleep came quickly when time allowed. One day AnnaBelle approached Adam with a request.

"We need laptops Adam. Those kids are not used to working. They are full of energy and bored to death. Laptops can be a great learning tool and the games can keep them occupied so they won't be so afraid. A couple of the kids have them and it is really causing problems." AnnaBelle was dressed in a double layer of sweat clothes at the breakfast table.

"Take them all away then, so nobody has one." Adam did not want to go out in this hostile, alien environment. "It's pitch black outside and it's only middle morning now. Everything is covered with ash and its fifty-fricking degrees *below* zero out there. It is just too damn dangerous." Adam was adamant.

But AnnaBelle was insistent. "Mr. Michelson, the bus driver, said he'd drive." It always worked to shame Adam into doing something. If the old guy would go, Adam would come around.

"Shucks, AnnaBelle. OK, but if we don't make it back, it's your fault." Adam stormed into the basement and out into the compound to find Mitch Mitchelson.

"You certain you know what you're doing girl?" Debra was seated at the table with AnnaBelle. "Maybe shaming Adam into going out in this isn't the best thing to do?"

"Those kids are driving me crazy. They don't know how to entertain themselves. They spent their entire lives glued to a TV set. Most of them are city kids that never did an ounce of work in their lives. How hard could it be, run into town, grab some games, run back? Why is everything so difficult? I've got to feed the baby." AnnaBelle shuffled off into the house.

"She's going to get that boy killed." Debra mumbled to herself.

Chapter 73

"We've got a real problem John." Ken had found John down in the meat room.

The floors were red tile and the floor was all sloped to drain to a central drain. The ceiling and walls were covered with white FRP for easy cleaning. Several three-quarter inch green hoses were coiled along the walls to wash down the whole area. One wall was lined with stainless steel tables. On the tables were large pieces of raw beef in various stages of being cut up and processed. Just off of another wall were stainless tables where the beef was being wrapped and then taken to one of several locations for storage. In the center of the room were several band saws and grinders, all needing to be washed. John was wearing a white cap and white gloves with an apron that covered his clothes and hung to his knees. There was a chain around his waist from which suspended a black plastic device that held several blood covered black handled knives of various sizes and a honing steel. His white gloves and apron were covered in blood.

"Let's get out of this refrigerated room, my fingers are numb." He led Ken into an adjoining room. The doorway was composed of several 12-inch wide heavy clear plastic strips suspended from the top of the door that hung to the floor and overlapped; allowing the temporary passage of personnel but not of much cold air.

John sat down in an office chair and propped one leg up on the desk. He motioned for Ken to take a chair. "Ready for a cup of coffee?" He asked.

"I'm ready for a drink." Ken replied.

"Oh, hell. What's up?" John asked. He desperately wanted a cup of coffee but this sounded serious.

"You know how we keep hoping the ash will stop but it just keeps on falling, looks like it might be letting up."

"That's good news. Isn't it?" John was confused.

"That part's good enough. And the temperature has been hovering down around sixty below for several weeks."

"We've known that," John countered. That beef we're cutting up is headed straight outside. The freezers in here won't work when it's that cold outside. Where's the bad news?"

"Remember when you were worried that that cold might dip so far south that the oxygen level might drop? Well, it seems to be happening." Ken's voice was shaking. We've done a pretty good job of holding back the ash that killed a lot of people. We did a pretty good job of holding back the cold that killed a whole lot more. But this." He sat down and put his head in his hands.

"What do the learned science men have to say?" John asked.

Ken took a moment to pull himself together, then began. "Even if all the ponds freeze and all the plant life here in North America goes dormant, there is a lot of water and plant life down in the warmer climates. That vegetation has always kept the atmosphere breathable. The scientists think that the oil spill in the Gulf covered more surface area than we originally thought possible. They have cut a lot of trees, John. The rain forests have just been decimated, turning the lush green tropical rain forests into poor cropland. People didn't get the memo, John; that things people do half way around the world can come back here and haunt us. We die if the oxygen level gets much below 19 percent; we're there."

"So, why aren't I having trouble breathing?" Ken.

"Because the atmosphere in the tunnels and in the house are being supplemented by those big oxygen generators we bought. They use electricity to separate oxygen and hydrogen from water and add the oxygen to the air we breathe, just like in a submarine. It doesn't take much oxygen to supplement this small environment but outside it's getting really bad. The scientists are afraid that it might drop below 16 percent; that is what it takes to sustain combustion. If the fires go out, we die. It is that simple." Ken put his head back in his hands.

"Do we all just drop to our knees then and pray for a speedy death?" John was more serious than he wanted to admit. This whole ordeal was taking an emotional toll on everyone.

"Right now the seasons should be changing. We can't see it, but this old Earth is getting nearer to the sun every day. The scientists feel that since the ash is nearly done then perhaps all of the eruptions have ended. That means the ash particles that are blocking the sun will begin to settle out of the atmosphere. That will let the sun shine through, the phytoplankton will bloom and flourish, and the atmosphere will come back. Our hope is that it already has begun and we are feeling the worst of it right now." Ken at least sounded hopeful.

"What do we do?" John asked.

"I'm worried about the fires tonight, if they go out, with the temperature the way it is, we're done for. I would like to see everyone get comfortable in the greenhouses, where the oxygen levels are fairly high anyway; and spend the next two nights. That way I can adjust the oxygen concentrators toward the generators. The air will get a little thin in the outer parts of the compound for a couple of nights." Ken seemed worried that John might refuse.

"I guess go ahead and do it. What happens if this doesn't work?' John hated to ask.

"We all get very tired, go to sleep and never wake up." Ken stood and left the room

Chapter 74

"Why was I not told?" John was furious. He seldom raised his voice but when he did, people shrank back.

"I guess I didn't think." AnnaBelle was in tears.

"Fifty below temperatures, zero visibility; and you conned Adam into going out in this for a few lousy video games. Medicine or something vital, I might understand, but video games?" John began to pace the control room.

The control room was one of the intermodal containers located in a central location near the intersection of the two main isle ways. It was the center of activity for all that went on in the underground complex. It was better lit than many of the units with desks and computers along both long walls and an isle down the middle. John was now pacing back and forth in that long isle.

Susan and Jerri heard the commotion from down the hall and came to see what was wrong.

Susan had seen John in this mood on several occasions so when the two entered she sort of pushed Jerri forward.

"What's wrong John?" Jerri asked meekly.

"That daughter of ours," and he looked at Susan, "conned your son," he looked at Jerri, "and the father of our grandchild into driving into town to gather laptops for the children."

"How nice." Jerri added.

"Nice!" John nearly lost his temper.

"Surely he didn't go alone, did he?" Jerri added.

"No," John started pacing again. "He took a hundred-year-old bus driver with him."

"Who took a hundred-year-old bus driver where?" Ken was passing and heard the ruckus. "Why are you crying AnnaBelle?"

Susan walked over and took his arm. "John made AnnaBelle cry because he's worried about Adam."

"And why should he be worried about Adam?" Now Ken was becoming worried.

"AnnaBelle thought the children needed some laptops, so she asked Adam to go into town and get some.

"Not today!" Ken became anxious. He began to pace the room.

"What's so special about today?" Jerri asked.

"The oxygen level is low, they could die." Ken stated.

"But I feel fine." Susan added.

"Round everyone up and split them up into two groups, have them bring sleeping bags or blankets and pillows everyone is spending the next two nights sleeping in the greenhouses." John commanded. "Come on Ken, let's look outside and see if we can see Adam."

The two men ran down the aisle way toward the airlock.

Chapter 75

Bennett had it all planned out. He was surprised that these people didn't think it was necessary to lock doors. It wasn't that the locks weren't locked it was that the doors didn't even have the capability to be locked. He was free to travel unchecked throughout the complex and no one asked any questions. He was the one who planted the bug in AnnaBelle's ear about getting the video games for the kids. He was the one who convinced Mitch that it would be a safe walk in the park. These people were so easy, so easily manipulated.

Justin was the target for Bennett's revenge. If not for Justin, he would have been on an island safe from all this misery. But, he had a plan. There was a separate duct that fed into the heating system of the main house. This was done so that the oxygen generator and the complex heating units could be directed toward the house. The Williams and Thomas families would be the only casualties and he intended to destroy any evidence. Of course, the way the world was going now, there might not be anyone left to care.

A pin-hole leak was all that he needed. It had taken several days but by working very slowly and using a straight pin as a drill bit he had managed to create a small drip in the condensation line from the furnace. The line was under no pressure, but had constant flow and this gave him the drip, drip, drip, that he needed.

This would act as a timing device so he would not be near when the event occurred. Cyanide gas was deadly and he wanted to be well away. The plan was that the drip drip drip would fill a catch pan and when the pan was nearly full, it would over balance and spill into the bottom of the filter rack where the crystals would be waiting. The cyanide gas would be brought into the duct work and fill the house; bringing an unfortunate end to anyone sleeping there. He needed the pan to fill in two to three hours that would be enough time for an alibi. This required that he resize the drip hole twice, but it was ready now. Once those families were out of the way, he would be in charge again. He considered that maybe he should wait until the worst was over. These people did a lot of work that he couldn't do himself. Ultimately he decided, the sooner the better.

He opened his briefcase on the cot and checked to see that the little crystal canisters were still dry and intact. He must not let the crystals get wet. Patrick could be the guard. "How you doin' in there Patrick? Still all dead and covered in plastic? Good, good. Sucks to be you. It won't be long now." He shut the briefcase and slid it back in the overhead rack above his bed. He finished just as there was a knock on his door. Because of his evil temperament and his general attitude of superiority, no one objected to his taking a unit all to himself.

Jerri was at the door. "Mr. Bennett, John is asking everyone to please bring a sleeping bag or blanket and pillow to one of the greenhouses. I won't go into great detail with most people, but you're an engineer and will understand. He said the oxygen level outside is getting critically low and we need to concentrate the oxygen generators on the generators if that makes sense?"

"Perfectly my dear, things are becoming quite complicated," he began to gather a blanket and pillow. He looked into the air, "Not tonight Patrick, maybe tomorrow." Jerri looked puzzled but led the way to the greenhouses.

Chapter 76

"It's ten below in the airlock, John. We can't open the big door, not even for a minute. Let's suit up." Ken walked to a set of lockers; each had a name on it. Inside were sets of innerwear and outerwear, base layer gloves and mittens, balaclavas; which were like a head and neck hood with a face hole, goggles and boots. "This set is rated at sixty below John, and it's no colder than that outside and the ash is starting to lessen. Adam's stuff is missing." Ken suited up.

John suited up as well. The outer man door opened inward and it was a good thing. A little pile of gray ash fell inward onto the floor. Footsteps through the ash showed where two others had gone before.

The ash was no longer falling but the sky was still black. "Let's walk up toward the road." It took an effort for John to be heard through the mask of the balaclava. Ken nodded in agreement. The ash was difficult to walk through and made a little dust cloud as Ken slid his way through it.

"We are lucky there is no wind." John thought to himself.

After a great deal of effort, they stood at the top end of the parking lot. Both men were bent over trying to catch their breath.

"This was really stupid, Ken." John wheezed.

"Good way to have a heart attack, that's for sure. I'm worried about that old guy Mitch. Bet he doesn't make it back." Ken was finally able to stand up. "We're not going to be doing any good up here we better get back slowly."

"Wait, do you hear something?" John pulled back the balaclava to expose his ear to the cold. "I definitely hear something, shine both lights over there."

Both men pointed their flashlights in the direction of the noise. Soon they were rewarded with the sight of two pinpricks of light coming from the direction of the town. The noise got louder and louder.

"Noise must travel well in cold climates." John volunteered. "I'd have never heard that on a normal day.

The points of light got bigger and closer and the noise of the four-wheel drive pickup got louder. The two men stepped back and pointed their lights at the ground. The red 1993 pickup came to a stop right in front of them. The engine was quiet but there was a noise coming from the inside of the cab. Adam and Mitch were singing loudly, something about fifty-seven bottles of beer on the wall.

Adam looked at the two men and waved, he made the motion of trying to roll down the window but it was frozen shut. He opened the door. "Climb in the back and we'll take you to the airlock." He shut the door again. Soon, the singing recommenced. Luckily, the tail gate opened. It was difficult with all the heavy clothing to hop up on the tailgate but they managed. The bed of the truck was filled with big boxes that contained small boxes and one box filled with bottles. Everything was covered with a layer of ash.

Adam drove slowly back to the compound not wanting to stir up a dust cloud. He parked in front of the big double overhead door and waited. Mitch jumped out of the passenger side of the truck and motioned for John and Ken to stay where they were. He went into the man door and returned a moment later with a large aluminum grain shovel. He slowly and carefully scooped up shovels full of ash and deposited them away from the door entrance. Soon he had removed a section of ash the width of the shovel all along the base of the big door, he returned to the man door and soon the overhead door was rising. He stopped it just high enough to allow the truck cab to enter and as soon as the truck was through, he closed the door again. Shortly after the door had opened two large blower heaters kicked on and began to warm the room.

These continued after the big door was shut, but before the room was warm, they flamed out. Ken and John started to have trouble catching their breath. Adam was standing beside them and gave each of them a small cylinder with plastic tubing attached.

"Use these." Adam demanded.

They tore off their balaclavas and masks, and put the little hoses over their heads, attaching the plastic piece under their noses so they could breathe deeply.

John noticed that both Adam and Mitch were wearing these little bottles around their necks and had the breathing apparatus attached under their noses.

"I like to died by the time we got into town, thankfully Adam knew where the medical supply store was, and we picked up some of these." Mitch motioned toward the little bottle.

"I was having trouble breathing, so I put one on too. Is there something wrong with the air?" Adam asked.

"I'm afraid so Adam. That's why we were so worried about you two." John answered.

"We don't have enough of these for everyone, what's going to happen?" Adam was thinking of AnnaBelle and their child.

"We have moved everyone into the greenhouses for tonight. We are directing the oxygen concentrators toward the greenhouses and toward the central heating system. Did you notice those heaters flame out? They used up all the air in this sealed room. Our only hope is that the ash has cleared south of here already and that the sun is shining and whatever green things have survived will have started doing their oxygen thing." Ken explained.

"And if they haven't?" Mitch asked.

"When the oxygen generators can't keep up and the O2 level gets too low for humans, we will all fall asleep and eventually die. Then the oxygen level will lower to the point where it can no longer support combustion." He pointed up toward the heaters. "And our corpses will freeze."

"The Earth will slowly right itself, the sun will come out, the plants will grow again, the eggs will hatch, and the earth will get along quite well without humans to pollute it. Just like with the dinosaurs. Thomas once said, we might not be able to destroy the planet, but we can sure make it a place where humans can't live anymore. What you got in the truck, Sparky?"

"After Mitch and I discovered we couldn't breathe and fixed that little problem, we did an experiment to see if alcohol would freeze. Turns out the higher proof bottles don't, but the beer and wine don't do so good." He reached into the box, removed a bottle of high proof bourbon and handed it to Ken. Ken held it in his mitten-covered hand.

"We'll sip this after it warms up a little." He said.

"We warmed one already, but it's still pretty cold." He handed the opened bottle to John. John approved the label and, after taking a long pull, passed it over to Ken, who also took a long drink.

"That's plenty of that," Ken coughed, "we've got work to do." He patted Adam on the shoulder and opened the man door into the complex. The warm air rushed into the doorway and rose to the ceiling while the cold air of the air lock rolled down the aisle way.

"How was it out there?" John asked Adam.

"Bad, really bad." Adam admitted.

"Wasn't nothing alive." Mitch added. "Not man, nor beast."

"We drove all over, John. Any building with a flat roof is collapsed. Most buildings with low-pitched roofs are collapsed. There is no sign of any kind of life. The power failed, and then the natural gas failed. What the ash didn't kill, the cold did and if anyone by some miracle was able to survive; this low oxygen will finish them off. It wouldn't surprise me if we were the only humans left alive. How rare would it have been for more than two places like this to have been built? You saved us John." Adam began to unload the boxes from the truck onto a four-wheeled cart. He thought for a moment. "Maybe."

"You can bet the government survived. They have hollowed out mountains, where they can hide. That is just what we will need, a whole new generation of people who don't know how to do anything except how to take bribes." Mitch made a spitting motion as he helped to unload the boxes. "Those are the greedy self-serving bribe taking sons of bitches that got us into this fix. Better not take the booze to the children. I wonder how their hollow mountains did against a hundred feet of ash. I wonder how their mountains did against those damn earthquakes."

Chapter 77

AnnaBelle apologized to Adam for trying to get him killed. He accepted her apology then wallowed in the hero worship that was poured on him by a grateful group of children. There were plenty of laptops to go around, even enough for any adults that wanted them. And there was a year's supply of batteries that the cold didn't hurt.

"Did you somehow pay for these?" asked AnnaBelle.

"Your dad probably owns most of those stores, besides everybody's dead. Oops." Adam was sorry he had said that.

"What do you mean everybody's dead?" AnnaBelle was shocked.

"It's not a secret, I thought you knew. Nobody outside could have made it." Adam was blunt.

"Guess I have been so busy with the baby, I didn't pay attention." She began to cry.

"Will this nightmare never end? It seems like we've been cooped up here forever." She complained through the sobs.

He took her by the arm and led her down the aisle way. "You've got to hold it together for the kids. It won't do them any good to see an adult breaking down like this."

"But, I don't want to be an adult." She cried harder still.

He held her until the sobbing stopped.

"I'm OK now." She hurried back to finish passing out the games. "Now, you kids find a nice comfy spot to relax, we're going to spend some time with these nice green plants. They need our breath to help them grow. That's why talking to plants makes them green, see?" She blew gently on a few green leaves. The kids began to do that as well.

"Make them stay in here." Adam told her as he went down the aisle way to find Ken and be of the most help.

"Run through the complex and make sure everyone is in the greenhouses." Ken told Adam. "Then run through the house and make sure everyone's out of there. I'm going to see that all the livestock gets brought into the corrals closest to the center, maybe they'll get enough oxygen. If not there's nothing else we can do. Tell everyone in one hour the air at the perimeter won't be fit to breathe."

Ken ran down the aisle way toward the corral. He satisfied himself that all the animals were as close to the aisle way as possible. He hurried back and shut the big double doors that had never been closed before, shutting off the complex from the arena.

He checked the south greenhouse to make sure the vents were open and supplying good air. Then he stopped at the panel room and shut off all the unnecessary loads. The generator speed dropped to near idle. All the lights except for the emergency lighting went out. He found his way to the north greenhouse and sort of counted heads. Everyone was present and accounted for. Jerri motioned for him and he saw that they had made a comfortable place for him to sit, with a nice cushion to sit on and a big reading pillow. When he sat down, he noticed that he was situated between Jerri and Susan. Jerri laid a video game on his lap and he nodded. Then he took Susan's hand in his right and Jerri's in his left. He had done all he could. Now, all he could do was pray. He began to say a few prayers in his mind. He fought the sleep his body needed. He knew that there was a good chance that if he went to sleep he might never wake up. He went to sleep. In his mind, he heard the generator fail.

Chapter 78

He knew he was dreaming. Ken heard footsteps running down the aisle way. The door to the greenhouse burst open. Debra was out of breath. "The sun, I saw the sun!" Maybe it wasn't a dream after all.

Ken rose and every muscle ached.

John was first out the door followed by the ladies. They followed Justin down the aisle way toward the arena. He opened one of the double doors and cool air rushed in. Cool, not cold.

"As soon as the sun came out it must have warmed up 50 degrees. It's still around zero but there's still little wind and the sky is clearing." He ran to the big overhead door and opened it. It was morning and the sun was shining. The world was covered by a layer of grey ash, but to see the sun and feel its warmth brightened everyone's spirits. Everyone from the complex came streaming into the arena. The children were laughing again and wanted to run outside.

"It looks like we lost some sheep and a few cattle overnight." John observed.

"All the chickens are alive and accounted for," Jenny said as she came running up.

Richards followed behind with a baby chick in his hand. "We've had thirty five new hatchlings in two days. I thought this baby might like to see the sun."

"It could have been a whole lot worse." Susan commented.

Everyone agreed. There were hugs and kisses of thankful gratitude.

"Don't let the kids out in this ash, they can play here in the sun, but don't let them breathe that nasty stuff. We need to figure out a way to dispose of it, the stuff can't be good for the soil. If the wind kicks up we need to close that door. Let's go do some planning." He and Ken walked into the compound discussing the future.

"Can we sleep in our own beds tonight?" Susan asked out loud.

"Count on it." Ken replied loudly.

Bennett smiled.

Chapter 79

The briefcase was caught on something up there. Bennett was in a hurry and didn't want to try to find a ladder. So, he tugged and tugged. Finally, the little nail that was holding it broke free and the briefcase came loose with such force that it came free from Bennett's hands and flew across the room, hitting the corner of the dresser. It fell to the floor. He laid it on the floor and opened it to look for damage. The corner of the dresser had knocked a triangular hole in the side of the briefcase right where the tar covered bird piece was. He lifted the piece and noticed a crack in the acrylic. "You're alright Patrick, still all dead and covered in oil, still all dead and covered in plastic, still sucks to be you." He put the piece back in the briefcase and closed the lid. He failed to notice the loose crystals from the damaged container.

"We don't have much time," he said to himself as he carried the briefcase down the aisle way. Part of his job description was to put the vent valves back the way they were so that the heating units could warm the house. Everyone was going to be sleeping in their own beds tonight. He had just thirty minutes to get the water tray all set up and balanced. He would need to make sure the filter pan was good and dry, then set the pan under the drip, then sprinkle the crystals into the filter pan. Two hours later when everyone in the house was good and asleep, the pan would tilt, the crystals would become wet, the gas would be released, and the ductwork would carry the cyanide into the house. By morning, he would be as shocked as everyone else and reluctantly take charge. He had been working this angle in other people's minds since he came to this terrible place.

He made sure that no one was in the aisle way when he entered the fan room. He placed a chair against the doorknob, so he wouldn't be disturbed. Then he checked to be sure that the filter pan was good and dry. He checked the drip to be sure it was going to fill the little pan. Everything was good and ready.

He laid the briefcase on the floor and spoke to the bird. "Well, Patrick, you stupid, dead, oil-covered bird, it won't be long before I'm back in control again. Won't that be good?"

He knelt to open the briefcase and detected the slightest whiff of bitter almonds. Then he noticed that one of the canisters was open and the crystals had spilled. The last thing he ever saw was the wet crystals. He collapsed, his head landing in the open briefcase— a drop of moisture oozed from the crack in the statue onto his lifeless cheek.

Chapter 80

"Tell me the whole story about Bennett. I just caught the tail end of it as you were telling Jerri." John sat in a chair in the office area and put his leg up on the desk. The whole family was taking a much-needed break.

Susan brought him a cup of steaming coffee. He closed his eyes to listen. "Proceed." He said.

Ken held his cup out to Susan who refilled it. "I couldn't get the door to the air handling room open. I pushed and pushed and it wouldn't open. I couldn't figure out why, so I got Adam to help me and we pushed and pushed and finally we broke the chair that had been propped under the door handle. Bennett, you remember the oil guy, was laying on the floor, dead, with his head in a briefcase. Inside the briefcase were three cans of the chemicals the Nazi's used in the last war, and that." He pointed toward the filing cabinet where the statue of the dead bird was on display. It appears that somehow the acrylic surrounding the bird had cracked. There must have been some moisture still trapped inside and the moisture escaped through the crack and got those crystals wet, producing a gas that killed him. Looks like the bird got his revenge.

"Sweet," John said. "What did you do with the body?"

"I guess we'll bury it up on the side of the hill." Ken said.

"Get the padre to say some words, would you. I didn't much care for the guy myself; world's a better place without him. What was he doing in there anyway?"

"The way things were set up, it looks like he had created a leak in the tubing that was to have wet those crystals after a period of time and released cyanide gas into the vents."

"Which vents?" John asked.

"The vents that feed the house." Ken replied

"You mean that son of a bitch was trying to kill all of us in the house?" John was aghast.

"Guess he was planning to take over the compound. He had mentioned to a few people that he was the only one qualified to take charge if anything happened to us." Ken shrugged his shoulders.

"That piece of shit. Don't tell the padre anything about this. Feed the son of a bitch to the hogs." John sipped his coffee.

"John!" Susan exclaimed "you can't mean that, he was a fellow human being, even if he had some evil in him."

"Fine," You're digging a big hole to bury all that ash in, aren't you Ken?"

"We're scraping all the ash off, we have to wet it first so it won't cloud up; then we use dump trucks to haul it down stream and we're burying it under a few inches of dirt so we won't worry about it with a wind storm. The ground is still frozen, so we're having a pretty easy time of it."

"So, throw the body in with the ash, no headstone. Bennett was responsible for the deaths of millions of innocent people; he doesn't deserve a headstone.

He looked at Susan. She knew this was the best she could expect and she agreed. She said no more.

"Found any more people alive, now that the radios work again?" John asked.

"The ham guy readjusted his antennas after the ash storm and he said he talked to one guy down in New Mexico that lived in some cave. The guy was fifty-two with a wife and three kids." Jerri said. "He thinks there surely are others he just hasn't got hold of yet."

"You know how we have been talking about the need to repopulate the planet, right?" Jerri asked. She walked over to John and held his arm. She looked at Susan and winked. Susan walked to Ken and took his hand. They both spoke in unison. "We're pregnant."

Ken and John were trying to figure out what to say when the door burst open.

Dr. Nubury, the "spermmeister" entered the room. "I need to speak with you people. It's of vital importance."

"Very well doctor, what is it?" John sat on a chair and let Jerri set on his lap.

"May I use this white board?" Without waiting for a reply he began to erase the daily menu from the board.

"We are well on the way to resurrecting our herds. All of the cattle are bred and will soon calve. The same can be said for the sheep and goats and rabbits and chickens. By using frozen eggs and sperm, we will be able to repopulate most of the species we cherished that were lost. The animals will be fine, but not the humans."

"As you know, we may be the last surviving humans. We have an overwhelming duty to preserve the species. We also have an opportunity to create a new civilization. It will take generations, I grant you, but if we approach this in the proper way we can alleviate a lot of what was wrong with us before the event. If you discount those of us who are too old— myself included— that will leave less than sixty human females of childbearing age. Fortunately, most of them are Millennials. In order for the species to survive, it is imperative for every female to bear as many offspring as she can; with each child from another gene pool. I have gone through the health records of the children and there are only two with problematic genes. Both are female, and they can be implanted with fertilized embryos from others. Now, I have laid out a plan here that will be the best roadmap for the continuation of the species.

AnnaBelle interrupted. "So, doctor, while your machine was doing the analysis, generally speaking, that is to say as a rule; the machine would not allow the pairing of family members specifically brother and sister, for example.

"I'm glad you brought that up." The doctor knelt down beside his briefcase and consulted a file folder. "I remember there was an issue that concerned you and your husband, Adam wasn't it?"

"Yes, Adam." She replied in a worried voice.

There was absolute silence in the room. You could hear a pin drop.

"Ah, here it is, your children will have a better than average chance of having a photographic memory."

"Then we are not siblings?" She held her breath.

"Certainly not. We would have been informed by the program."

"Adam's not my brother? Adam's not my brother!" She ran over and embraced Adam, who had a puzzled look on his face.

There was an audible sigh of relief from the gathering.

"Why would there be a doubt?" The doctor looked to the group who shrugged their shoulders.

"Finally, for you ladies here, I think it would be best for the species if you, Mrs. Williams were to bear a child with Mr. Thomas; and you Mrs. Thomas to bear a child with Mr. Williams. Why are you laughing? This is serious science."

The End

Please visit www.millennialark.com

There was absolute silence in the room. You could hear a heartbeat.

"Someday your own children will have a happy and average marriage, having a photographic album..."

"But we were not siblings?" She held her breath.

"No, and no! We would have been brother and sister."

"No, we are not brother and sister," said Jasper. She could hardly restrain Albun, who had a puzzled look on his face.

The musician and his wife glanced from the...

he would like to be a doctor. The doctor broke [to the group] who sat in thoughtful silence.

"If things would lead as they? think, it would be best meeting each of you, Mrs. Williams who to have a child with her Thomas, and you, Mrs. Thomas, to bear a child with who... What is so serious about... in anything?"

The End